THE
HOME
I KNEW

ALLY LEE

ROSE VALLEY

This one's for my wine lovers and those who feel like they never belong. I couldn't forget about you.

1

SIENNA

I didn't always work at Monroe. In fact, I wanted to work at a more local vineyard near my home. I'm a sommelier. I love my job, but Monroe Vineyards is *way* out of my league. The brand of wine, my co-workers...the clientele.

I take another look at the merlot bottles that sit in inventory. I recognize a few of the names, but the one that's standing out—Dragon Lily—is a new one. I admire the design: a baby dragon emerging from a lily. It's cute, but the meaning behind it boggles me.

Is the wine spicy?

Does it have a hint of sweetness with a kick at the end?

Is it made with fermented dragon fruit?

So many questions. And not enough time.

I'm super scatterbrained, and it doesn't help that I'm worried about my trainee coming in and asking me about the difference between a red and white. I chuckle at that. She seems like a smart girl, but the questions she's been asking leave much to be desired.

Why are you chilling the white wines but not the red?

What are wine flights?

Wait, so you can't fake vertical IDs?

I'm sure her interview went well. My boss told me she's majoring in viticulture and enology. And she scored decently on the winemaking test on her first day. I'm just concerned about how well she will keep up within the first week. Judging by her questions and difficulty on differentiating the wines, the jury's still out. And it might screw us up for the upcoming busy season.

It's almost summer, and that's the prime time for Monroe. It's only May. Yet we've already had a few slight rushes the last few weekends. We've had some wine run out already. Our clients love our pinot noir and Riesling.

"Sienna! Are you done counting inventory?" my boss, Mr. Stevens, shouts from up front.

Crap. I tally the merlots and pinot grigios and close my notebook.

Running back up to the front, I see my trainee talking to him, and their gazes land on me, my boss frowning.

"Everything okay?" I warily ask. I was gone for about ten minutes. What could've possibly happened? I look around the lobby, but everything looks to be in place.

"Everything's fine, Sienna. Except for the fact that Ashley told me you forgot to give her a name badge and show her around the facility."

I frown. "Um, I thought I *did* show her around the facility."

He cocks an eyebrow at me. "So our new hire is lying, then?" *Yes. Obviously.* I give him a pointed look, but he's not budging.

Sighing, I put my notebook on the desk and motion for her to follow me. "Let's look around, Ashley," I deadpan. She gives me a gleeful smile as Mr. Stevens walks off.

I bring her to the backroom where the wine inventory is. We stop in front of the pinot grigio shelf, and I point to a Tilted Molasses bottle.

"This isn't as popular at Monroe, but you'll see a lot of the younger crowd sampling it. It's our most expensive pinot grigio at $150 per bottle. They never purchase it, but they like it because it's fruit-forward," I explain.

Monroe is very popular with the wealthy due to our close proximity to the Monroe Country Club. The country club was founded by William Monroe in the 1800s, and this vineyard was founded by his great-great-grandson William Monroe V back in the 1990s. Because of how high profile the area is, we've had famous actors, musicians, models, and moguls frequent the winery.

I walk past the shelf and open the back door to the vineyard. I show her the expanse rows of vines. She gapes at the land as we overlook the highway. It truly is a beautiful view. I wouldn't have it any other way.

"This is beautiful," she says in awe. I nod, taking it all in myself. It's a sunny day on a Saturday morning. We should start picking up around mid-afternoon since we have live music starting soon.

I bring her back inside to the lobby and search through the desk drawer for badges. I pull one out and give it to her to write her name on. We usually order them, but this is her second day, and we don't have time. Soon, she's going to be shadowing me as I write the wine list for Monroe's bistro today.

"So what brings you to Monroe? Why did you apply?"

I ask because I'm genuinely curious. I love wine. Probably more than anyone else here. But I'm always interested in learning what others love about it.

"I want to be a sommelier. Like you." She smiles. "But I'm not as...*fluent* as I can be in terms of knowing wines." I can't hold in the snort that comes out. She has an embarrassed smile. "Look, I know you don't like me. Not a lot of people do. I mean, I'm beautiful, and I don't come off as the smartest girl. I would hate me too."

I'm immediately put off by the comment. Did she really call herself beautiful? "I never said I didn't like you."

She raises an eyebrow at me. "I'm not an idiot. You gave me the stink eye when I told Mr. Stevens you didn't show me around."

"Because you told Mr. Stevens I didn't show you around," I deadpan.

She rolls her eyes. "You showed me around the *lobby*. That's it. That's not the same thing."

I shake my head. I'm not interested in the semantics. Sighing, I pull out my notebook and create a loose list of what wines we should pair with food at the bistro.

"I'm gonna create a list for today's lunch. This is what your job will be once you're bumped up. Usually, they let you know what's on the food menu for the day. As the sommelier, you'll use your expertise to decide which wine would pair well with the selections. Then you'll *create* that wine list. Got it?" She nods and gives me a small smile.

A few hours pass, and it's already noon. Ashley is organizing the wines in the backroom, and I'm on the phone ordering more bottles of pinot noir.

"We probably need three more boxes of the Damsel in Distress. Okay, thank you." I'm writing down what other bottles we need when a deep voice sounds above me.

"Excuse me? I'm looking for a Calvin Stevens."

"Sorry, sir. Just give me one minute," I say, holding a finger up. Whoever Mr. Deep Voice is can wait a few seconds.

Then a husky laugh rumbles through my core. "Honey, I only need five minutes of your time."

Sighing, I put my pencil down and look up, gaping at what I see.

A chiseled face smirking down at me. His golden blond hair is the first thing my gaze goes to. Medium-length waves with stubble on his chin. It's like looking at a young Matthew McConaughey. His piercing ocean blue eyes send a jolt of excitement through my body. What the hell?

I clear my throat. "What can I do for you, sir?" My voice cracks.

He chuckles again. "Mr. Stevens, babe?"

I cock an eyebrow at him. Babe? If another jolt of heat didn't run through me, I'd be annoyed. "First and foremost, I'm not your '*babe.*' Secondly, hold on." His smile grows, and I pick up the desk phone, dialing 1.

Mr. Stevens picks up on the second ring. "Sienna, is everything all right?" I almost ignore the question when Mr. Deep Voice winks at me.

I frown, clearing my throat again. "Everything's all right, sir. You just have a guest here looking for you." I look down at his hands and almost shiver at the veins popping out from them.

*I wonder what those long fingers can do...*Down, girl.

"What guest? We don't open for another fifteen minutes. Did you open the doors early?"

I cock an eyebrow at that. "Someone probably let him in."

Mr. Deep Voice beckons me forward. "Tell him William is here to see him," he says, grinning.

4

Clearing my throat, I manage to say, "He said his name is William." He nods his head and mouths *Good girl*. I could vomit...if he weren't so hot.

Just then, Mr. Stevens lets out a loud gasp, freaking me out. I wait for his response, but it doesn't come. I'm about to ask if he's okay when he clears his throat.

"William is here! Wonderful, I'll be right down." And then he hangs up. That was fucking weird.

"Mr. Stevens said he'll be right down, sir. You can sit in one of those chairs." I go to finish writing down what needs to be in inventory, but I still feel him staring down at me. I look up and, yeah, he's still there. "Can I get you anything else, sir?"

He tilts his head and sizes me up. I frown. I don't like being under a microscope.

"What's your name?" he asks curiously. His lip quirks, and my eyes are instantly drawn there. There's a mole above his lip. His face is freaking beautiful. Wait, he asked me a question.

"Sorry, what?"

He laughs, and I love the sound. "Your name."

"Sienna," I say slowly.

He smiles, and his eyes scale down my body again.

"Cute name for a cute girl." I cock an eyebrow. This model thinks *I'm* cute? Did I step into a parallel dimension? I look around to make sure, and he laughs again. "What are you doing?"

"Just making sure I'm not being punked."

"What would I need to punk you for?" I cock an eyebrow. There's no way he thinks I'm cute.

"You just seem like a guy who has a...*type*."

He chuckles. "You figured me out, babe," he mocks.

"Look, Mr.—"

"Will," he interrupts.

I narrow my eyes, making him smile again. "It's been a pleasure, but Mr. Stevens said he'll be down in a minute. Maybe you could sit and wait for him."

He's staring at me, making me uncomfortable. Why are we doing this? I have a job to do, and I got him what he needed. He's making this weirder than it needs to be.

Finally, he nods and walks over to the closest chair. I make another phone call and order a few more boxes of our Fiery Stone Rosé.

Mr. Stevens finally makes it down, and he's dressed differently. He's wearing a perfectly tailored suit. I frown.

He walks over to Will, who jumps up and greets him. "Ah, William. It's so great to see you, son. We have your party decorations set up in the banquet room. Will your mom and dad be joining us as well?"

Oh, he's having a party here. So he *is* rich. It costs $10,000 to book the entire banquet room. If it weren't for the fact that he's wearing cargo shorts and a gray hoodie with flip-flops, I'd think he were just a hot delivery man.

"No, they're both out of town on some business trip. They'll be back later. Just in time for the dinner," he says, and his persona is different. He's talking like a businessman now, and it's kind of...sexy. Clearing my throat, I finish writing up inventory.

"Oh, Sienna! I'm sorry, where are my manners? This is William Monroe VI."

My stomach drops, and my heart stops. I slowly look up to find Will smugly smiling at me. Monroe, as in...

"William Monroe? That's a familiar name," I deadpan, making his smile bigger.

Mr. Stevens gives me a confused look. "Yes, Sienna, this is William V and Lily's son."

William V and Lily Monroe.

The owners of this vineyard.

For fuck's sake, I just told off their son.

2

WILL

The hot girl with the equally hot attitude is staring daggers at me, and it's the most beautiful thing. Those piercing brown eyes make me harder than I don't know what.

She's not my usual type, but I might have to rethink that notion. I always go for blondes. Will Monroe has a thing for blondes. Maybe a redhead here and there, but none of them turned me on more than the smoking hot brunette standing in front of me. Her skin is a chestnut color, and she's more petite than the girls I usually date. And the fact that she's glaring at me makes me smile harder.

"It's like you can't get rid of me," I joke. I've known her for maybe thirty minutes, and I can already tell staring at her is my new favorite thing to do. Each eye roll she gives me makes me fantasize about her doing the same thing when I'm inside her. Clearing my throat, I adjust the situation in my jeans.

"Yeah, it's quite fulfilling," she mocks. Story of my life.

Because nothing is as fulfilling as standing next to her right now. And I'm the heir of Monroe Vineyards. I wake up in my California King bed with that thought in my head every day, and not even that is as fulfilling as smelling this girl's perfume. Goddamn, what is that scent?

"You smell really good, Sienna. What's the perfume you use?"

She looks up from the party favors on the banquet table to give me a bored look. Her disdain for me is the cutest thing I've ever seen. I'm not used to this kind of reaction, and I have to say, it's a breath of fresh air.

"It's called lotion, Mr. Monroe."

Okay, I need to nip that in the bud right now. "You don't like calling me Will?"

"Calling you by your first name is a bit unprofessional, don't you think?"

I gape at her. "Who the fuck cares? It's only you and me here," I say more aggressively than I want to.

She flinches. "You're a *client*. Not to mention a *VIP* client. That'd be inappropriate."

I frown. Is she for real right now? Sure, I'm rich, and this is my parents' winery. But she can't be a regular person for five minutes?

"Me being a Monroe doesn't change the fact that I'm a person," I snarl.

She cocks an eyebrow. "Well...yeah, you're right. But Mr. Stevens—"

"Fuck that. If you want to, call me Will," I offer.

She stares at me before hiding a smile. Shit. What's her smile look like? I have to see now. "Okay. Mr. Monroe," she jokes.

I narrow my eyes at her, but mini-me is rock hard yet again. "You're a real comedian, you know that?"

She shrugs and places a wine glass near a metallic dinner plate.

"I have my moments," she admits, tucking a strand of hair behind her ear. She's beautiful. I'm tempted to run my hands through her hair, but I restrain myself.

"How come I've never seen you before? I'm here every weekend." I'd notice someone like her.

"I'm a sommelier, so you'll only see me behind the counters, spewing my knowledge on wine."

I raise an eyebrow. "A wine connoisseur. That's pretty hot."

She rolls her eyes, but I don't miss the smile that touches her lips. Those lips I can't stop staring at. Perfect and kissable.

"Yeah, I actually wanna be a winemaker. Maybe even own my own winery one day."

I tilt my head at her. "That's pretty ambitious. How'd you get into wine?"

She freezes.

Like, she actually freezes in midair.

I frown as a look of terror spreads across her face. What the fuck did I say? "It's...kind of a long story," she mumbles.

Well, *that* wasn't alarming. I'm about to ask to hear the story, but a small voice sounds from the doorway to the banquet room.

"Sienna—Oh, sorry! I didn't know we had a guest."

I turn to find a blonde with a banging body staring at us. My eyes land on her tits, and *man* are they an impressive pair. I go back to her face and tense when I lock eyes with the same ones I stared into when I screwed her.

Ashley fucking Westbrook.

What the hell is *she* doing here? Damn, she still looks hot as fuck. I'm mesmerized until Sienna clears her throat next to me. I turn to find her smirking.

"Mr. Monroe, meet Ashley. Ashley, meet Mr. William Monroe VI."

I look back at Ashley, and she's grimacing at me. "Oh, trust me, I know Will Monroe," she sneers.

I gulp. "Ashley. Nice to see you again, doll."

She rolls her eyes, walking over to us. "Yeah, for lack of better wording."

"Am I missing something here?" Sienna has a look of concern on her face.

"Oh no, nothing at all," Ashley mocks. "The famous Will Monroe can do no wrong."

Sienna still looks confused as hell. Then a knowing grin stretches across her face. "Wait a minute," she says, humor in her voice. "He smashed and dashed you, didn't he?"

Ashley and I both flinch. Our non-answer makes her laugh. *Hard.* But it's still a beautiful laugh. I find myself smiling at her. "Your laugh is beautiful," I say in awe.

This makes her stop, confused eyes staring back at me. For a second, we're having a brief staring contest. She's truly a pretty girl.

Then Ashley clearing her throat interrupts our moment.

"Don't get involved with him, Sienna. He'll pump and dump you like nobody's business."

I roll my eyes. She's being dramatic. She had to know we weren't going to make it past one night of fun.

"Wasn't gonna," Sienna mumbles, pulling a wine glass out of a glass rack.

"Never say never, babe."

She slams down the wine glass and faces me. I gulp as she meets my gaze, clearly annoyed. My eyes do a quick glance down her body and land on her breasts. *Fuck*, they look great. The perfect handful. I then glance at her slightly wide hips. Damn, what I would do to this centerfold body.

"Are you done ogling me?"

My eyes shoot back up to hers, and she's glaring at me. I only smile. "I wasn't ogling you," I lie.

"That's not what your groan said." I gape. Did I really groan?

"I hope I didn't interrupt anything between you two." Ashley's annoyed voice makes me turn around, and I find her glaring at us. Well, this is uncomfortable.

"No, Ashley. You weren't interrupting anything. I'm trying to help set up Mr. Monroe's—"

"Will's."

"*Mr. Monroe's* banquet dinner tonight." She ignores me. It only makes me smile bigger. Soon, she'll know I have something for lippy girls.

Ashley has a bored expression on her face. "Is there anything else you need me to do? I finished organizing the wines in the back." I raise an eyebrow and look at Sienna.

"You can go on a lunch break. Did you want something from the bistro?"

"Not really. Can I go off the vineyard to get lunch?"

"Sure, just be back before 4 p.m."

Ashley nods, glares at me, and walks off. I look back at Sienna as she continues setting down wine glasses.

"She works under you?"

"She's training to be a sommelier. If you ask me, I'm not sure how well she'll do." She mutters the last part before looking up, realizing what she said. "Shit, I did *not* mean to say that."

I just stare at her and then laugh. "You don't think she's gonna do well?"

She bites her lip, and my eyes follow the action. "I mean...she just has so much catching up to do. She did well on her pretest, but she keeps asking questions that even a general tasting room attendant would know," she jokes.

I laugh. "Well, maybe give her a chance." No matter how much she hates me right now. "She's learning from the best, so I'm sure she'll do fine."

She narrows her eyes at me. "Are you fucking with me?" Mini-me twitches again. If she says that word again, I might bust in my jeans.

"Absolutely not. Anyone with a prickly personality and such dedication to their job can achieve the impossible."

She just stares at me before rolling her eyes. "You're an asshole," she laughs. I just smile and continue watching her.

In fact, that's what I do for the next few hours. I sit in a banquet chair and just watch her set up the party decorations across the room. I want to believe she doesn't notice me watching her, but I think she knows. Loose waves falling over her shoulder, the focused dip in her eyebrows when she adjusts a wine glass or plate, the pleased grin she makes when everything's in its place. She looks so in her element. Like she enjoys working here and doing stuff like this. And *God*, it's a turn-on.

It's 4 p.m., and it's time for me to go back home and get ready for tonight. It's my birthday dinner. I'm turning twenty-six, and my parents decided to throw me a birthday bash at Monroe. I wanted to spend it downtown, but no chance of *that* happening.

"Dude, what are you still doing here? Your party's at 5:30 p.m." My best buddy Collin walks into my house without knocking. It fucking pisses me off when he does that.

"Can you get into the habit of knocking? If my parents were here, you'd be shot down already."

He rolls his eyes, throwing his tuxedo blazer on the couch. "The Monroes won't shoot me. I'm family to you guys."

"More like a pain in our asses," I mutter. I'm adjusting my bowtie and combing through my hair when I hear the fridge open and close. Collin walks out with a can of beer.

"When are your parents back, dude? They're gonna miss their son's birthday."

I'm annoyed at the question, but for the wrong reason.

This would be the fourth birthday in a row they missed. This one was their idea, so I hope they don't miss it.

"They said their plane lands at 6 p.m. So they might be a little late."

He nods his head and takes another swig.

I run upstairs to my bedroom and pick up my phone, flinching at the number of texts I have already. Twenty messages from friends coming to the party. But I only zero in on the ones that matter.

> **KAYLA:** *Hey, Monroe! What time's the birthday thing again?*
> **WILLA:** *Connor's pissing me off right now, so we might be a little late, Monroe.*
> **CONNOR:** *Willa's b-ing a drama queen rn. We might b a little l8, dude.*
> **MASON:** *Hey, sexy. I'll be waiting in the lobby if you're not there yet.*

I chuckle at Mason's text as I put my phone in my back pocket. I run back downstairs to find Collin downing another beer.

"Can you stop drinking my dad's beers? He's gonna think it's me, *again*."

He sighs, standing up. "It's only a Utopia. These things are $70 a pack. Highly doubt your dad will care. Calm down."

Ignoring him, I put on my tuxedo blazer and look at my watch. It's 5 p.m. already. Shit.

"I'll meet you at the vineyard, bro. I gotta go."

He nods, and I run off. He usually locks up when I'm not home. That's how close we are.

I smile as I pull out of the driveway. Twenty-six. *Let's do this.*

"And we present to you the birthday boy!" the DJ shouts into the microphone, followed by a room full of cheers.

I stand and walk up to the front of the banquet hall, sitting in the birthday throne. The DJ puts a crown on my head.

"If anyone would like to make a toast to the birthday boy, make your way up front!"

A crowd of people suddenly rush up. I smile at the sight. I'm not a narcissist, but I love that there are people who actually have nice things to say about me. Even as a spoiled dude, I have friends who care.

I look around the room and admire the amount of people who were able to make it. Everyone...except my parents. My birthday party's almost over, and they couldn't even be bothered to show up. What happened to their plane landing? What happened to *'Don't worry, son, we promise we'll be there this time'*? Both lies, I guess.

I can't even focus on the fact that Collin's now at the microphone, motioning to me. Everyone in the crowd is smiling, but my attention on him is in and out.

"...and even though you said your sister's off limits..."

For fuck's sake, he's talking about my sister. I roll my eyes. He's had a thing for her for as long as I can remember. She couldn't make it tonight since she had a last-minute sorority event pop up, but it still makes me uncomfortable that he's bringing her up in a room full of people.

"...you're one hell of a dude, Monroe. Happy birthday, fuckhead!"

I roll my eyes, but everyone cheers as he hands the microphone back to the DJ. Next is Willa, and as she walks up to the front, I scan the crowd to see if maybe I missed my parents. But my gaze finds the little minx I met earlier.

Sienna.

My gaze zeroes in on the hot little number she's wearing. A little red bodycon dress. She's standing at the entrance of the banquet hall holding a clipboard. She's not looking at me, but she's writing stuff down as people walk in. *Meet my gaze, babe.*

"Will's been one of my good friends since the day we could walk..."

She finally turns toward the stage, and a jolt of heat shoots down to my crotch when I see her face. Shit. She's gorgeous. My eyes land on her bright lips. The color matches her dress very well. Her hair is in Hollywood-style curls.

I have to have my hands on her.

"What would we all do without you, Will? I don't know..."

She's still not looking at me, and my heart starts beating. I'm not taking my eyes off her until she meets my gaze.

"You're now twenty-six and on to do great things..."

She's still looking around the room and writing stuff down. What could she possibly be writing? Guest count? Updates on the event?

"Hopefully you'll find the girl of your dreams..."

And hopefully she'll find me, too.

But first I need her to look me in the eyes. My gaze is still on her. And the miracle finally happens. She finds me onstage, and my breath hitches. She looks me up and down and gives me a small smile. I wink at her, and she rolls her eyes. I'm still staring at her. Unfortunately for me, her eyes are back on the clipboard.

"Happy birthday, Will. May you continue to further the Monroe name!"

The loudest cheers tonight happen right then. Willa bows and hands the microphone back to the DJ.

"Thank you everyone for your words about the birthday boy! Now, if *said* birthday boy will get down and have a dance with a girl of his choice. Choose wisely because we're all watching," he jokes. I laugh, hopping down from the stage.

Any girl I choose? I could ask Mason to dance, since she can't stop drooling over me. We had a thing two years ago after flirting a bit in high school. But would that be a wise choice? Most likely not.

No one's even watching me anymore. They all head to the dance floor, finding partners. I look around the room for a friend or someone I know. Everyone has a dance partner. *Tough luck.*

Why are you kidding yourself?

Sighing, I search out the only girl I really want to see right now. She might think I'm a pain in the ass, but I'll do whatever I can to prove to her that I'm not. I walk up to her as she writes on her clipboard. As I get closer, I get a better look at her dress. *Fuck*, she's hot. Her rack peeks out from the top a bit, and her hair is beautiful.

"Don't *you* look like a sight for sore eyes tonight."

She jumps, meeting my gaze. She's frowning as she looks around the banquet hall. "Uh, Mr. Monroe. Can I help you?"

"First of all, you can stop calling me Mr. Monroe," I offer. She rolls her eyes and looks back down at her clipboard. "Come dance with me, Sienna."

Her eyes shoot back up to me. "What?"

"I want you to dance with me. You look gorgeous tonight, and I need an excuse to touch you."

She flinches. I might be coming off aggressive right now, but I'm very attracted to this girl.

"That's not appropriate," she croaks. I smile. I got to her. Taking the clipboard from her, I offer my hand to her.

"We're way past that. Come dance with me."

She looks down at my hand like it's a bomb about to detonate. She swallows and looks around the hall again. What's the problem? Does she think I'm punking her *again*?

She sighs, straightening her back. "Okay, Will. *One* dance," she retorts.

Smiling, I lean in to her. "We'll see about that," I whisper. She stiffens as I pull her to the dance floor.

3

SIENNA

I'm dancing with Will Monroe. I was *coerced* into dancing with Will Monroe. This has to be a prank. Otherwise, he's lost his mind. There's no way a guy like Will is into me. He's the heir to the one of the most popular wineries that happens to be in the already-exclusive Rose Valley, Kentucky. This doesn't feel like a legitimate situation.

Even as we're dancing, there are eyes on us. Nothing looks judgmental, but...it just feels odd.

"You're still stiff," he chuckles above me. The laugh makes me shiver. I need to get ahold of myself. Reactions like this are not healthy.

"You're still weird," I retort.

He pulls back, looking into my eyes. *God*, those piercing eyes.

"What's going on in that pretty little head of yours?" Those same eyes are still piercing into me. I swallow. His eyes scale down my body.

"I'm just confused about why you asked me to dance," I whisper. I look around, and only a few eyes are on us now.

"Because I wanted to." I look back up at him, and all I see is sincerity. There's something in his eyes that tell me there's nothing to worry about. There's a sense of security that makes me a bit uncomfortable. "You thought I was joking earlier. I think you're absolutely gorgeous."

"Will—"

"Go on a date with me."

My eyes widen, and my heart beats faster. "Will, I can't do that."

"Sure you can. Are you a coffee or ice cream girl? Dinner girl?"

An heir is asking me out. My head is reeling from the reality of this. "I'm a whatever-you-can-afford kind of girl."

He cocks an eyebrow, giving me a smirk. "That's a very dangerous thing to say. I'd take you to Italy if I wanted to."

For a moment, I think he's joking. But he's not. His gaze remains sincere.

"Will, I really can't go out with you."

"Why, Sienna? What's wrong?"

I swallow. "I've never gone out with a rich guy before." Let alone a rich guy whose family owns half of the small town of Rose Valley.

"It's just a date, Sienna," he whispers. "I'm not asking you to marry me." I laugh, and so does he. He's right. I'm overthinking. He's looking into my eyes. "So what do you say?"

I let out a sigh. "One date."

He narrows his eyes. "What if I like you?"

I cock an eyebrow. "Not possible."

"I'm thinking it's *very* possible."

I gulp at his hungry gaze. "We'll go on one date for now. I'm not a gold digger." Thank God my skin is darker because he can't tell my face is heating right now.

"I never thought you were one. If you were, who the fuck cares?"

I almost laugh. "You would date a gold digger?"

"If I liked her, sure. But it's rare that I'll ever come across one. Look at me. I'm fucking gorgeous."

I gape at him. Then I laugh. Loudly. I've never heard a guy say this. I open my eyes to find him smiling at me.

"I can't believe you said that," I continue, laughing.

He's staring at me in awe. Again. "*Gosh*, your laugh is gorgeous."

My laughing slows down. I can't tell if he's being genuine right now. I could tell before, but these are the words of a player.

"Thank you," I croak.

He's staring at me before clearing his throat. "How does Monday sound? Are you available?"

"I have a...meeting."

He cocks an eyebrow. *Please don't ask.* "Okay. Tuesday?"

"Tuesday's fine, Will." I just want this conversation to be over.

He gives me a big smile before hugging me again.

It's all fun and games up until Mr. Stevens appears at the entrance. My eyes widen as I watch him scan the crowd. Looking for me, no doubt. Crap. I pull away from Will.

"What's wrong?" I turn to look at Mr. Stevens again, and his gaze follows mine. He rolls his eyes. "Have to get back to work?"

I nod. "He's gonna be upset if he sees me fraternizing with the wealthy," I joke.

He frowns. "Let me talk to him."

My body tenses. "No, please don't do that. I'll just...talk to you later?"

His eyes dart across my face. Then he nods, letting me go. "I'll get your number later," he pledges, winking. Rolling my eyes, I walk back to the entrance.

Mr. Stevens' gaze lands on me. "Finally, Sienna. Where have you been?"

Letting a hunky heir feel me up on the dance floor. No biggie. "I was checking to make sure the tables were cleared for dessert."

He doesn't look convinced for a second. But he nods and motions for the food runners to come in with cheesecake. I look back to the dance floor. I'm expecting to find Will dancing with another girl, but his eyes remain on me. The intense gaze makes me swallow. He gives me a knowing smile before disappearing into the crowd.

In less than 24 hours, I met the son of William and Lily Monroe, and he asked me on a date. That doesn't just happen in life. I'm just a sommelier. A normal girl. What the hell does he want with *me*?

"Sienna, Sienna, Sienna. I thought you were smarter, girl."

I turn around to find Ashley looking at me, disappointed.

I frown, pulling her aside. "What?"

"I saw you talking to Will."

I cock an eyebrow, swallowing. "Yeah, we were just...hanging out."

She gives me a look of disbelief. "Don't get involved with him."

A wave of heat hits my cheeks as I turn back to the dance floor, seeing him dance with a few guys. "There's nothing going on. We were just being friendly," I lie. "What makes you think I would get involved with him?"

Her eyes narrow at me. "You were *dancing* with him. And the entire room witnessed it." *Of course they did.* "He asked you on a date, didn't he?"

I flinch. "Um...how did you know that?"

She gives me a small smile. "Let me guess: He asked you on a date, and you said yes. He's gonna take you out, maybe invite you back to his house—or if he's feeling gentlemanly, he'll drop you off at your place and ask to come up for a nightcap. Am I getting warm?"

I'm stuck gaping at her. "Um—"

"*Then* he'll convince you to get naked. You two have sex. And the next thing you know, you won't hear from him again."

I clear my throat. "It's just one date, Ashley. I told him that."

"One date is all he'll need, babe," she says, concern in her voice.

I let out an annoyed sigh. I look back at the floor, and he's still dancing with his friends, a few girls joining in. The sight stings...and I have no idea why. This isn't good. I shouldn't get attached to a guy like Will Monroe. Ashley's right. He even admits to being the ladies' man he is.

I turn back to Ashley. "Thanks for telling me," I sigh.

She gives me another small smile. "You're welcome. I might be stuck-up, but I watch out for my friends," she says, giving me a hug.

My heart swells. I'm suddenly looking at Ashley with new eyes. She didn't have to warn me about him. And yet, she's standing here, giving me a hug. She pulls back, her gaze landing on the dance floor. "If you want, I can go and tell him the date's off. Better me than you."

I laugh, following her gaze. "Sure. I need to look at inventory in the back anyway." And I don't need to deal with a confrontational Will right now.

She nods and walks in the direction of the group of dancing bodies. Sighing, I rearrange the dessert plates on the buffet table and continue writing down wine inventory. I've yet to finish taking down what wines we need.

I walk out of the banquet hall and head to the back. I need to distract myself with work. Staying up-to-date on wine inventory should be my priority right now. The summer season will be here soon, and we're not going to be any good if we're low on the good stuff.

I'm counting the cabernet sauvignon bottles we have when the door to the backroom opens. I let out a sigh of relief. The talk with Will went well.

"Ashley, thank you so—Oh, what are *you* doing back here?"

Will's angry face pops up in my line of view. He's standing at the door, staring at me. I swallow at the fiery glare.

"I knew you'd be back here. The better question is, what are *you* doing back here?"

I cock an eyebrow at him. "Um, I'm working."

Which he won't allow to happen, it seems. He inches toward me, and I back into the shelf. He stops about a foot from me, still angry.

"You're a smart girl," he starts.

I frown. "*Some* might agree with you."

"I'm not in the mood to play games with you right now," he snarls.

"Look at that, something we can agree on," I deadpan. "I'm trying to get some work done so I'm not behind."

He pulls the clipboard from me and throws it on the shelf, making me flinch. "Work can wait," he whispers. His smoldering gaze practically melts my panties.

I swallow as he puts his hands on the shelf behind me.

"Will—"

"I asked you on a date. We agreed on Tuesday. I told you I find you *excruciatingly* hot. I even asked you to dance. Your dress has me rock hard," he states plainly. I flinch at the last part. His eyes go down to my boobs peeking out from the neckline.

"Four of those are true," I croak.

"Four?"

"I doubt my dress has that effect on you."

He gives me a mischievous smile. "Are you asking to find out?" I go to get around him, but he refuses to move. "Answer the question, babe," he growls. I have no idea what the hell is going on right now.

"Will—"

"Five out of five are true. Yes or no?"

"Judging by your intense glare, I'm guessing yes," I retort. My brain is mush right now. I can't focus when he's only inches away from my face.

"So if five out of five are true, why the fuck did Ashley just tell me you want to cancel our date?"

I flinch. Shit. This is definitely about me. I gulp and tread lightly. "Because you have a pattern, Monroe boy," I retort, trying to stand my ground. And failing.

"Excuse me? Come again?"

I gulp, straightening my shoulders. "She told me about the little *plans* you have for girls you take on 'dates.' Are you *that* horny?"

He flinches. "What the hell are you talking about? Plans?"

"You ask girls out, have sex with them, and then never call them again. She told me all about it."

For a second, he just stares at me. I hold my breath, wondering what he's going to do next. Why is he so silent?

Excruciating seconds go by before he laughs.

He fucking laughs in my face.

"Sienna..." he says, his laughter keeping him from talking.

"What's so funny?"

His laughing slows down. "You're taking advice from Ashley Westbrook. The girl who I never *took* on a *date*," he emphasizes.

I'm left puzzled. "Wait, what?"

He lets out another laugh that turns into an amused grin. "Ashley and I never went on a *date*, babe. We ran into each other at a bar back in college, and she brought me back to her place. Yes, we had sex. But that's all it was. *Sex.* She even said she wanted a one-night stand, so I took her at her word."

Again, I'm left puzzled. And mildly annoyed. "I-I'm confused."

"So am I," he says, chuckling.

"So...you and Ashley *never* dated?"

"Ashley Westbrook made it clear she didn't want a relationship with anybody. We talked about her misadventures in college, only running into guys who wanted to date her. But she wasn't looking for that. So she told me she wanted a no-stress, no-pressure night of fun. That's what I gave her."

I let out a groan, lying against the shelf of wine. "Why would she lie to me, then?"

He lets out a sigh. "Maybe she wanted to date me," he jokes. "I don't know."

"So she would ruin any chance of me dating you? That's silly."

I look up, finding him smiling at me. "You wanna date me?"

I flinch, silently cursing myself for not choosing my words carefully. "That's not what I said."

A glimmer shines in his eyes. "Yes, you did. You like me," he says.

"I don't know you."

He cocks an eyebrow. "You'd know me a lot better if you'd go out with me Tuesday."

I roll my eyes. "I don't need to know you any better to figure out you're a ladies' man. Maybe Ashley misled me, but I know we'd never work out."

He flinches again with a hurtful expression. "Why would you think that?"

"Something tells me you're a tits guy—"

"I am," he says, shrugging.

I frown. He doesn't get it. "We're already incompatible in that regard."

He's gaping at me. "I'm so lost," he says, shaking his head.

"You were staring at Ashley's boobs," I deadpan.

Confusion etches his face. "Her boobs are fucking huge. What do you expect? And..." He clears his throat. "You're forgetting that I've seen her boobs before, so of course my eyes immediately go to them."

I gape at his candor. "And my boobs aren't huge at all."

"Your boobs are still hot as fuck, sweetheart. Perfect, actually. Wait, why the hell are we talking about boobs?"

He shouldn't be in here. He's arguing with me when he needs to be in the banquet hall, celebrating his birthday. Not questioning me about why we wouldn't work.

I clear my throat. "My point is, I don't have your ideal body type or appearance in general. I can't go on a date with you, and you know that. It would be a waste of both our time." I can't believe I have to spell this out for him.

His eyes keep wavering between my eyes and my lips. "Stop writing me off. I've only known you a day, and it's already pissing me off."

"I'm just in touch with reality," I retort.

Anger flashes in his eyes. "Be careful what you say to me, babe."

"I'm not afraid of you." I don't know where this newfound challenging came from. I usually don't argue with guys about shit like this, but he's trying his luck.

"We're going on a date."

I flinch. "No, we're not."

He cocks an eyebrow. "You already said yes. So I'm taking you out."

"No the fuck you're not," I snarl. "We're not going on a date. I don't date players. And you, sir, are one."

I move to get around him, but his hands land on my hips. "I don't think you want to play this game with me," he warns.

"Are you threatening me?"

"When I tell you I'm gonna be inside you in the next five minutes if you don't stop backtalking me, honey, that's a fucking promise."

I flinch, and my core literally lights on fire. I gulp as his hands trail up and down my waist. "Your empty threats mean nothing to me," I whisper.

He smiles at me again and leans down, only a hair away from my lips. Shit.

"Keep backtalking me. I have time. This is my birthday party, but I will spend the entire night in this back room with you if I need to."

"You're crazy."

"Only for you."

Before I can say anything, his lips are on mine. His tongue trails along my lips, and I let out a moan. He growls, picking me up, my legs automatically wrapping around him as he slams me against the shelves. His hands squeeze my waist as our kiss intensifies, turning into a hungry one. I suck his tongue in, and he groans.

His hands reach my ass, squeezing each globe. He pulls away and starts trailing kisses down my neck. He bites me, and I squeeze his shoulders.

"We can't do this," I whisper, and his nibbling intensifies. His hands reach my ass again, squeezing harder.

"You're so fucking hot, Sienna." He kisses me again, biting my lip.

"So are you," I moan against his lips.

"I know."

I smile at his cockiness. His free hand reaches between us inside my panties. It cups my center, and I gasp at the sensation.

"Oh fuck, you're soaked, baby," he pants. He circles me, and I throw my head back against the shelf, not caring whether or not the bottles drop to the floor.

"I can't believe you're touching me right now," I breathe out.

"You feel phenomenal. Are you gonna let me inside?"

I shiver at the question. "No," I moan as he pinches my center. *God*, those fingers. Those hard, callused fingers.

"Please, baby," he begs.

"You have to earn it."

He groans again, pulling back and looking into my eyes. His frantic eyes dart across my face. "How do I earn it? Oh honey, please tell me how I can make the cut. You're so primed for me."

His words are going to send me over the edge. I just ignore his question and undulate against his fingers. "Are you a good boy?" He nods his head vigorously, and I smile. "Then you'll make the cut."

His forehead falls against mine as he continues rubbing me. "I'm not being a good boy right now?" He sounds so adorable.

"Good boys don't finger girls they don't know," I tease.

He kisses me and looks back into my eyes. "You let me kiss you, baby. It was game over after that," he jokes.

His smile makes me throw my head back again. *Fuck*, these fingers feel so good.

"I didn't let you do anything. You did it of your own volition."

"And you kissed me back."

"I don't reject kisses," I admit. Especially not from painfully hot guys.

"You'll be rejecting other guys' kisses now."

I smile at that. "Possessive, are we?"

He nods his head again, and his hand intensifies, making me whimper. "Fuck yes," he admits. "I know what your lips taste like now. They're mine," he growls, kissing me again, my arms instinctively going around his neck.

Suddenly, he hits a pivotal spot, and I mewl. "Oh fuck, do *that* again," I moan. He hits the same spot, and I cry out. If his hands have this superpower, I can only imagine what his...

"I love that sound," he growls. He hits the same spot, and I undulate faster. "Come on, baby. Let go. I want to watch you." I nod as I continue moving against him. "Talk to me. What do you need to get off? *God*, you're so beautiful right now."

"Just keep talking. Your voice is so hot."

He chuckles, kissing my nose. "I want to be inside you so fucking bad, you have no idea," he pants. "Fuck," he whispers, yanking the top of my dress down, exposing my boobs. His mouth latches on to my nipple, and I hold his head there.

"*God*, please don't stop," I whine.

He flicks his tongue over the tip, and his free hand pinches my other nipple, making me squirm. "When I come back here, I need you like this all the time."

"Like what?" I'm not even comprehending what he's saying anymore.

"Braless. Every fucking day. I'll come up here just to suck on these babies."

I moan again and throw my head back. His hand is still rubbing me, and his other hand is tweaking my nipple. "Will," I moan. "I'm so close."

He bites down on my nipple, lapping it with his tongue. I watch him, and it's too much. He latches his mouth around my nipple again and stays there, his hand rubbing my center over and over. His hand speeds up, and I rock against his hand faster.

"Come on, baby. Let me see you," he pleads. "We won't leave this room until you let go on my hand." I throw my head back, his words sending me over the edge.

It's a moment in time until I call out his name, and I see fireworks. My hips stop rocking, and I feel weak. My eyes are closed. My body is floating, and my breathing slows. I open my eyes to find him smiling down at me. It's not a smug smile, either. There's a new appreciation in his eyes. Something... vulnerable.

"You back with me?" He kisses my forehead as he palms my boob.

I give a weak nod, and he laughs. "That was...*amazing*," I swoon.

He chuckles again, the sound rumbling through me. "You know what this means, Sienna," he states. I frown, looking up at him. "We're going on that date."

"Actually, my post-nut clarity says I don't have to keep seeing you," I joke.

He growls, squeezing my thigh. "Sienna, I'm serious. I want to see you. I felt you on my *fingers*, doll."

I shiver again. "Will, I've only known you for a *day*. You don't think things are moving too fast?" Surely he can see the craziness in this.

"I don't think things are moving fast *enough*," he admits. I cock an eyebrow at him. "I like you, Sienna. A lot. Like 'I'm ready to make you *mine*' a lot. But you're hesitant. And I get it. This wasn't just a one-time thing, though. This only solidifies that I'm not going anywhere."

I shake my head at his words. He can't be serious right now.

"Will, you barely know me," I emphasize.

He shrugs. "I don't. But I also know that I like you. Your personality turns me on, and so does this centerfold body," he growls, making me swallow.

He's still holding me against the shelf. I clear my throat, signaling for him to put me down. He sighs and finally lets up. He tweaks my nipple again, making me shiver. I pull back to fix myself up, adjusting my dress.

He's looking at me as I comb my fingers through my hair.

"What?"

"You know this isn't over by a long shot, right?" I narrow my eyes at him. His eyes are pleading. I've never seen a guy look at me like this before.

I sigh, nodding my defeat. "Yes, Will. I know."

4

WILL

I still smell her on my fingers. It's the next day, and I refuse to wash my hands. She's the most beautiful girl I've ever seen, and getting her to let go like that has me attached. The fact that she *let* me is what's mind-boggling to me. She gave me the impression she was so hard-up, but that little minx can turn you on your head.

I'm packing clothes for my weekend trip to Miami when my phone beeps a text:

COLLIN: *Dude, are you ready to go or wut?*

I roll my eyes at Collin's lame-ass text. I was hoping it was Sienna, but the girl hasn't texted me at all since I gave her my number. It makes me sadder than I'd like to admit.

"William! Come downstairs for a second!" my mom calls.

I roll my eyes. I'm really not in the mood to talk to either one of them right now. They planned a birthday party and didn't even *show up* for the damn thing. Why would I need to talk to them right now?

Just go downstairs, you spoiled brat.

I jog downstairs and see my parents sitting down, concern etching their faces.

I frown. "Who died?"

They both flinch as they watch me walk up.

"Nobody died, honey. We just...come sit," my mom says, sighing.

Annoyed, I walk in and sit down. "Then what's wrong?"

They share a look before looking back to me. "I know this is your birthday weekend, and you wanted to celebrate more in Miami," my mom starts. I quirk an eyebrow. "But—"

"You can't go this weekend, son. I'm sorry," my dad says.

I'm gaping at them. Is this a fucking joke? "And why not?"

"Your sister is coming home tonight." I cock an eyebrow. I wait for them to continue. Dad clears his throat. "We don't trust her to be here alone. She got suspended from school."

I flinch. "Suspended? For what?" She had a sorority event last night. What could she have possibly done?

"She was caught doing...*unruly* things to a man at the event last night."

I close my eyes, trying not to laugh. God only knows what *that* means.

"I don't mean to make this weird, but how is doing...'*unruly*' things to a man on a college campus grounds for suspension?" If that's the case, literally everyone on campus would be suspended.

Mom cocks an eyebrow at me. "It was on a professor," she deadpans. "And he's been fired." I flinch again. *Yep. That'll do it.*

Sighing, I run a hand through my hair. "So what then? I'm supposed to babysit her this week? You guys are going out of town again or something?" No fucking surprise there.

"We are, but...we have to go out of town much longer this time."

I close my eyes. Of course they do. "For how long?"

"For about eight weeks." I flinch yet again. What the hell do they need to go out of town that long for? "There are investors looking to expand Monroe Vineyards internationally. So we're going to be in Europe for eight weeks, meeting with them."

I let out a resigned sigh. No matter how mad I am at my parents, Monroe Vineyards has been pretty successful. They have a vineyard in Sophia, Idaho and one in Napa Valley. If they're able to expand it to Europe, that'd be pretty awesome.

"Well, I can't be upset at that. So how long is Taylor gonna be home?"

They both sigh. "She shouldn't be home that long. She said she wants to transfer to Vanderbilt, but we don't trust her to be on a campus right now. She'll be home, working the family vineyard. So will you."

What the fuck? "Excuse me? What the hell does *that* mean?"

"It means you will be helping out during our most crucial season. This is the busiest time for our winery. Surely you didn't think you'd be sitting home and doing nothing."

Not *nothing*, but I don't want to work at the winery. What the fuck do I need to do *that* for?

"I don't even know the first thing about wine."

It's embarrassing to admit. I'm a golf guy. When I'm not traveling or doing business retreats with my parents, I golf.

"Then we will ask Mr. Stevens to have one of the sommeliers work with you on your knowledge in wine."

I cock an eyebrow at that. One of the sommeliers, eh? I know of one. The same one I had the pleasure of touching last night.

"No need. I know one of the sommeliers at the vineyard, actually."

My dad cocks an eyebrow. "Oh you do? Then that's perfect. You'll work with them this summer and immerse yourself in the culture. Plus, it'd be better to have two Monroes be up close and personal with our clients."

I don't care to consider what my dad is saying. Spending the entire season with Sienna? That sounds like heaven on earth.

"We leave later today, son. If you could go up there today and talk to Mr. Stevens about hours, then that'd be great."

Dad gets up when his phone rings, and I'm left with my mom giving me a small smile. "How are you holding up, William? How was your birthday?" I give her a pointed look, and she flinches. "I know, sweetie. We couldn't make it last night, and we're sorry. Our flight got delayed in California. You know we would've been there."

I'm tempted to roll my eyes, but this is my mom. She's a delicate flower. And I hate to make her feel bad. I just wish they were there. "I know, Mom. I had a good night, regardless."

I had a *great* night. I clear my throat when Sienna's moans play in my head.

"That's good, son. Your father and I will probably leave in the next hour or so. Talk to you soon?"

I nod, and she kisses me on the cheek before disappearing upstairs.

I guess I'm heading back to the vineyard today. I'm not sure when Taylor gets back into town, but I'm going back up to the vineyard to see my girl.

It's Sunday afternoon, and the winery isn't as busy as it was yesterday. Groups of young adults line the counter, ordering flights of wine. There are a few children running around outside, and there's live music playing.

I make my way up to the main area where I met Sienna. Hopefully, she's there. If Mr. Stevens is there, that'd kill two birds with one stone.

I open the door to the main area, and it's like the entire room's eyes are on me. Literally. I'm suddenly rushed at by a bunch of people.

"Oh my gosh, it's a Monroe! Dude, when does the next wave of Open Cupid Pinot Noir come in?"

"My sister *loves* the seasonal Apple Cider Riesling that you guys have. Is it in yet?"

"You're so hot! Will you go out with me?"

I laugh at the last question. I give everyone a nod and walk around to get to the desk. I walk up, and Sienna's eyes widen when she sees me. Fuck yes, she's here.

"Hey, cutie."

She looks around nervously. "Will, what are you doing here?"

"I had to make a surprise trip up here. Is Mr. Stevens around?"

She narrows her eyes before picking up the phone and calling him. I look around the lobby and observe the reserve wines that line the shelves. I have so much to learn this summer.

I look back to Sienna, and she's staring at me. "He'll be down in a minute." She looks down at her notebook, but I'm still hovering above her. She looks back up at me. "Can I help you with anything else?"

"What's your name?"

She rolls her eyes, and I laugh. "You're so annoying," she chuckles.

I reach for her hand, and she just looks at it. "Let's go on a walk," I offer.

She frowns at me. "Mr. Stevens said he'll be down in a minute."

"It'll just be for a few minutes. Besides, isn't it your lunch break?"

She shrugs. "I don't really take lunch breaks," she mutters.

I cock an eyebrow. "Let's change that." I walk behind the desk and find the *At Lunch* sign.

She frowns at me. "Will—"

"It's just a walk, babe. It doesn't have to be longer than you want it to be."

She bites her lip again, and I'm tempted to kiss those lips.

"Only for a few minutes."

I nod and reach for her hand again. She sighs, taking my hand, and I relax at the warmth.

When we walk toward the lobby door, I hear a door shut behind us and find Ashley's gaze on us. Her eyes widen at Sienna's hand in mine. Sienna quickly lets go, but I grab it back. It's time we made some things clear.

"Ashley, it's actually good you're here. I wanted to talk to you. Sienna and I are kind of a thing now. I'm sorry if I hurt your feelings back in college, but I think it's shady that you lied to her about me taking you on a *date* and then leading you on."

She narrows her eyes at me, her cheeks turning red. "We had drinks at a bar, Will. That's called a date to most people."

"We ran into each other *at* the bar," I deadpan.

But she just waves it off. "Oh, semantics. I just didn't want Sienna to go through what I went through with you. That's all."

My eyes are bulging out of my head. "You told me you just wanted casual sex. Am I missing something here?"

"You didn't give it a chance for it to be something more! I still wanted to hang out, Will."

"Guys, can we not do this? People are staring." Sienna nudges my side.

I let out a breath, my shoulders relaxing. "This is stupid." Ashley flinches. "Look, I'm sorry again if I hurt your feelings. But we have to move on. Can we do that?"

She grinds her teeth, still glaring at me. Her eyes waver between me and Sienna. "Sure," she growls. "But give me time. I...need to get used to seeing you two together."

Sienna tenses at my side. "What? No, we're not tog—"

"Thank you, Ashley."

And with that, we're walking outside. I don't have the mental capacity to argue with her right now. She can deny our chemistry all she wants. I'm not giving up on her just yet.

"Do you think we should cool it with her around?"

"Do you *want* to cool it with her around?"

She's biting the corner of her mouth. "I...just don't wanna start drama. Especially if you guys were a thing, you know?"

"We weren't a thing. I don't know how we got here, but I promise you, it was just one night. Literally. We didn't even talk or text *before* that night. We knew of each other because *everyone* knew each other at the University of Louisville."

She looks uncertain. "I just don't—"

She yelps when I pull her against me. We're in front of a tree now, my arms caging her in. She's looking up at me with wide eyes. Her outfit's cute today. She's wearing a slightly opened plaid shirt, jean shorts, and brown boots. A typical Kentucky girl.

"Stop fighting me," I tell her. "Ashley and I were never a thing. I promise."

She peers up at me, nervous. Then she gives me a small smile, warming my heart.

"Okay, Will."

I let out a sigh of relief. Thank God we got that out of the way. Now we can move onto more pressing matters.

"I had a good time last night," I whisper.

Her smile grows bigger as she wraps her arms around my waist. "I hate to say it, but I actually did too."

I laugh at her candor. "Why do you hate to say it?" I ask, tucking a strand of hair behind her ear.

"I try not to fraternize with the enemy," she jokes. If her voice didn't crack, I'd think she were kidding.

"I'm hardly the enemy, Sienna. Stick around a few more months. You'll like me more than you want to admit," I say, kissing her. She pulls me closer as I nibble on her neck. She smells so fucking good.

"Mr. Stevens is coming this way." She stiffens in my arms. But I don't pull back. I move my hand to the inside of her camisole. I groan, feeling her bra underneath. *Lace.*

"This bra is hot as fuck. But I thought I told you to go braless when I come here."

"Will, Mr. Stevens—"

"Can wait a few seconds. Answer my question."

"You didn't ask a question." God, her personality. I tweak her nipple, and she falters in my hands. "Fine. I didn't know you were coming here today."

I smile against her neck and kiss it. "You're forgiven. Besides, I'm pretty good with bras anyway." I pull away, and she's giving me a confused look.

"What does that—"

"William! What are you doing here?"

I turn to find Mr. Stevens at my side. He looks bewildered at what he's seeing.

"My parents wanted me to speak with you," I say, moving away from Sienna.

He folds his arms across his chest. "What about? Is everything okay with the vineyard?"

"Everything's fine, sir. They're going out of town, and my sister's coming back home. When they're gone, they want me and Taylor to work the vineyard this summer."

His eyes widen. "What?"

"Will?" Sienna's breathless voice sounds behind me. I turn to her, and she looks heartbroken. I frown.

"What do you mean 'work the vineyard'?"

Sighing, I put my hands in my pockets. "They want us to help out. Dad thinks it'll be good for business if there are two Monroes managing it and helping out."

He gives me a look of understanding. "That makes sense. So how do *I* fit into the picture?"

"Well, we need to get our hours worked out. Taylor will be back home, so she has free time. You know I golf, so I won't be around as much. But I'll try my best to help out."

"Yes, sir. Anything we can do, you let me know."

I smile. "Great. Taylor gets in later, so I'll meet you then." He nods and walks off. I turn to Sienna, and she still has the same look on her face as before. "What's wrong?"

She clears her throat and walks away. "I have to get back to work," she mutters. What the fuck?

"Hold on. What happened here?"

"Nothing, it's just...*this*"—she motions between us—"can't happen. I'm sorry." She walks back up the hill to the main area.

I run to her side, stopping her. "Wait a second, did I do something?"

She crosses her arms. "What was your plan in talking to me? Was this just your way of banging the help? You sleep with me, and then you dump me when you get ahead at the vineyard?"

I flinch. "Whoa, let's take a step back here. First of all, I don't need to sleep with you to get ahead, babe. My family owns this vineyard," I argue, making her flinch. It sounds bad, but it's the truth. "Second of all, I don't see you as the help. I don't even see you as a girl I want to bang. I just see *you*."

She has tears building in her eyes, and it confuses the fuck out of me.

"I let you finger me," she mutters. I hate the wave of heat that hits my cheeks.

"And it was the best experience I've ever had with a girl," I whisper. She looks up at me. "Sienna, I really like you. I don't know why I have these strong feelings for you, but I don't wanna let this go."

She looks uncertain before sighing. "Can you promise to maybe *not* kidnap me from my desk again?"

I snort before saying, "No."

"Will—"

"I don't make promises I can't keep. If you want no PDA at work, I can promise that. It'll be hard." This makes her chuckle. "But I can promise it. No kidnapping you on breaks? I can't promise that, honey."

She gives me a small smile before nodding. "This is so weird," she whispers.

I frown at her. "What's weird?"

"I don't date."

"What do you mean?"

She starts to speak but stops herself. "Nothing. Look, I have to go back to work."

"Wait, what time can I pick you up on Tuesday?"

She turns around with a confused look on her face. "Pick me up? Why would you do that?"

"Answer the question, babe," I say, smiling.

She returns the smile, rolling her eyes. "Six is fine, Will."

I give her another smile, and she walks off, giving me a perfect view of her pert ass.

5

SIENNA

Will Monroe is working his family's vineyard this summer, and there's not a damn thing I can do about it. I won't be able to avoid him or brush off his advances.

You don't do a great job of that anyway, Sienna.

I groan at the memory of what we did two nights ago. I let the bastard touch me. And not only did he touch me; he got me off. And that's not a normal thing that happens to me.

Sienna Durham does not let guys out of her league touch her.

And yet she did.

The memory refuses to leave my brain. Even now as I'm sitting in my therapist's office. It really should make its way out of my head. Because now I'm squeezing my legs together as she checks in on me.

"How are you holding up, Sienna?" my therapist asks as she writes in her notepad.

As best I can, I want to say. But that's not the answer she's looking for. Mostly because it's not an accurate one. I've had the same therapist for ten years, and she can read me better than anyone. *I* wouldn't believe I'm okay, and neither would she.

"I'm doing how I always am, Ms. Spencer," I relent.

She gives me a reassuring smile before crossing her legs. "How's the winery job going? Is it helping you any?"

"I've asked for more hours, and I've gotten them. So there's that."

She gives me an easy smile. "That's not what I'm asking you, dear."

I let out a shaky breath before saying, "We got more merlot in. Merlot's my favorite wine, you know," I laugh. "Cherry Orchards in particular is my favorite. It's made with notes of vanilla. Vanilla in general is supposed to calm you, and that's exactly what it does for me—"

"Sienna," she stops me. *"That's not what I'm asking, honey."*

I let out another shaky breath. "Then what are you asking?"

"Is working at Monroe helping you any?" When I don't answer, she asks another daunting question. "Have you been taking your anxiety medication?"

I look down at my thumbs, twiddling them. "I've been on and off with it," I mumble.

Her disapproving sigh makes me look up. "So the winery's not helping you then."

I roll my eyes. "Sure it is. Wine works better for me than my medication. My nightmares have stopped."

For the most part. I still have dreams about my mom, but ever since I've been working at Monroe, it's slowed down a lot.

"But you weren't prescribed wine."

"I know that, Ms. Spencer," I deadpan.

There's a moment where she just looks at me. It makes my skin crawl. She crosses her legs in wonderment. "Tell me more about the winery. I understand it's like a club for the wealthy?"

"You could say that. I've actually met the owner's son."

"Really?" she asks in noticeable awe. "Isn't Monroe a very promising winery?"

"Yeah, I've heard rumors about there being an expansion internationally. I'm not sure how true that is, though."

Mr. Stevens was talking to William Monroe V a few weeks ago about European investors—and even Australian investors—being interested in expanding Monroe.

"Well, that's pretty cool. How's the son? Is he nice?"

I freeze at the question. He's more than nice.

Nice enough to get you off in an inventory room.

I shake my head of that nonsense. I shouldn't be sitting here, thinking about how talented Will's fingers are.

"He's...fine. Um, I don't know, he sort of asked me on a date," I mumble.

Her eyebrows shoot up to the sky. "*Really*?? Well, that's great, Sienna! Are you going?"

I close my eyes at the question. "I don't know yet. It's kind of... weird."

"Why is it weird?"

"We just don't seem like we would mesh well," I croak.

She gives me an amused smile. "If he asked you out, he probably thinks otherwise."

"No, it just means he wants to put my job in jeopardy." She gives me a confused look. "I'm a sommelier at Monroe. His family *owns* Monroe. And within thirty-plus years, so will he. I don't like wasting my time."

And I don't want to. I go on dates with guys I know I'll have a chance with.

"You're definitely overthinking this. I think you should go. It might be good for you," she says way too cheerfully.

"Good for me how?"

She gives me a pointed look. "Ever since you started taking care of your dad, you've been a recluse. I understand you want to focus on caring for him, but you're *twenty-three*, dear. There's nothing wrong with going on *one* date." Is she my therapist or my dating coach?

"My dad requires my attention," I retort.

It's been two years since he was diagnosed with Parkinson's disease. My mom is gone, and there's no one to take care of him. I can't afford a nursing home since all of my money goes to rent and paying Dad's medical bills.

"I understand. But take advantage of your youth, Sienna."

I flinch. "What does *that* mean?"

"I just mean, it's okay to have a social life—"

"I know that," I retort.

She gives me a sad smile. "Your mom would want this," she whispers. The mention of my mom makes my breath hitch. I try not to think about her. Her bloodied smile was the last thing I saw before that Tahoe hit us. We were in a red sedan. The memory is still vivid in my mind. "Sienna?"

I snap out of it, clearing my throat. "You're right," I croak. Maybe I need this. Thinking about my mom is a recipe for disaster. The anxiety medication has done zilch for me. Though...as I think about her, my breathing nearly falters.

"You were thinking about your mom again."

I nod. "Yeah, I just...get pensive whenever she comes to mind," I mumble.

Her sad smile returns. "I know," she whispers. "Get back on your meds, dear. I understand you work at a winery, but you need to take a break from drinking. Alcohol and anxiety medication do not mix."

I've heard this mantra before, and I don't need to hear it again.

"I *know*, Ms. Spencer."

She tilts her head at me before writing down more notes. I've learned to hate that notepad. I don't take too kindly to people judging me, and that's the impression I'm getting from Ms. Spencer. Today, more so than ever. I clear my throat and wait for whatever intrusive question she's going to ask me next.

Before I know it, my session for the day is over, and I'm on my way back to Louisville. The drive is about thirty minutes, and I take in the scenery on my way. The water is beautiful and expansive, and the ranches are to die for. I smile as I pass Monroe Vineyards. It sits atop a hill, and I admire the string lights that line the pavilion in the distance. There's something comforting about the view. It's peaceful. It's festive in a way. It's my safe place.

It's my home.

The home I know.

The home I can't wait to move up in.

The great thing about the vineyard is that it looks great on your resume. If I can become a winemaker or even *assistant* winemaker, that would open up so many doors for me at higher vineyards. Working at a major vineyard in Europe is one of my big goals after looking in Napa Valley. The wine industry in the romance-speaking countries is booming and has been for a while now. *What I would give to work at a vineyard in Greece...*

My fantasies are cut short when I turn off the engine to my Mini Cooper. I grab my bag and walk the street to my building.

Jeez, it's so fucking hot.

It's not summer yet, but the weather is so telling. The walk to my apartment is brutal up until I open the door to the lobby. I wave to our concierge, and I'm on my way up to my loft.

When I open the door, I find my dad turning on the stove with a bowl of vegetables next to him. The sight freaks me out to the point where I throw my purse down, shut the door, and rush over to him.

"Dad! What are you doing? You shouldn't be cooking."

He gives me a bored look. "Oh stop it, Enna. You harp like my grandmother."

Rolling my eyes, I take the spatula from him. "Dad, stop it. I'll cook dinner, okay?"

He waves me off and stumbles as I walk him to the couch in the living room. I'm not risking him getting hurt in the kitchen. His tremors have slowed down a bit from this morning, which is good. But I still don't trust him with things like cooking or driving.

"You can't keep babying me, honey. I can take care of myself."

He'd like to think so. I'm not even letting him go to the bathroom by himself. The stubborn man won't let me get him a cane or wheelchair, so I lead him around whenever I can.

"If you'd stop being so stubborn, I'd loosen the leash a little bit."

He narrows his eyes at me. "You won't even let me drive."

"You're right. Because you're stubborn."

"Stubborn how?! My doctor has said *many* times that people with my condition can and *do* drive safely even *after* diagnosis."

I nod as if I'm hearing him out. But I'm not listening to his nonsense. "Yes, Dad. But until you can prove to me that you can take care of yourself, I will be nagging you."

He gives me a mean glare. "I can't prove it if I'm not given the opportunity, hun."

I'm already in the kitchen, chopping up the vegetables.

"You slipped in the shower, and I had to take you to the hospital last week. You've yet to prove to me you can take care of yourself."

He's silent for a few minutes, and it almost worries me. I turn around, and he's still glaring at me. I smile at him. He can be annoyed with me and complain all he wants. Until I can afford a caretaker for him, I *will* be a pain in his ass.

"So how was your day? Were you approved for disability yet?"

Ever since he'd been diagnosed, it's been hard getting him approved for disability insurance. Dad was laid off from his trucking job shortly before he was diagnosed due to cost reduction.

It was the weirdest time when I was seventeen. He could barely pay for college, and we had to scrape from both of our savings just to get by. Luckily, he was able to get unemployment benefits, but once he sort of lost his sense of smell and we got him diagnosed, we wanted to get him disability. And...it's been difficult. With his early symptoms, he got denied. Even now, at Stage 3 Parkinson's, they're giving him a hard time.

"I haven't gotten any notification yet," he mumbles, turning on the TV.

I let out a sigh, pushing the vegetables into the pan. "I'm sorry, Dad."

"It's okay, honey. I've been handling myself well up until this point. I can go longer."

The words make me frown. "Dad—"

"And I've already been talking to a realtor for you," he interrupts, making me freeze.

"What do you mean?"

He lets out a sigh and turns the volume down. "Honey, you're twenty-three. You work a good job, and you're on your way to do what you've always wanted to do," he whispers.

"What are you saying?"

He lets out a shaky breath. "There's a nice one-bedroom apartment on Apple Street, and your tour is at 1 p.m. tomorrow."

My eyebrows shoot up. "What? Dad, you can't just do things like that without asking."

"Just like you hold my hand everywhere without asking?"

I glare at him. "That's not the same thing."

"Sure it is," he retorts. "Look, I know you feel it's your responsibility to take care of me after...you know," he croaks.

My throat suddenly feels tight. "Dad..." I whisper.

"You have to go your own way, hun. Miranda isn't coming back. I wish she was." He has a troubled expression on his face. "But she's not. And it's not your fault, doll."

"I know, Dad."

Tears are already brimming in his eyes, and it breaks my heart to see. I swallow past the lump in my throat and continue cooking the vegetable stew.

"Which means you have to live your life."

I shake my head at the thought. I can't leave my dad alone. I wouldn't forgive myself if I left him. He doesn't have Mom. I'm all he has left.

"Can we talk about this another time?"

He gives me a sad smile before nodding. "Sure, honey. But your tour is still 1 p.m. tomorrow. The pictures look beautiful. Let me know how it goes."

I want to argue with him, but it's no use. He's stubborn. That's how I got the way I am. But I hate the thought of leaving. For over ten years, Dad's been my crutch, my safe place.

Then came Monroe Vineyards. The place that became my second therapy. I've had two channels for that. Once I leave my dad, there will just be Monroe. And how long will that remain my home? It's hard to tell.

Get out of your head, Sienna.

Clearing my throat, I ignore my dad's remark and continue with dinner. I can argue with him after the tour. If I hate it, I can always tell him. But there's a little voice in my head that's telling me...this just might be what I need.

6

WILL

"**Y**our rank has been pretty good lately, William. Are you sure you don't want to compete?"

I'm putting my club back into my golf bag when Coach asks that. I'm absolutely certain I don't want to go professional. Or rather, it's not *smart* if I go professional right now. If I have to help out at the vineyard this summer, I'm not going to have enough time to be on the course in my family's country club. Which just fucking sucks.

"I'm not sure I'm open to the idea right now. Mom and Dad want Taylor and me to work at the vineyard."

He gives me a look of understanding. "That makes sense. I just think it'd be silly to waste your talent. Singleton Athletics has been trying to get you to go professional for the past two years."

I roll my eyes. "If they can offer me more than a sponsorship, then I'd be open to the idea. But it's not something I can pursue right now."

Imagine if I'd go professional. I fucking love the sport, but I'm not sure if I'm great enough to compete with the Bryson DeChambeaus or Brooks Koepkas of the world. I have a hefty swing, but if I ever wanted to compete, I need to practice a lot. And I can't do that this summer.

"Look, son. You have an indescribable talent. I've been training you since you were a kid, and I think you're ready."

"Coach—"

"*But*," he emphasizes, cutting me off, "I understand your dilem-

43

ma. If you ever change your mind, the Harvey Invitational is in August, and I can sign you up."

"The Harvey Invitational?" That's one of the biggest golf tournaments on the West Coast. The purse is usually lower than the bigger ones, but it's not chump change. It's held at the Scottsdale Golf Course in Arizona.

He gives me a knowing smile. "Yes, it's in August."

I narrow my eyes at him. "What's the purse?"

"$600,000."

Well, fuck me. That's pretty damn good. On second thought, maybe competing doesn't sound so bad after all. Playing the sport I love professionally?

"I don't know, Coach. Can I let you know after this season? It'll be hectic this summer."

"No worries, son. Just let me know before July."

He walks off, and I'm left staring after him. Six hundred thousand as the prize money for my first golf tournament. For fuck's sake, how can I turn that down?

❧

The drive to Sienna's apartment is beautiful. She lives in downtown Louisville near the stadium. I was expecting her to live in Rose Valley, but judging by her hesitance to even *talk* to me, I had to rethink that assumption.

I'm conflicted. Because I like her. A lot. But I barely know her. But I *also* can't deny our chemistry. And it doesn't help that she's hot as hell. *The circle her lips made when I fingered her…*

I grip the steering wheel harder, but it doesn't do anything to stop the throbbing sensation in my crotch. I need to get a grip and just focus on our date tonight. Thinking about how beautiful she is when she's worked up isn't helping.

I'm thankful when I reach her complex. I get out of my car and walk inside to get her. The lobby is nice. The concierge gives me a curt nod before looking down at the monitors in front of him.

I'm off the elevator and walking down the hallway when I see her leaving her apartment. My steps slow as I take her in.

Oh fuck, she's gorgeous.

Her hair is in waves as usual, and she's wearing a white off-the-shoulder sweater and denim shorts. My eyes trail down to her sandals and zero in on the colored toes. Pink. I smile at the color.

I look back to her, and she looks nervous. So fucking cute.

"Hey," I say, hands going around her waist, making her yelp.

"Hey," she says, giggling.

"You look beautiful. As always."

She rolls her eyes, prying my arms from around her. "I look normal."

I ignore her. "Ready for dinner?"

Her eyes brighten. "Yes, I'm starving actually. I've had a long day."

"Did you have another meeting today?"

She stiffens beside me, and I look at her. "No, just a day full of apartment hunting."

"You're moving?"

"Yeah," she mutters.

"Why? This complex looks really cool."

"Long story," she sighs.

I stare at her for a couple of seconds, and she gives me a small smile. I let it go for her sake since she doesn't seem comfortable talking about it. We're inside the elevator, and my natural instinct is to grab her hand. I slide my fingers through hers, and I'm surprised to see her not flinch. She actually relaxes, and it makes me smile.

She briefly lays her head on my shoulder. "How was your day?"

"It was all right. I just golfed all day, really."

"You golf too? You really *are* a country club boy," she jokes.

"I *live* in a country club, hun."

She rolls her eyes. "Yeah, *please* don't remind me."

Her disdain makes me frown. "What's wrong with country clubs?"

"Nothing's wrong with them. But it just reinforces the notion that you're out of my league."

My eyebrows shoot to the roof. "I beg to differ on that."

"It's the truth," she says, shrugging.

"I think you're more in my league than you think."

"That doesn't even make sense."

I just stare at her before saying, "I don't think about screwing girls often."

She flinches, looking at me with wide eyes. "Will, what the hell?"

"What?"

She cocks an eyebrow. "Why would you say something like that?"

I open the door for her to get in. "Because it's true."

"So you're hoping this night ends in a fuck? That's it?" Her hurt eyes are piercing into me. That's not what I meant.

"No, Sienna. I'm hoping this night ends in you not writing me *off*."

"That's not the message you just sent."

I actually agree, but I'm not a wordsmith. Sighing, I shut her door and walk around, getting inside.

"I don't just think you're hot, babe. Your personality turns me on. A lot. And a girl who loves wine? I think I might've hit the fucking jackpot."

She chuckles, muttering, "You didn't hit anything yet."

"Sienna," I start as she turns back to me. "I'm not good at this, okay? I don't...go on dates."

She just stares at me before her face softens. "I can tell."

I laugh, running a hand through my hair. "I don't mean to make you uncomfortable. If I do, please tell me so I don't fuck this up."

She looks at me again. "You're taking this seriously, aren't you?"

I don't know if I am. All I know is, I like talking to her. Being around her. Hell, fucking *smelling* her. Looking at her is a bonus, too. She's the total package.

"I just wanna be around you more. Call me a weirdo, but I'm not afraid to admit that."

I hold my breath as she stares at me again. It feels like a century. My eyes zero in on her eyes, her lips, her nose. Something to signal an agreement. *None of those things will signal an agreement.*

Then her lips slide in a smirk. "Let's go to dinner, Will."

The satisfaction I feel might be unreasonable, but I don't care. It just feels good to hear her say that.

I'm driving to a bistro downtown when my hand lands in her lap. She's wearing jeans, so I only feel the denim under my hand. Again, she doesn't flinch. She's just looking out the window as we pass by greenery, lights glimmering in the city. It feels...right.

We finally make it to The Botanical Bistro, and I get out to open her door. She's laughing at me when I open it.

"Aren't *you* a gentleman."

"I do what I can." She smiles, and I reach for her hand again. She looks at it like it's a puzzle. "It won't pop out at you, babe."

She laughs again, accepting it. "I just never thought you were so...touchy," she jokes.

"I'm not usually."

Her gaze meets mine, and something changes in it. I'm hoping she sees how serious I really am. She clears her throat and motions to the restaurant. "Let's go inside?"

I nod and lead her in. We're greeted by a blond hostess, her eyes on the computer, but her attitude bright nonetheless.

"Welcome to the Botanical Bistro! Is it two tonight?"

She types something on the computer, but I stop her. "I have a reservation at seven for Monroe."

Her eyebrows shoot up, a look of confusion etching her face. Then realization replaces it. "Oh, Mr.—"

"Yes, Will Monroe."

She swallows, the blood rushing out of her face. "Right, yes. Let me lead you two this way."

I motion for Sienna to go, but she gives me a confused look. Smiling, I gently pull her with me. We arrive at a table near a window, and she puts down two menus as I pull Sienna's seat out. She sits down, and I sit next to her.

"That was weird," she says as the hostess walks away.

"Yeah, it was." I shrug it off.

She gives me a knowing smile. "Could it be because you're famous?"

"I'm not famous," I laugh. "I'm just a Monroe."

"Right," she mocks. "Because Monroe around here is a *very* mainstream name."

I smile, looking at the wine menu. "It actually is, babe."

"You're stubborn."

"Not as much as you."

She rolls her eyes. "I'm not stubborn."

"Babe, you're stubborn."

She laughs and continues looking at the menu, and I just look at her. She's stunning. Her button nose gives her a girlish appearance, but her high cheekbones give her a striking look. Her eyes are a beautiful brown, and they're almond-shaped. Finally, my eyes zero in on her pink lips. I smile at her.

She looks up and meets my gaze. "What? What's wrong?"

"Nothing," I say, clearing my throat.

She frowns at me, and I feel my face heat. It's embarrassing how much I enjoy looking at her. "I'm thinking a bottle of merlot. Do you like merlot?"

I smile at her. "Merlot's perfect. I didn't know you liked red wine."

"Sure, I love red wine. I prefer it to anything else," she admits.

I asked her before about how she got into wine, but she didn't seem to want to answer it. I'm about to ask her, but our waiter arrives before I can. I order a bottle of merlot, and he walks off, my attention back on her.

"You told me you want to be a winemaker."

She nods. "Yeah, I studied viniculture at Louisville State."

"There's a degree for *wine*? I had no idea."

Her laugh is music to my ears. "Yeah, it's not a popular degree obviously. But...wine helped me throughout my teen years."

I frown at that. "You drank wine as a *teen*?"

Her face is somber now, the smile no longer there. "Yeah, I needed to. Or else I would have lost my mind." Her forceful laugh does nothing to stop my mind from racing. What does she mean?

"Why would you lose your mind?"

"It's nothing," she says quickly.

I just stare at her, but she doesn't look like she wants to talk about it. The look concerns me, but I can't push her. She needs to be ready when she wants to be.

I reach out and hold her hand. "Hey." She looks up at me. "Whenever you're ready, all right?"

She gives me a small smile before looking down at the menu. Our waiter is back with a bottle of Cogburn Merlot, and he's pouring our glasses. We order dinner and we're saying *cheers,* looking outside minutes later.

The rest of dinner went better than I expected. We're outside of the restaurant, holding hands.

I push her hair back, and she's looking up at me. "I had fun," I admit.

She smiles, closing her eyes, my hands running through her hair. "I did too, Will."

My eyes gloss over her lips. "You know what this means, right?"

She swallows, her smile slowly diminishing. "No, Will. What does it mean?"

"Your 'one date' proposition doesn't hold."

"Will—"

"I want to take you out again, Sienna. And I'm going to."

She shakes her head. "We *can't* go out again. It just doesn't make sense."

"*What* doesn't make sense?" I'm getting frustrated with her shooting me down every second.

"Us. I only go out with guys I have a chance with." Her voice wavers.

I frown. "You don't think you'll have a chance with me?"

She shrugs. "I don't know. I just...don't like wasting my time."

I only stare at her. There's nothing I can do to convince her. Except prove it to her.

"Usually, I'd argue. But I won't tonight, Sienna."

She has skeptical eyes. "You won't?"

I laugh at her confusion. "No, I won't. I can just prove it to you," I say simply.

Her non-answer is enough answer for me. She knows what I mean. Sienna's a hesitant girl, and words won't change her mind. I'll have to show her through actions. I have no problem with that. I'll do whatever I can to ease her mind.

I open the door for her, and she slides in, as I shut it closed. I walk around and get in, peeling out of the parking lot seconds later. My hand finds its way back to her thigh, and she doesn't move to push it off. She's looking out of the window once again, exploring the scenery outside.

I'm outside of her apartment complex an hour later, and I start to get out, but she stops me. "It's okay, Will. You don't have to walk me up."

Not a fucking chance. "Babe, I'm not letting you walk up by yourself."

She gives me an amused smile. "It'd be very hard to rob me when the lobby is ten feet away and the concierge works 24 hours," she jokes.

I roll my eyes but can't keep the smile off my face. "Fine. Let me know when you're safe."

She rolls her eyes. "I promise I'll text you."

She moves to get out, but I stop her too. "Wait, um...can I kiss you goodnight?"

Her eyebrows shoot up. "You're *asking* to kiss me? This coming from the same guy that basically devoured me at his family's winery?"

Chortling, I lean in. "I didn't devour you. I just...took what was mine."

Her face goes serious, and she swallows. "Then why don't you take what's yours again?" Her whisper is a mere memory.

I'm on her seconds later. Her lips move against mine, and the simple movement makes a jolt of electricity shoot down to my crotch. My hand is on her neck, pulling her closer, nipping at her lips. Her tongue seeks entrance, and I open wider to accept it. Growling, I pull her onto my lap, and the kiss turns hungry. It's sloppy kisses as my hands make their way up her sweater. They find her boobs and gently squeeze, making her moan again.

She pulls back, her breathing erratic. "Wait, we can't do another episode in your car."

Smiling, I kiss her again. "Why not?" I'm kneading her breasts, the globes fitting perfectly in my hands.

"Because I wasn't expecting this."

"So?"

"*So* making out doesn't qualify as a goodnight kiss."

I try to consider what she's saying, but I'm thinking with the wrong head right now. He wants in.

"Baby, I'm *really* hard right now."

She swallows, quickly glancing down. "No sex," she whispers.

"I know, I know. I have to earn it." I painfully remember. My other hand reaches down and gently squeezes her hip.

"So...good night?" A small smile touches her lips.

I laugh, nuzzling my nose against her neck. "You're killing me here." I trail kisses up her neck as I continue kneading her breast. She's moaning again, and I immediately mourn for my tiny head. Groaning, I pull back. "You have to stop moaning, babe, or you won't leave this car tonight."

She laughs, laying her forehead against mine. "Good night, Will."

Sighing, I give her a peck and pat her butt. "Good night, babe."

Fixing her sweater, she gets up and leaves my car. I watch as she walks inside and disappears into the lobby. Letting out an annoyed curse, I put my car in drive, and I'm on my way back to Rose Valley. Action or not, I still want nothing more than to see her face again.

"Dude, where have you been? I haven't seen you since last week."

Collin runs up to me on the course the next day. I'm pulling my golf bag from the cart when he stops next to me, out of breath.

"I should ask where *you* have been." I look down at my watch. "It's almost 12 p.m. I thought you would've been ready to go *way* before I even made it."

He rolls his eyes, setting his bag down. "Sorry, dude. My dad's been giving me a hard time about the resort. He wants me to help run it when he goes to Dubai, but there's a slim chance I will," he jokes.

I roll my eyes. Collin Fairchild is the son and heir of Thomas and Catherine Fairchild. His dad inherited Fairchild Hotels, which had been passed down in their family for centuries. Arthur Fairchild started the hotel in London in the 1892, and now it's a household name. With more than 30 hotels around the world, the Fairchild Resort at Louisville is the go-to resort in Kentucky.

"Sounds like what my parents want me and Taylor to do."

He takes out his golf club before looking at me again. "What do you mean?"

"They're spending time in Europe this summer, so Taylor and I have to manage the winery while Mr. Stevens handles the other day-to-day operations."

"Taylor, eh?"

My eyes shoot to him and immediately despise the smug look on his face. "Dude, let it go. She's my little sister."

He rolls his eyes. "You're a buzzkill."

"No, I'm her big brother," I mumble.

He sets his ball up to tee off while I stand and watch him. We'll continue this conversation later. While I love Taylor, she's not a great choice for Collin. He may act like a playboy, but he has hearts in his eyes. My baby sister loves the single life. She won't return his feelings.

When we finish at this hole, we make our way to the next one. There are eighteen holes in our country club, and it takes about four hours to get through them all.

"Where's Connor? He couldn't make it today?"

"He went to the beverage cart long before you came. But I don't know where he is now."

Almost as if he heard us talking about him, Connor shows up at my side as Collin polishes his club.

"Sorry, guys. I saw Mason and Kayla at the cart."

My heart stops. "Mason? The girls are out golfing today?"

He shrugs as he sets his bag down. "Yeah, she said her horse guy cancelled on her today. So they're doing a last-minute girl's golf thing." He waves it off.

I forgot all about Mason. Shit, I hope I don't run into her.

"You look like you're freaking out," Collin remarks, an annoying smirk on his face.

"I'm not freaking out."

I'm definitely freaking out. After my birthday party, she got annoyed with me for leaving the banquet hall and not telling her where

I disappeared to—a steamy session with Sienna. I was doing my best to avoid her since then, but it seems like I won't be able to do that today.

"It's okay if you're freaking out, dude. Mason's a bit...forward, if you ask me," Connor laughs. *Yeah, no shit.* "You seemed preoccupied at your party, anyway."

My eyebrows shoot up. "What?"

"The girl in red? Come on, dude. You thought no one saw you?"

I shrug, setting my ball up. "I didn't really care."

"Really? You didn't care?"

I frown at Collin. "Why would I care?"

"I don't know. She was cute, but...she's just not your usual type," he says, his face reddening.

"She's not, but she's definitely the hottest and most interesting girl I've met," I croon. I'm setting my ball up, but I feel eyes on me. I turn to them, and they're both smirking. "What?"

"You like her," Connor remarks.

I feel my face heat. "So? Is it wrong to like a girl?"

"No, but it's obvious you like her for more than a night of fun."

"Can we not do this? We're golfing."

And talking about Sienna isn't helping. Because the thought of her makes a jolt of heat shoot through me yet again.

They both shrug, and I let out a sigh of relief as I practice a few swings. I take a swing and watch as the ball flies, happy with the distance. I turn to them, and they give me looks of approval.

Hours later, we finish the course and head to the vineyard for wine. *And for Sienna.* I don't know if she works on Wednesdays, but I'm hoping she's there.

I'm parking in the lot and walking up the hill with the guys when I see her leading a group of people to the pavilion. My eyes zero in on her white camisole, blue jeans, and pink sneakers, and I can't help but smile. Such a simple outfit, yet it looks pretty on her. She doesn't see me, so we head up to the lobby and wait for her.

"Dude, why are we just sitting here? Can we go to the bistro already?" Collin asks.

"Because I'm waiting on someone," I deadpan.

His eyebrows shoot up. "Can we meet them at the bistro?"

"No."

He throws a temper tantrum, and I only laugh. Seconds later, Sienna's walking up with the group, and her eyes widen in surprise.

"Will! What are you doing here? Are you working today?"

"No, babe. We just wanted to get drinks after a long day of golfing."

Her eyebrows shoot up, and she turns to the group. "Can you guys wait for me in the inventory room? Count how much pinot noir we have left."

They all nod and walk past us, looking at me in awe. But my eyes are still on her, and she seems frazzled. She looks at Collin and Connor, confused.

"Would you like to join us for drinks?"

She flinches. "What? No, I can't fraternize on the job."

Before I can respond, Collin's already on his feet.

"Hi, gorgeous. I'm sorry, Will's too elite to understand the concept of reality. I'm Collin, by the way. Collin Fairchild."

Those eyebrows rise again. "Fairchild. As in—"

"You got it," he interrupts, taking her hand and kissing the knuckles.

"Okay, enough of that." I push him away, a knowing smirk stretching across his face. Sienna still looks confused. "Sorry, babe," I whisper.

"It's fine, but...I can't drink with you. I'm working, and I don't know them. No offense," she says.

"None taken," Connor laughs.

"Just one drink?" I ask.

She bites the corners of her lip, contemplating. I hold my breath, hoping she accepts.

"I'm sorry, Will. Not today," she says, walking around me.

I watch as she disappears into the inventory room. Well, that sucked. Someone clearing their throat makes me turn around.

"So *that's* the girl in red," Connor remarks.

I let out an annoyed sigh. "Yes, that's Sienna."

He lets out a whistle. "I like her already, dude. Rejected *The* Will Monroe for a drink? It's almost a miracle."

Rolling my eyes, I motion them to the bistro. "Eat shit, dude."

7

SIENNA

Will isn't making this easy.

Why is he here right now?

Maybe because this is his family's vineyard?

It shouldn't make me this uncomfortable, but I wasn't expecting to see him today. Mr. Stevens told me Will and his sister will start working this Friday. So I was prepared to see them on...you guessed it: *Friday.*

Stop making this about you, Sienna.

He said he only came up here to get a drink, so I shouldn't be overthinking this. Surely he didn't even care if I was here or not. Happy with this reasoning, I continue counting bottles of wine while the new set of summer interns finish up moving extra bottles to the backroom.

I set my notebook on the lobby counter and make a call to order more Syrah when someone clears their throat, signaling for me to look up.

"Sorry, just give me—Oh. Hello."

I find a blond girl with bright blue eyes and an equally bright smile. She has her hair in a loose side braid, and she's wearing a T-shirt dress.

"Hi! Is Mr. Stevens here?"

"Uh, he's off today. But I can make an emergency call."

"Oh no, I'll catch him later. I just...really need to talk to him about my hours. My brother's making me work the same hours as him, but I'm not as enthusiastic to be working at the place that I was practically raised in," she complains.

I frown, taking a good look at her. Same nose, same eye shape, same fucking beautiful looks.

"You wouldn't happen to be Taylor Monroe, would you?"

Her smile grows brighter. "In the flesh. Can we save autographs for later, though? I didn't bring my lucky pen."

"Lucky pen?"

"Yeah, it's pink. And it writes pretty darn well," she remarks.

I laugh at that whimsical answer. "Uh, well I'm not looking for an autograph. You just remind me of someone," I joke.

"So you've met my brother."

I laugh. "You could say that."

Her eyebrows shoot up, and almost on time, he shows up with his friends following suit.

"Taylor? What the hell are you doing here?"

She rolls her eyes. "Looking for Mr. Stevens, Willy," she deadpans. "Calm your tits."

"You're supposed to be at fencing practice."

I whip my head to him. Fencing? Who the hell *are* these people?

"Shocker, I didn't wanna go," she deadpans.

I snicker, making Will briefly glance at me before glaring at his sister. "Taylor, if Mom and Dad call me and tell me your coach said you didn't show up—"

"Willy, there are hungry children overseas. There are more pressing issues to worry about."

I think I love this girl.

"Hey, Taylor. It's good to see you," his friend Collin says. I look at him, and he looks *way* too happy to see her.

She gives him a friendly wave. "Hi, Fairchild," she says absently. "Look, I'll make up practice later, okay? I just need my hours changed. I don't want—or *need*—to be working overtime at this place."

He lets out a sigh, rubbing his temples. "We'll talk about this later, Taylor." He looks at me. "You've met Sienna," he points out.

She looks visibly confused. "Sienna?"

"The girl you were just talking to," he deadpans.

"Oh, hot stuff behind the counter," she exclaims before turning back to me. "Yeah, she's awesome. Why?"

"Don't run her off with your craziness. She's one of the good ones here."

My face heats, feeling eyes on me. Taylor looks between me and Will, suspicious. "Why would I run her off? And why would you care? No offense," she offers to me.

I snort. "None taken."

"Yeah, Will. Why would you care?" Connor asks.

"Because she's one of the good ones," he repeats, gaze still on me. He's giving me a stare that's way too torrid for the public.

I clear my throat and look away, finding Taylor giving me a knowing smile.

"I get it now. Okay, Willy. I won't run her away," she says.

He visibly swallows, looking away. "Good. Now, go home. Or anywhere but here."

She nods and gives me another smile before walking off. Now there's just us three.

"That was really unnecessary," I mumble.

"Sienna—"

"This is my *job*, Will. What if she tells your parents you have a crush on the help?"

His eyes flash. "You and I both know this is more than a crush," he growls.

We share a brief staring contest before Collin clears his throat behind Will. I look back down at my notebook. This is why I told him to keep things professional. Now three different people know there's something going on between us.

"May I just ask, what the *hell* is going on?"

"Nothing."

"Everything," he says at the same time.

"Well, *that* was telling. Since my best friend has a crush, though, I never introduced myself. Connor Hansen," he says, holding his hand out to me.

"Uh, yeah. Sienna Durham. Nice...to meet you," I croak.

His blue eyes brighten, a smile stretching across his face.

"Nice to meet you. Are you joining us at the Monroe-Szuch Black Tie Gala next Saturday?"

My eyebrows shoot up. "Um, no I wasn't planning on going," I laugh. I look at Will, and he frowns at that.

"Surely Will would like you as his date."

"Um, that'd be silly—"

"Silly?" Will's hurt expression catches my gaze.

"Well...yeah," I chuckle nervously.

He lets out a sigh before turning to his friends. "Guys, I'll meet y'all later for dinner."

They both give me a knowing smile before walking away. When they're out of the lobby, he turns back to me, a confused look on his face.

"What?"

He takes his cap off, running a hand through his hair. "Sienna, Sienna, Sienna. What am I gonna do with you?"

"I don't know what you wanted me to say," I whisper.

"You say yes, dammit," he bites out.

"Will, it's a *gala*. Why would I show up there? I'm not rich."

He flinches as if I've slapped him. "It's not only for the rich."

I cock an eyebrow. "Who's all invited, Will?" He opens his mouth to argue but closes it in defeat. "Exactly."

"Sienna, I'm inviting you as my date. It's my family's annual charity event, babe. We collaborate with the Szuch family. All proceeds go to help less fortunate little girls in Louisville get horseback riding lessons."

I gape at him. "That's...actually kind of sweet."

He shrugs and puts his hands in his pockets. "It's pretty cool. Why don't you wanna go with me?"

"It's not that I don't wanna go, but...that's somewhere I'd feel out of place. I wouldn't get along with anyone there."

"How do you know that?"

I scoff. "Hmm, let me guess, I'm not rich, and I'd be showing up with a high-profile heir. Not to mention, I'm not the type of girl people would expect you to show up with."

He frowns. "Who the fuck cares?"

"Your family," I deadpan.

"My parents are in Europe, and even if they were here, I literally couldn't give a shit."

I roll my eyes. He's not getting it. "Will—"

He cradles my face, peering down at me. "Sienna, I can't keep fighting you. I can't make you, but I'd really like you to go with me," he whispers.

I look up at him and fear the sincerity in his eyes. Swallowing, I nod. "Okay," I whisper. "Okay, Will. I'll go with you."

His eyes dart across my face, a smile growing across his face. "Yeah?"

I nod my head, and his smile grows brighter. "Yes, Will. I'll go with you."

He nudges his nose against mine before brushing our lips together. His hands go around my waist as he pulls back.

"This Friday will be a week."

I frown. "A week of what?"

"One week since I've asked you what your name was," he says, his nose still nudging mine.

I only laugh. "A week since you've been a pain in my butt."

He laughs and stares into my eyes. "And I don't regret it."

I only stare up at him, really looking in his eyes. The same cocky guy I met a week ago is being affectionate with me, a mere employee at his family's winery.

This can't go anywhere.

Surely it can't go anywhere.

A small part of me tells me I'm wasting my time. And then the other part tells me I have nothing to worry about. Only time will tell.

And time is not exactly friendly to me. Dad scheduled another apartment tour for me tomorrow morning, and this alone should make me mad. But Ashley calls, telling me she needs help with her sommelier certification course. And I basically have no time to be mad at Dad.

You're off the hook this time, Pops.

Minutes later, I'm driving up to Rose Valley and shocked to be driving to Monroe Country Club. For fuck's sake, does *everyone* live in this club? I had no idea Ashley even lived in here. Is she an heiress of some sort too?

"No, my parents are corporate lawyers. I'm living with them until I finish grad school."

She's packing a bag of notebooks and pens as I look around her room. She has a king canopy bed with pink linens and a quilt. Her room is very expansive with a wooden desk and laptop, a flatscreen TV, and a huge walk-in closet.

"Not to intrude, but if you're rich, what makes you want to work as a sommelier?"

She tucks a strand of hair behind her ear and picks up her purse.

"Rich people can be ambitious too, you know."

I only smile. "I never said they can't."

She shrugs. "I just love the cultivation of grapes. I'm not really into winemaking, but I love the varying tastes and how it makes me feel. I feel...at home when I'm drinking a nice glass of malbec," she jokes.

I just stare at her. "At home. That's how I feel when I talk about wine. I definitely feel at home when I drink merlot. It helps with my anxiety," I say before thinking.

She's looking at me, confused. "Anxiety?"

Clearing my throat, I walk to her door. "Ready to go?"

She stares at me before relenting. We leave and drive her dad's golf cart to the clubhouse. We pull up, and I'm gaping at the mansion in front of me.

I've been to many clubhouses growing up. I dabbled in tennis in middle school, so I practiced at some upscale country clubs. But this takes the cake. It's like a miniature white house, with a resort-style pool on one side and three tennis courts on the other.

We walk inside, and the hostess leads us to a window table. I look around the dining room, my eyes landing outside on the golf course. The window's huge, so I can see the land for miles. The sun shines bright on the sod, and I'm in awe.

"Can I start you ladies off with a glass of wine?"

I jump at the man's voice behind me. I turn to find a tall Adonis peering down at us.

"Just a glass of malbec for me. Brontis would be great," Ashley says, pulling out her notebooks and ID. She motions for me to give her my ID, and I hand it to her. She shows them both to him, he nods, and his eyes land on me.

I take my ID back, as I clear my throat and look at the wine menu.

"How are your merlots?"

"Do you have a vineyard in mind?"

I shrug. "Anything from Napa or an Australian vineyard is fine."

He flashes a bright smile. "Well, Associa is a great merlot if you like a bit of a full-bodied, cherry flavor with a hint of vanilla. The vineyard is in Victoria, Australia."

Music to my ears. "Great, a glass of that will be fine." He nods and walks off. I turn to find Ashley smiling at me. "What?"

She shakes her head nonchalantly. "Nothing, I just admire your taste in merlot. It's too...subtle for me."

I raise my eyebrows at that. "I wouldn't expect anything else from a girl who loves malbec. Plum is an intense flavor."

She smiles at me. "Touché."

Moments later, he arrives with our glasses, and we nosedive into studying. She asks me questions about how long the test is and what all she needs to know.

"If you want, I can get you a practice book for the test."

She shakes her head. "That's not necessary."

"It's not an issue. I'm your supervisor, so I can definitely get that for you."

She looks like she wants to argue but doesn't. I begin quizzing her on the difference between white and red wines. She's definitely improved from her first day. She passes with flying colors, and we move on to the different white wines.

I'm telling her about wine tastes and aromas when a familiar group of people walk in.

The rich kids of Monroe Country Club.

And one of those rich kids is Will Monroe.

He's laughing at something Collin says, and there's a very beautiful blonde on his arm. Like *strikingly* beautiful. Clearing my throat, I turn back to Ashley, who's staring at me.

"Everything okay?"

"Everything's fine," I lie.

She doesn't look completely convinced. She turns around and looks at the group before turning back to me, rolling her eyes. "You're upset Will's with Mason," she points out.

"What? No. I'm not upset. We're not dating."

She laughs in disbelief. "It's okay to be upset about it."

"I'm not upset. They're probably just...hanging out." Yeah, low chance of *that*. "Look, it doesn't matter, okay? We're not...exclusive."

She narrows her eyes at me. "Why the hell would you agree to be in a non-exclusive relationship with Will Monroe? Are you a masochist?" Then something dawns on her. "I don't know why I'm surprised. This is totally his M.O."

I'm starting to regret my decision about not believing her. "Can we get back to studying, please?"

She gives me a small smile. "I'm serious, though. It's okay to be upset. Just...don't get in too deep with him. He's gonna break your heart."

"I'm not getting in too deep with him. We're not together, so I don't care *who* he sees," I lie.

She's not buying it. "I definitely think it bothers you, Sienna."

Sighing, I put my pencil down. "Will Monroe and I are not a thing." I look back in his direction before meeting Ashley's narrowed eyes. "And the fact that he's with her proves that. Can we move on?"

She gives me a look of disbelief. I hold my breath, waiting for her to tell me that she doesn't believe me. But she shrugs and continues writing in her notebook.

I look back at the group, and Will's eyes are on me now, heat coursing through my body. He looks like he's seen a ghost. Clearing my throat, I look back down, feigning notetaking. But I already feel a presence above me. Closing my eyes, I look up. Will and his friends are already at our table.

He gives me a small smile. "Sienna, I didn't know you'd be here." His gaze lands on Ashley and narrows. "Ashley."

She cocks an eyebrow. "Monroe."

He rolls his eyes, gaze landing back on me. "You didn't tell me you were coming tonight."

"Why would I tell you that?" I ask, swallowing the lump in my throat.

"Who's this?" the bombshell beside him chirps.

"Just an employee at the vineyard. I've been helping him learn more about the wine business," I answer for him.

His gaze is piercing into me, but I do my best to ignore it. "Can we talk?"

Hell no. "I'm actually busy right now. Ashley needs my help. I'll tutor you on wines later."

Collin and Connor laugh as a hurt expression spreads across Will's face. Why is he hurt? He's the one that has a disgustingly beautiful blonde on his arm.

"Sure, yeah. Tutor me later," he mumbles, walking off.

I watch as they leave, and Collin gives me an approving smirk. I try to hide my smile, my attention back on Ashley. She's giving me the same smirk.

"You can be a bitch when you wanna be."

I shrug in faux ignorance. "I do what I can."

She shakes her head, and we're back to studying.

8

WILL

She was at the clubhouse last night. For fuck's sake, my stomach dropped when I saw her. Her sad eyes play through my head throughout the day. I never wanted her to see me with Mason. It wasn't even what it looked like.

Collin and Connor swindled me into dinner with Mason, Willa, and Kayla. Willa invited her because we had a thing. *Had* being the operative word. If 'having a thing' is even the right word for it.

Mason was hanging on my arm when Sienna saw us. It wasn't meant to look like an intimate thing. She was a bit tipsy. I asked her to hang on to my arm because she was wearing heels, and I was helping her stay upright.

Mason has high alcohol tolerance, though. She looked fine when I was at dinner, but she started tripping over herself in the dining room when she stood up. Her hanging on my arm I'm sure didn't look the greatest in Sienna's eyes, though. *Shit.* I need to make this right with her.

I'm walking into the lobby with my sister the next day. Sienna's writing something down in her notebook, completely oblivious to the world around her. She has her hair in a messy bun with an oversized sweatshirt.

I walk up to the counter, but Taylor stops me. "If you brought me here to harass the staff—"

"I'm not harassing anyone," I retort.

Sienna's head suddenly pops up, her gaze landing on me. She gives us a confused look before putting her notebook away.

"Um, hey, guys."

Taylor gives her a friendly wave before scowling at me and walking toward the banquet hall. Sienna's eyes follow her for a second before landing on me again.

"Sorry, she's...an interesting gal," I remark.

Her eyebrows shoot up. "You're telling me." She grabs a set of keys before walking to the inventory room. I find myself following her. Once we're in the back, she lets out a resigned sigh. "Will, why are you following me?"

"Can we talk?"

She laughs, grabbing a case of Dragon Lily. "You asked me that last night."

I run a hand through my hair. "Yeah, that's true. Look, um... about last night—"

"Can we not do this? It's not a big deal," she mumbles, walking past me. I follow her back to the lobby.

"What do you mean?"

She sets the case on the lobby counter. "You were hanging out with people last night. You don't have to explain it to me."

"Well yeah, but...it wasn't what it looked like."

She gives me a once-over before counting the bottles in the case. "It looked like you were with friends."

I let out a sigh of relief. "Yeah, exactly. It was just a dinner with my friends. Mason showed up—"

"The blonde?"

I flinch at the interruption. "Yeah, she's an old friend from high school. We sort of had a thing..." She visibly stiffens. "But it's all in the past. I promise."

"Okay."

I frown at her. "That's it?"

She's not looking at me. "That's all there is."

I just stare at her. That can't be all she has to say. "Sienna—"

"It's not a big deal."

It's bothering her. I round the counter and reach for her hand. "Come with me," I whisper.

She slouches, annoyed. "We can't keep doing this."

"Doing what?"

"You can't keep stealing me while I'm at work," she jokes.

I smile at her. "Sure I can. Don't you get off at four?" I look at my watch. "It's 3:30, babe."

She bites her lip, contemplating. "I have thirty minutes left."

"Sienna, come on. Let's hang out today."

Her eyes widen in surprise. "W-What? No, we can't hang out."

"Why not?"

"I'm really tired because of the study session with Ashley last night, and I had an early morning, touring another apartment," she moans.

Hugging her to me, I revel in how good she feels.

"So let's just hang out for an hour or something. You like ice cream?"

She's gaping at me. "Ice cream."

"Yeah, it's pretty popular. It's like a sugary dessert." Smiling, I reach down and cup one of her boobs, her body stiffening. "Much like these babies."

Her eyes widen as she looks around the lobby. "Will, you're touching my boob. In public."

I swallow, kneading one. "Mm-hmm, that I am."

"Will," she gasps.

"Yeah?"

"Let go of my boob," she whispers.

"What if I don't want to?"

"Will," she warns. Sighing, I drop my hand and hug her closer to me. "And did you *really* just call them a sugary dessert?"

"I did. As in the phrase 'sugar tits.'"

She flinches. "You really don't have a filter."

"I don't. Seriously, though, Sienna, let's get ice cream. Then I'll take you home."

She's pondering, and I'm holding my breath. For fuck's sake, I'm standing here, waiting for a girl to make up her mind about a date. If I saw myself back in college, I'd laugh.

Letting out a breath, she nods. "Okay, yeah. We can do that."

Smiling, I give her a peck on the lips. "Awesome. I'll meet you outside."

She walks in the backroom, and I'm left staring at her ass. And Taylor chooses the perfect time to tease me.

"*Sooo.* You have a thing for the *sommelier,*" she singsongs as she walks up.

"And what if I do?"

She shrugs, her hands in her sweatshirt pockets. "Nothing, it's just that you're a pro at keeping your foot in your mouth."

"And you're a pro at keeping other things in yours," I retort.

She flinches. "Wow, Willy. That's low. Even for you."

"You still didn't tell me why you made a pass at your professor."

Her nose scrunches up. "'*Made a pass*'? What are you, fifty?"

"You're dodging."

She rolls her eyes, but her face reddens. "It wasn't a big deal. He's...hot."

I just stare at the girl known as my sister. "You like older men?"

"No! He's twenty-eight, for fuck's sake."

I give her a smug smirk. "Again, you're into older men?"

Her glare is the only response I get, but Sienna walking out has my full attention. She has her hair down, waves falling over her shoulder. Her eyes land on Taylor when she stops in front of me.

"Miss Monroe, nice to see you again," she says with a friendly wave. Taylor gives me a confused look.

"Sienna, this is my sister. You can call her Taylor."

She gives an apologetic smile. "Sorry, force of habit."

Taylor chortles, shaking her head. "No worries, girly. You can always call me Taylor. Or Tay. Whatever works."

Literally no one calls her Tay. "Or Taylor is fine."

I earn Taylor's annoyed look. I reach out for Sienna's hand, and she just looks at it. Her eyes go back to my sister, and she looks as if she's about to bolt.

"Um, Will—"

"She already knows."

She frowns. "She knows what?"

"That he likes you," Taylor offers.

"Oh, um, okay," she laughs nervously.

"Ready for ice cream?"

Taylor pipes up beside me. "Dude," she scoffs. "You're taking her to get ice cream?"

"Yes, and you're not going." I turn back to Sienna. "Come on."

She lets out a shaky breath and holds my hand, my body relaxing at the touch. We walk to my car, and I'm on my way to the house to drop Taylor off.

Minutes later, I stop in front of the house and turn to Taylor.

"Hop out, kid."

She rolls her eyes, reaching for the door. Then she stops. "Wait, can you unlock the wine fridge?"

"I don't condone underage drinking," I deadpan.

"I'm twenty-one, stupid," she retorts.

Grunting, I open the door to get out. "Fine, but don't go too crazy." I turn to Sienna, and she's staring up at the house in awe. I smile at her wonderment. "Are you okay, babe?"

She quickly snaps out of it, looking at me. "Yeah, I'm fine," she laughs nervously.

She looks off out her window, and I'm left staring at her.

"You can come in if you'd like."

She looks at me with wide eyes. "What?"

"Come inside. I just need to unlock the fridge, and then we can go."

"Okay, then I can just stay here. It's rude to go into your parents' house."

"Sienna, it's fine. Come on, babe."

She gives me an annoyed look before taking off her seatbelt. I smile at the small victory. I'm learning very quickly that she likes to put up a fight, but I can ease her mind.

We walk inside, and Taylor skips to the basement. Rolling my eyes, I follow after her, but I stop when Sienna stiffens next to me.

"Is everything okay?"

She bites the corners of her lips. "I really don't know if I should be...walking into your house."

"What do you mean?"

"Will, this is a fucking mansion," she blurts out.

A chuckle slips out. "Yeah, most of the homes in this country club *are* mansions, babe."

"Ugh, this is just so weird. I'll just wait for you on the couch," she mumbles.

I smile at her. She's so stinking cute. She slouches down on the couch, looking around the living room. I'll talk to her about this later.

I go downstairs, finding Taylor staring at me with her hands on her hips. Rolling my eyes, I whip the key out and unlock the fridge. I pat her head, and she grumbles at me.

"No partying," I scold.

"Yeah, yeah, just go on your date." She waves me off.

I roll my eyes and run upstairs to find Sienna still on the couch. But she's now looking at her phone.

"Ready to go?" She looks up at me with worried eyes, and it makes me frown. I'm immediately kneeling in front of her. "Babe?"

She swallows, an unreadable expression etching her face. "Uh, Will, I can't go get ice cream with you."

I flinch, my eyes still on her. "What? What do you—"

"An emergency just came up," she blurts out.

I'm immediately on high alert. My eyes dart across her face, but I don't know what I'm looking for. "Is everything—"

Before I can finish, she bolts past me. I follow her outside, and she opens the door to my car. What the hell is going on?

"I just need to go home. I'm so sorry," she says, her voice wavering.

I'm in the driver's side in a second. "Baby, what's wrong?" She's looking forward, a scared look on her face. My hand rests on her thigh. "Sienna?"

"Um, there's just been a terrible emergency that I need to take care of."

I frown at that, but because of the intensity in her demeanor, I don't ask another question.

I'm on my way back to her apartment, the drive incredibly tense. My hand is still on her lap, and she wipes her face. Shit, she's crying. My hand squeezes the wheel in response.

I pull in front of her complex, and she slips her seatbelt off.

"Thank you, Will," she mumbles.

I stop her before she reaches the door handle. "Sienna, what's going on? Is everything okay?"

"Yes, just...someone I know has an emergency I need to take care of," she says, sniffling.

I wipe the tears from her eyes. "How can I help?"

"You can't," she retorts. "It's not your problem to fix," she whispers.

"Sienna—"

Suddenly, her phone rings, and she picks it up, her breathing labored. I watch her as she quivers in her seat. The sight scares me.

"Hello? Yeah, is he okay? Can I talk to him?"

I frown as worry continues to etch itself across her face. Who is she talking to?

Who is *he*?

"Shit, right, he can't talk right now," she mumbles. "Okay, thank you so much again. Is he awake, at least? Okay, tell him I love him and I'll be right up." She hangs up and gives me an apologetic look. "Look, I have to go."

"Who was that on the phone?" I bark.

She's frozen, her eyes staring up at the apartment complex. I'm holding my breath, waiting for a response.

"My boyfriend," she mumbles.

And with that, she bolts out of my car, running inside, as if what she just said didn't break my heart.

9

SIENNA

"The world is your oyster, Enna. Never forget that."
I smile at my mom as she pours another glass of merlot. I'm sitting with her in the living room as she sets the glass down and pulls out a paintbrush from the rainbow water on the coffee table.

I tilt my head at the unfinished painting. "What is it, Mom?"

She hums, running the paintbrush over the white canvas.

"It's not quite finished yet, honey. But soon? It'll be a gorgeous vineyard. One that you will learn to love someday."

"What makes you say that?"

"Because for so long it's been my home. There's something about grapes and the green earth beneath us that makes the earth go round."

That alone speaks for itself. I watch as she paints terrain on a thin line across the canvas. Soon, there's the sun and lines of vines stretching across a green field.

"It's beautiful," I revel.

She hums, pleased with her work, dipping the paintbrush in the water.

"I grew up at a vineyard in Lawrenceburg. There was something welcoming about the culture. I couldn't drink as a kid, but I loved dancing across the pavilion. Then, when I got older, I experimented with red wine. It's good for the heart, they say. And boy, were they right."

I frown at that. "What do you mean?"

72

"Well, wine is romance, dear. There's something romantic about the way tastes dance together in a good glass of wine. There's something passionate about it. Whether it's a good blended wine or a good pairing with wine, you're always satisfied." She turns from the painting to me. *"You'll learn to love wine, doll. You're too young, but I just know it."*

I shrug. "I don't know about that. The smell of alcohol isn't exactly my favorite."

She gives me an endearing smile. "It's not about the smell. It's fermented grapes, so most people will be more drawn to the taste. That's the most enchanting thing about wine. One good glass, and you'll fall in love."

"Ms. Durham?"

I snap back to reality, finding a tall doctor standing over me with a clipboard in his hand.

Clearing my throat, I stand up. "Yes, that's me. How's he doing?"

He looks at his clipboard. "He's doing as well as he can. He's in good condition right now, but we think we're gonna keep him for a few days."

Well, that's not what I was hoping to hear. When I heard my dad had a seizure, I was scared for his life. I walked into the room, and he was sitting in a chair, dazed and confused, a paramedic standing over him. Thank God I asked one of my neighbors to check in on him, or this could've gone an even worse way.

"How long is a few days?"

He looks at the next page on his clipboard. "Perhaps until Monday." Well, fuck me. "We've been checking his vitals, and he's on the right track. But his tests show that he's been dehydrated."

I raise an eyebrow at that. "Dehydrated? How is that possible?"

"I'm not sure. Have you considered hiring a home health aide? I understand you work a lot during the day."

I let out a shaky breath. "We, um, can't really afford that right now."

He gives me a look of understanding. "I see. Well, we're going to monitor him for the next few days."

Sighing, I hug myself to calm down the flood of emotions steam-rolling through me. "How much is five days' worth of hospital? I'm only a sommelier, sir. I can't afford this."

He cocks an eyebrow. "Do you guys not have insurance? Disability?"

I swallow, shaking my head. "It's been...difficult, getting him approved for it."

"Well, that's strange," he says, looking at his clipboard again. "It says here he was diagnosed with Parkinson's about five years ago."

"Yeah, there's some weird thing going on with his insurance company. He got laid off from trucking years ago, and..." I trail off, not sure what else to say.

"I understand, dear. Look, I'll do my best to take care of your dad and get him back on his feet. For now, go home and get some rest."

I shake my head. "No, I'm staying here with him."

He gives me a concerned look before nodding his head and disappearing into the hall. Letting out a shaky breath, I make a call. This is the only person I can call right now.

The phone rings three times before it's picked up. "Hello?"

"Ashley?"

There's a moment of pause before she talks again. "Yeah. Is this Sienna?"

"Yeah, it's Sienna. Look, I'm not sure if this is fair to ask of you, but are you able to cover for me today?"

"Is everything okay?"

I inhale and exhale carefully. "I have a family emergency," I say, my voice breaking.

Her breath hitches on the line. "Oh my gosh, sure, I can help. What do you need?"

"I just need a break from work. I'll send you the menu for tomorrow. Do your best to do wine pairings. If you need help, I'm a phone call away."

"Sure, yeah! Um, aren't Will and Taylor starting their first day tomorrow?"

My heart practically drops at the mention of Will. I tried to avoid his hurt eyes earlier. I lied and told him my 'boyfriend' had an emergency I needed to take care of.

74

Why the hell would you say that?

If he ever found out about my family baggage, it would've been the end of us anyway. I'm my dad's primary caretaker, I have severe anxiety, and I'm a working class twenty-three-year-old girl. Surely he didn't think this would work out.

"Yeah, they're starting tomorrow. I'm supposed to be training them, but obviously I won't be there," I mumble. "I'll work on some training packets tonight, and I'll email them to you."

"Sounds good, girly." She pauses for a second. "Are you sure you're all right?"

For some reason, the simple question makes more tears brim in my eyes. Sniffling, I wipe them away. "I'm doing as best as I can. Talk to you later?"

"Talk to you later, love." And with that, she hangs up. I'm left staring at the floor.

Where I do go from here?

Pack a bag for a few days?

Bring a bottle of wine to help myself cope?

Maybe that's what you need.

Clearing my throat, I get up and decide that's *exactly* what I need.

It's the third day, and I decide I'm *not* okay. Dad's sleeping in the hospital bed, and he looks like he's doing well. But I'm not. He had a seizure. Under my lack of supervision. Which means it's my responsibility. Not to mention, he's been dehydrated. Why wasn't I aware of that?

Because you were spending too much time with a rich boy.

I groan, snuggling further under my blanket. I hate how uneasy I feel. My eyes are on Dad, suddenly waiting for the last shoe to drop. This isn't the first time he's had an accident. But this is the first time he's had a major thing like a seizure happen. I hate this feeling so much.

I think back to the accident. The accident that's essentially my fault. Dad was drinking, and Mom wanted to drive. But the need for her to read me a story before falling asleep on a long road trip from Tennessee mattered more. I didn't want her to drive because I wanted to hear her voice. And it resulted in her death. The tears are back and now streaming down my cheeks.

I'm reaching for a tissue when my phone rings. I frown at the unknown caller ID. Who could be calling me right now?

Just answer the damn phone.

Sighing my frustration, I clear my throat and pick up. "Hello," I croak.

"Hey."

I freeze as Will's voice flows through the phone, sending a shiver up my spine. I wasn't expecting to hear from him.

"Oh...hey," I say, clearing my throat again.

"Did you block me, babe?"

Shit. I *did* block him. I was worried he would try to convince me to change my mind, and evidently...I was right.

"Will—"

"It's okay, Sienna." There's a moment of pause on his end before he lets out a sigh. "You haven't been at work lately. Yesterday or today," he points out, but his voice is soft. Not the normal cockiness I'm used to.

"Yeah, I'm still dealing with the emergency, unfortunately," I mumble.

"Ah, right. The *boyfriend,*" he bites out, making me flinch.

I swallow, choosing my words carefully. "Will, about that—"

"What's he like?"

I frown at the question. "Um, what do you mean?"

"You know what I mean, Sienna," he whispers.

My breath hitches. I look at my dad, and he's still asleep. "Will—"

"Does he satisfy you?"

"Sure he does," I croak again. Why am I doing this?

"That's good," he chirps. "Does he appreciate you?"

He can be a pain in my ass, actually. "Of course he does."

"Of course he does," he repeats. "With that confidence, I can't compete with that, huh?" The emotion in his voice is so evident. I didn't mean to hurt him.

"I don't know what to say," I whisper.

He lets out a sigh. "Don't worry about me, Sienna. I'm...happy for you. And I'm sorry about the emergency. Are you sure there's nothing I can do to help?"

"No, Will." My voice wavers. "There's no need for that. But thank you."

He's silent again for a few seconds. "It's okay if you need help, Sienna. I'm always willing to help. I want you to know that."

"I know you are, Will. I know."

He sighs again. "Okay, then. Before I go, I just have one more question." I swallow, waiting for it to come. "Does he touch you?" His voice is deeper now. Cocky, passionate Will is back.

"Sure he does," I lie.

He clears his throat. "Does he touch you like *I* touch you?"

I close my eyes, dreading that question. There's no way I can answer that.

"Will—"

"Does he?"

I sigh, ready for this conversation to be over. I can't sit here thinking about this when I've ruined any chance of dating him. Much like I expected I would.

"No, Will. I don't think *anyone* will touch me like you do."

His breath hitches, and I hold my breath, waiting for his response. He wanted me to be honest, that's the God's honest truth.

"Take care, Sienna," he croaks.

"Take care, Will." My voice breaks. I quickly hang up before I break down on the phone. I hate that this happened. I wasn't expecting to hear from him, and that call just made it worse.

Why did he have to call me?

I pull the blanket over my shoulders more, but it does nothing to stay there. My sweatshirt is too bulky for this tiny blanket. But if the only thing it provides me with is the thing I'm currently lacking—comfort and security—I'll take it.

The weekend's almost over, and I go back to work tomorrow. They've discharged Dad from the hospital early, so you can guess how happy I am to be dragging him into his bedroom. His bed is messy, but I manage to quickly pull the covers back and set him down.

"Will you stop? I'm not an invalid," he mumbles.

I scoff. "Says the man who can barely take care of himself."

"I *can* take care of myself, Enna. So what? I don't drink water. I was doing just fine without it for years."

The irony makes me snort. "Yeah, I'm not listening to any more of what you have to say. Lie down and get some rest."

He mumbles an unintelligible insult. I ignore it and slide his legs under the covers. He settles into his pillow, and I leave him to rest.

I have so much to catch up on for work. Mr. Stevens decided to take time off since Will and Taylor are managing the winery this summer, so there's bound to be tasks left for me when I get back.

I'm pulling out my notebook full of wine inventory. It definitely needs to be updated. I pull out my cell and call Ashley.

She picks up on the first ring. "Oh my gosh, thank *God* you called," she groans.

I frown. "Is everything all right?"

"No! Who knew Sundays get busy?"

"How busy are we talking?"

"There's a line of people that stretches outside of the lobby."

Shit. That means the summer rush is beginning. Sighing, I throw my notebook in my purse.

"Don't freak out, okay? I'll be there in thirty minutes. Have Will or Taylor work their Monroe magic," I joke.

She laughs. "Sounds like a plan. See you soon." She hangs up, and I'm grabbing my keys, leaving to head to the vineyard.

I make it there in record time, and I briefly eye the parking lot. It's already full. *When it rains, it pours.* I manage to find a spot, and I'm running uphill to the lobby shortly after.

The wave of people that I come across when I open the door is definitely anxiety-inducing. Taking a deep breath, I make my way through the crowd, and Ashley's worried expression is the first thing I see. She's on the phone, and when she sees me, panic across her face, she hands it to me.

"So sorry, we're dealing with a bit of an emergency. We'll call you back soon." I hang the phone up, and she has a horrified expression on her face. "Who was that?"

"A wine club member wanting to order wine," she cries.

Oops. Well, there are other matters to tend to right now.

"I'll handle this crowd. It looks like a group of recent Bellarmine grads. I knew they were bound to come in at some point. Work with Will and Taylor on talking to them outside while I handle orders."

She frowns. "Oh, uh, Will couldn't make it in today. But Taylor's outside working her magic."

My mind is reeling at the first thing she said. Will's not here? *Why's that?*

Clearing my throat, I banish the thought from my head. "That's fine. Go join her."

She nods and scurries outside, some of the male guests in line watching her go. Rolling my eyes, I motion for the first guest to come up to the counter. They order a bottle of rosé, and I look under the counter to find no wines whatsoever. I run to the back and grab a case.

Hours pass, and the crowd calms down. I finish up the last two guests in line, and they all settle in the outside pavilion, some scurrying into the banquet hall. I let out a sigh of relief.

I walk to bring a case of wine back to inventory, and Ashley appears, following me.

"How did you do that?"

Chuckling, I set the case down on a shelf. "I've been dealing with the young crowd here for two years. They usually starting trickling in around the same time during the summer months. They're a docile group for the most part."

She lets out a sigh as we make it back to the lobby. "I was *not* expecting that. I was the only person here for like an hour, until Taylor showed up."

"And you handled it like a boss," a familiar voice chirps.

Taylor struts in, her blond hair flowing over her shoulders, in a comfortable get-up of a white camisole and jean shorts.

Ashley rolls her eyes. "Whatever, I'm not used to girls snapping at me because I'm '*moving too slow,*'" she air quotes. "*I'm* usually the one who snaps at someone because they're taking too long."

I laugh, pulling out my notebook. "You poor thing."

"Where have you been, girly? I haven't seen you in two days," Taylor announces.

I stiffen. "Um, just dealing with some...stuff."

She looks unconvinced. "What *kind* of stuff? My brother's been a wallowing mess."

I swallow and open my mouth to say something, but Ashley beats me to it.

"She's been dealing with a family emergency."

"Ashley," I warn her.

She looks at me, confused. "What? It's true. Will can wallow to someone who cares."

"*Family* emergency?" She chuckles. "That's not what Willy told me."

I cock an eyebrow at her. "You know about that?"

"Of course I do." She shrugs. "We talk about everything."

I glare at her. "So why did you—"

"Because I wanted to hear the truth, and what he told me just didn't sound like it."

I flinch at her candor. The little bitch.

"Well, now you know the truth. My dad had an emergency, and I've been helping him with it."

"Why did you lie to Will?"

That's a stupid question. *But is it?* "Can we not do this?"

Ashley pipes up. "Oh no, we're doing this." My gaze shoots to her. "What? I may not like him, but I need to hear this explanation. Wine anyone?"

Taylor squeals. "Oh, a glass of Riesling for me, please."

"You got it!" Ashley disappears into the inventory room.

"Why are y'all doing this?"

"We're gonna sit here and talk about why you told my brother you have a boyfriend," she says simply.

Just hearing the words again is silly. Did I really tell him that? What a dumb lie to tell a guy I obviously have the hots for.

I clear my throat. "There's nothing to talk about."

She gives me a look of disbelief. "Girly, I'm not stupid."

I open my mouth to respond, but Ashley bursting through the doors with two bottles of wine and three wine glasses distracts me.

"So it looks like we'll be drinking some Toffee Rivers and Hognoff today!" Her and Taylor's squeals make me jump. These girls are super dramatic.

"We can't drink on the job," I groan. I could get fired since I'm technically overseeing them.

Ashley rolls her eyes. "Stop it with the rules. No one here cares. Look around." She motions outside and in the banquet hall. "These people are getting drunk themselves." She pours Riesling into Taylor's glass and merlot into ours. She winks at me.

"Now why did you lie to my brother?" Taylor is no nonsense.

Sighing, I take a begrudging sip. "I didn't mean to, but...I just didn't feel comfortable telling him about my dad." I shrug.

She frowns, taking a long sip. "Why not?"

"Because it's none of his business, and he likes to offer to help with stuff." Which I appreciate, but I'm not a charity case.

She shrugs and gives me a look of understanding. "That's my brother, the hero. But why isn't it his business? Aren't you guys... kind of a thing?"

I flinch at that. "What? No. We were just...having fun," I lie.

Or at least I think I am. I don't fucking know. I like him, but it just can't go anywhere.

"*He* doesn't seem to think so."

My gaze whips up to hers, and I look at Ashley. She rolls her eyes and pours another glass.

"Will doesn't know what he wants. He has a type. I'm just...not his type," I joke.

Ashley rolls her eyes. "Will you stop it? Anyone with eyes and a *brain* can see that guy has heart eyes for you."

"Well...yeah. Anyone's *bound* to have heart eyes for something that's new and exotic."

Taylor frowns. "Where's this coming from? What did Will do to make you think he's not into you?"

I let out a shaky breath and take another sip of merlot.

"He didn't...*do* anything. I'm just looking at it from a different perspective, you know? I don't date guys for short-term. And he probably doesn't seem to like me as a long-term thing. A lot of people are fine with doing that, but I'm not."

I jump when Taylor's hand covers mine. "I get it. But why are you assuming he only sees you as a short-term thing? You don't know what's going on in his mind," she explains.

Biting the corner of my lips, I look at them both as they stare at me, waiting. I really don't know what to say.

"This entire conversation is silly," I laugh. "I barely know the guy. Why am I expecting him to know if he likes me for long-term? I'm sorry."

Ashley frowns, dancing the stem of the glass between her fingers. "Why are you sorry? That's a valid feeling. Especially where Will Monroe is concerned."

"Will you lay off my brother? It was many moons ago, Ashley. Let it go."

"First of all, it wasn't many moons ago, it was four years ago. Secondly, it doesn't change that her feelings about womanizer Will Monroe are valid."

Taylor faces Ashley, hands on her hips. "You shit on him every chance you get! And you're not making matters better by feeding Sienna bullshit. Maybe he actually likes her for long-term, and she's overthinking."

"So you're saying I'm not allowed to be hurt because Sienna is our friend?" Ashley asks incredulously.

"I'm *saying* you weren't completely forthcoming about your intentions with my brother. You told him you weren't looking for a relationship and were looking for fun, right? That's what you guys had: *fun.*"

"He didn't give us the opportunity to turn it into something *else*, Taylor. That's my point," Ashley retorts.

Taylor rolls her eyes and turns back to me, taking another long sip of her Riesling. "Look," she says to me, "ignore Ashley and her mourning of her fake almost-relationship with my brother."

"Bitch," Ashley mumbles.

"I think it's really unfair for you to assume that Willy doesn't like you for anything more than sex. You went on *one* date with him and concluded that."

I roll my eyes. "I *know* all of that."

"Do you?" She gives me a pointed look.

Shaking my head, I finish up the glass. "My mom always told me when I was little, wine is romance." My gaze is on the empty glass. "That someday I'll find my home with my favorite wine. But she didn't mean only wine. She told me I would find the love of my life *doing* what I love. Drinking what I love. There's something enchanting about sitting down, drinking a nice glass of wine, and sharing it with the person you love." I pour another glass as they just stare at me. "Excuse me for wanting that Hallmark romance, but Will can never offer me that."

Ashley gives me a small smile, but Taylor gives me a look of pity.

"It breaks my heart that you think so low of my brother," she whispers.

"I'm not thinking low of him. It's just...how things are. I can't satisfy him long-term, Taylor. When he first met me, he couldn't take his eyes off Ashley's boobs."

Ashley rolls her eyes. "Oh my gosh, not this again," she groans.

"Yes, this again."

"So he stared at her tits." Taylor shrugs. "They're a nice pair."

Ashley raises an eyebrow. "Thanks."

"I occasionally stare at a girl's ass if it's nice enough. What's the issue?"

I just stare at her. "Are you a lesbian?"

She rolls her eyes. "No, girly. I like men. My point is, sometimes we stare at things because they're attractive or they're hard to ignore. So Will stared at her tits."

"You're forgetting he saw these tits back in senior year," Ashley remarks, making me flinch.

I roll my eyes as Taylor gestures as if to say *case in point*. "See? It was basically like déjà vu."

This conversation is fucking stupid. "I still don't get your point."

"My *point* is you're being a drama queen. I'm sure Will thinks your tits are just as great. And look at you. You're *gorgeous*. Stop being stupid."

I should appreciate her compliment, but I can't bring myself to do it. I can't risk a change of emotions. He may like me now, but he'll decide I don't make him happy two months from now. It's not worth the risk.

"Thanks for the pep talk, but I'm just not feeling it."

She sighs, leaning on her elbows. "You're stubborn, you know that?"

"Your brother actually notified me," I deadpan.

She stares at me briefly before sticking her finger in her glass, tasting it. "Well, this conversation wasn't very productive, was it?" I shake my head. "Guess not. Anyway, it's getting late, and I'm meeting some friends for dinner. Anyone care to join?"

Ashley looks to me for approval. I frown. "Why are you looking at me?"

"Do you wanna go?"

"I think she was asking you. I don't live in Monroe." I take a long sip of merlot.

"No, I was actually asking the both of you," Taylor says.

I frown at her. "Why would you invite me?"

"Because y'all are my friends. So I'll see y'all tonight?"

"Sure, we'll meet you around six," Ashley says, looking at her watch. Taylor gives a satisfied nod and skips off, leaving the lobby. I look at Ashley, who gives me a confused look. "What? What's the problem?"

"I can't go to dinner with Taylor Monroe. Or you. I don't hang with rich people."

She flinches as if hurt. "Why do you only see us as rich people? Why not just people?"

"Because that's not reality," I deadpan. "Rich people hang around their own for a reason."

"That's not always true. Just come to dinner, Sienna. It's not a big deal. We can get ready together."

I open my mouth to respond, but she's already off, leaving the lobby. I look down at my watch and see it's fifteen minutes past four. Sighing, I look up and see everyone's gone. Time to close up. If Ashley thought distracting me with a glass of wine would make me forget she was supposed to close, she has another think coming. She *will* be closing tomorrow.

I'm following her to the country club minutes after cleaning up and closing. Once we get to her manor, we make our way inside. I throw my bag on their coat rack as she leads me upstairs. We make it to her room, and she disappears into her closet.

"Um, Ashley? I don't have a change of clothes for a fancy dinner."

She quickly reappears, observing my T-shirt, jeans, and sneakers.

"No worries. I have something for you."

I frown as she disappears back into her closet. "If you say so. But...you're okay with letting me wear one of your precious outfits?"

"Why wouldn't I be okay with that?" her voice booms.

"I just don't tend to wear designer clothes."

She chuckles. "Don't think of it as wearing designer. Think of it as an opportunity to show your curves."

I frown. "What? What are you talk—"

She suddenly walks out with a knit turquoise off-the-shoulder bustier dress. I'm staring at it in awe.

I look up to see her bright smile. "You like?"

"That's *gorgeous*, Ashley. I can't wear that. What brand is it anyway?"

She looks at the tag and shrugs. "Balmain."

I gape at her. "I can't wear that."

"Why not?"

"What if I spill food on it?"

She rolls her eyes. "Just try it on, drama queen. This was too small for me, but I didn't wanna sell it. Try it on."

Sighing, I take the dress from her and walk into the bathroom. I look at myself in the mirror and admire how it highlights my hips—or lack thereof. Minutes later, I walk out, and Ashley looks up from her phone, a pleased smile on her face.

"Oh my *gosh*, girly! You look beautiful! You *have* to wear that tonight," she urges.

I look down at it, and it does fit me nicely. "I don't know...you don't think it's too much?"

"Are you kidding me?! No, this is perfect for Taylor's dinner! She's friends with some high-profile *trusties*."

I frown at that. "Trusties?"

"Yeah, like trustafarians," she explains.

I cock an eyebrow at her. What the hell is that? "I'm not sure I understand..."

"Kids who have trust funds," she deadpans. Oh. Well, that explains *that*. "You're gonna look so pretty, oh my gosh. Please wear it," she begs.

Sighing, I roll my eyes. "Okay, I'll wear it."

She jumps up and down, squealing. "Yes! Okay, what are we doing with your hair?" She gasps, making me jump. "You should do those curls you did at Will's birthday bash!"

The Hollywood curls? That's my staple for events.

"You don't think that's too formal for this?"

"No, it'll set you apart. Her friends are rich, but they have no sense of fashion. They all wear name brands, but nothing matches," she jokes. "You didn't hear it from me, but she's the only one with real style in that group."

I chuckle as she leads me into the bathroom. She pulls out a curling iron, and I use it as she does her makeup.

Minutes later, I'm putting on makeup, and she's straightening her hair. I can't believe I'm at Ashley Westbrook's house getting ready for a dinner with a Monroe. How did all of this happen in less than a month?

After we finish, I remember I left my dad hours ago.

"Hey, I need to make a quick call."

Ashley gives me a knowing look before finishing her mascara application. I pick up the phone and call Dad.

"Hello?" he groans.

I let out a sigh of relief. He sounds okay.

"Dad, it's Sienna. Are you okay? Did you eat?"

"I'm okay, honey," he says.

I smile at his annoyed sigh. "Okay, I'm just checking. Did you take your medication?"

"*Yes*, Enna. The doctor had me take all of that, so I'm okay."

"Good. Well, I'm gonna be out for a few hours hanging with friends. I'll see you later tonight."

"Friends? Aww, finally, baby! You're making friends!"

I roll my eyes. "Get some sleep."

He laughs in my ear, and I smile at the sound. "See you later, honey."

"See you later, Dad." I hang up and throw my phone in my purse.

Ashley gives me a nervous smile. "Is he okay?"

"He's good. I was just checking in on him."

She smiles and looks back in the mirror, primping. "Good. Because tonight is all about you getting out of your head."

Rolling my eyes, I apply my lipstick, and we're off to the clubhouse moments after.

10

SIENNA

The clubhouse looks beautiful tonight. The sconce lights illuminate the hallway as we close in on the host stand. Candles are set up on the stand, and the scent of vanilla floats through the air. We're greeted by a warm smile from the host.

She pulls out two menus and silverware rolls. "Is it just two tonight, Ms. Westbrook?"

"No, we're actually guests of Taylor Monroe tonight."

The hostess's eyes brighten as she nods and motions for us to follow her. We walk into a private dining area, and I marvel at the group we see. Taylor's hair is straightened, and she's wearing a pink low-cut maxi dress. One of her friends looks at us, and she follows their gaze, smiling a bright smile.

"Girls! You made it!" She rushes me, hugging me tightly. She then pulls back, and her eyes scale down my body. "Damn, girl. You look gorgeous! Highlighting the curves, I see."

I roll my eyes. "Ashley insisted on going all out tonight."

She looks to Ashley, eyes widening. "Ash, oh my gosh! Is that the new Pomriono line?"

"Yeah! It was a present from Dad."

They both squeal as I try to figure out what the hell the Pomriono line is. I clear my throat, and they both look at me.

"You ladies are just a sight for sore eyes tonight. Come meet my friends." Taylor pulls us toward the large table.

My pulse quickens as all eyes are on me. Everyone looks friendly, but a few eyes are staring daggers at me.

88

"Guys! This is Ashley and Sienna," Taylor remarks.

"We know Westbrook. Who's the *other* eye candy?" a deep voice asks.

I look at the source of the question, and my breath hitches at the model staring at me. His brown hair is illuminated in the light, and he's wearing a fitted navy polo shirt.

Taylor rolls her eyes. "The eye candy is Sienna. I just said that," she deadpans.

The supermodel gives her a fake pout. "Aww, don't be jealous that you're not the only hottie in here," he says, followed with a wink.

She rolls her eyes, motioning us to sit down. "Anyway, that's Cale. Don't worry, he's as stupid as he looks."

"Don't worry, she's as bitchy as she seems," he retorts.

Taylor doesn't acknowledge him. "We were just talking about you guys. Ashley and Sienna work at the winery."

I flinch. Why would she tell them that? Aren't these people 'trustafarians'?

An extremely beautiful brunette quirks her brow. "Work at the winery as what?" I don't miss her snide tone.

"Um, well I'm actually a sommelier," I manage to get out, hating my voice cracking.

She chuckles, tossing her brown locks over her shoulder. "So you're like a wine professional?"

I simply nod, and she gives a weird look at Cale and the blonde sitting on the other side of her. Is being a wine professional some sort of new thing?

"And what do *you* do, Westbrook? I didn't even know you were working a *job* now."

Ashley gives her a look of disbelief. "I'm a sommelier-in-training, if you must know."

"*Oh*," the brunette mocks. I frown at her attitude.

The blond girl next to her clears her throat. "That's actually pretty cool. You guys are really helpful when it comes to pairings."

I smile at her effort to defuse whatever tension is going on.

"Thanks. Yeah, it can be hard finding a good pairing with wine. I can always help if anyone needs suggestions."

"Well, we'll definitely look at *you* if we need help pairing food and alcohol," the brunette deadpans.

"Can it with the bitchery, Sadie," Taylor snarls.

Sadie rolls her eyes and plasters on a fake smile. "My apologies. I'm not myself without my Cosmo."

"You must need a Cosmo every fucking day, then," Cale jokes.

"Shut up, Cale," she retorts.

They spend the next few minutes fighting—and flirting—while Taylor introduces us to the other two people there. The blond girl's name is Willa, and the guy sitting next to her is her boyfriend Connor, who I've met already. Everyone seems nice, except for Sadie.

We're all eating dinner, Taylor's asking Ashley about the latest Birkin bag she got, Willa and Connor are all coupled up, and Cale's trying to make conversation with me.

"So, Sienna," he starts. "How do you know Taylor?"

"Oh, um, well she and her brother are working at the winery this summer. So I've been getting to know them." For lack of a better explanation. I've been getting to know Will *very* well.

Taylor intervenes as if summoned. "My brother has a thing for her," she remarks, making me flinch.

Sadie suddenly butts in with a look of disbelief. "Will Monroe? He has a thing for the *sommelier*?"

"Yeah, they were dating until Sienna rejected him." Taylor really needs to shut up.

Cale is easily impressed. "You rejected a Monroe? That doesn't happen every day," he snickers. "I think I like this girl."

"Yes, let's all applaud the girl who has no taste," Sadie remarks.

"This coming from a girl who prefers Cosmos over wine?"

She quirks an eyebrow. "I like something a bit stronger."

"Fair enough. But Cosmo? You had to pick the lamest cocktail there is? Why not an old-fashioned? Perhaps a Manhattan? You had to pick a pink drink?"

She flinches as Cale tries to hide laughter, and Taylor's smile grows. Sadie rolls her eyes and turns to Willa, exiting the conversation.

"Ignore her. She dated Will for a bit, and she has a wad in her panties over the fact he dumped her," Cale whispers.

I look at her. Will dated her? Well, that makes sense. She looks like Adriana Lima. *And* she's rich. But her attitude is annoying.

"Has Will dated *everyone*?" I joke.

He gives me an amused smile. "He's Will Monroe, rightful heir of a multi-billion-dollar vineyard. He's pretty powerful here, and he looks like a GQ model. I'd say he's dated his fair share of girls."

"I get it. That's kind of why I ended it with him."

He gives me a look of confusion. "You broke up with him because he's a Monroe?"

I nod, hating myself for admitting it. "That, and I don't really waste my time with guys out of my league."

Cale's eyes widen. "Out of your league? Have you *seen* yourself?" I frown as his eyes scale down my body. "You're a hottie."

I can't help the chuckle that comes out. This guy is virtually a model, and he says I'm a hottie. Yeah, whatever.

"Uh, thanks. But things can get confusing really fast. I only date guys who I see myself with long-term, you know? Will doesn't see me that way." I shrug.

He flinches. "What the fuck? He actually *said* that to you?"

No, Sienna's just being stupid. "No, he didn't. But I'm nothing like the girls he dates."

"I'll be honest, you're not," he chuckles. "But you're...different. Which is good. It's nice to see a girl who looks different. You're gorgeous."

I smile at him, and he returns it. Is he flirting with me or just being nice? I can't tell. His eyes seem genuine, but there's no look of attraction. Will made it clear just from his piercing eyes that he was attracted to me.

And speak of the devil.

Nervousness courses through me as he struts in with the blond girl from before. I think he said her name was Mason. She looks beautiful tonight. Her hair is in loose waves, and she's wearing a purple maxi dress. It looks radiant against her porcelain skin. It's hard to look away from her. Everyone here looks like a movie star.

It takes me a bit to notice Will's looking at me, and I don't miss the surprise on his face. Clearing my throat, I look back to Cale, who's giving me a knowing smile. What a night this is going to be.

"Will, you actually made it," Taylor says, surprised. *You and me both, sister.*

"How could I miss my sister's superficial dinner?" he deadpans.

I can't help but fight a smile. Also, superficial? How ironic is that comment? Look at the stunning girl on his arm.

Taylor rolls her eyes and motions for them to sit down. They take a seat at the opposite end of the table, and everyone goes their separate way talking. The server brings two opened bottles of wine, and I'm popping open the bottle of merlot.

"You're a merlot girl?" Cale asks.

I smile, pulling out the cork. "In the flesh," I joke.

He laughs, the sound creating goosebumps on my arms. "Merlot has an interesting taste to it."

"I like the vanilla. Black cherry and vanilla go amazing together."

His smile grows bigger. "What would you say I could pair it with?"

"Food or dessert?"

"Food. Then we can talk about dessert."

I smile at the potential of putting my expertise to use.

"Well, if you like steak, it pairs great with a filet. If you're just looking to snack, I would recommend maybe crackers and a raspberry preserve. But filet and lamb are both great to pair with this."

He's eyeing me appreciatively. "Interesting. What about dessert?"

"That's easy: chocolate. A chocolate mousse cake would be great with something like merlot. The smoothness fits very well with a good mousse."

He nods, hand resting on his chin. "So if we split a chocolate mousse cake for dessert, will you drink merlot with me?"

I guess I have my answer now. He's definitely flirting.

"I don't think your girlfriend would like that very much," I say, looking at Sadie as she talks to Taylor.

He looks at Sadie and then back at me, confused. "Sadie's not my girlfriend."

I cock an eyebrow. "She's not?"

He shakes his head, a pleased smirk growing on his face. "She's hot, but she's just a close friend. Well, a close pain in my ass, really," he jokes.

"You two bickering looked like an old married couple."

His chuckle rumbles through me. "It's all in fun. We've known each other since elementary school," he says, shrugging.

I nod, drinking my glass of merlot. They all seem to know each other really well. I look around, and everyone's up close and personal with each other. And then my eyes do the worst thing: They land on Will.

Whose eyes are staring daggers at me. I flinch, staring back. Why's he looking at me like that? He looks between me and Cale, obviously upset.

Cale's sigh grabs my attention. "Someone's jealous," he whispers.

"Who's jealous?"

He cocks an eyebrow, and my gaze follows his back to Will. "Something tells me he has more than just a '*thing*' for you."

I shrug. "He's with Mason. It doesn't matter," I manage to lie.

"He's not even looking at Mason. She's too busy talking to Sadie."

I frown, my head whipping to Mason. Who is in fact talking to Sadie. Of course, they're friends. It's like watching two Victoria's Secret models talk to each other. And that just annoys me more.

"Like I said, it doesn't matter. We're not a thing anymore."

He smiles, drinking from his glass. "I guess it's settled then. We're sharing a mousse?"

I stare at him, waiting for the punchline. But when it doesn't come, the laugh that comes out is very intentional. Somehow and somewhere, I've stepped into the twilight zone.

"I guess we're sharing a mousse."

He gives me his brightest smile and taps Taylor's shoulder. "I think I wanna marry this girl," he jokes.

Taylor looks at me, confused. "He's kidding," I reassure her.

She rolls her eyes and moves closer to me. "Cale talks out of his ass a lot, so don't mind him."

"Don't be mad, princess," he jokes.

But again, Taylor ignores him. "Are you having fun yet?"

At first, I thought I wouldn't. But I actually *am* having fun. Everyone seems super nice, apart from Sadie. But that's just typical. I've dealt with my fair share of mean girls. I'm twenty-three. I don't care to entertain that.

"I actually am," I laugh. "I wasn't sure if I would."

She squeals and hugs me, making me yelp. The Monroes are touchy people.

"I'm so glad!" Then she suddenly gets secretive. "Are you okay with Will being here?"

I flinch, the same nervousness coursing through me. "Yeah, why wouldn't I be?"

"He told me he wasn't gonna show up tonight. So this is a bit of a surprise." She laughs nervously.

I shrug. "It's nothing I can't handle. We're not dating, Taylor."

She cocks a perfectly shaped eyebrow. "Well, yeah, but...he's been staring at you for the last thirty minutes."

I look back over there—stupidly—and he's still staring at me. What the hell is his problem? Does he not want me here? Mason suddenly turns to him and says something, turning his gaze off me.

"He probably doesn't want me here. It's okay, I don't mind," I lie.

She gives me a small smile and gently squeezes my arm. "If he makes you uncomfortable, let me know. I'll pull him aside."

Thank God for Taylor's meddling. But I wouldn't want to get Will in trouble. I'm essentially the misplaced guest here. She shouldn't have to scold her brother for simply being here. What's more, he wasn't expecting me to be here. So of course he's caught off guard with my presence.

The dinner ends a few hours later, and we're all trickling out of the dining room. I give a hug to Taylor and say my goodbyes to everyone—everyone except Will, Mason, and Sadie.

Ashley and I are laughing about the craziness of dinner when someone shouts after me.

"Sienna! Wait up!"

I turn to find Cale running toward me, and I am very confused by it. I look at Ashley, and she has a surprised smile on her face.

He stops in front me, catching his breath. And then a smile stretches on his beautiful face. "Sorry," he laughs.

"No worries," I say, chuckling.

He stuffs one hand in his pocket, running the other one through his hair. "That was fun, huh?"

"Yeah, it was fun," I say awkwardly.

Ashley suddenly speaks up. "I'm gonna...wait in the car." She gives me a wink and walks off.

He briefly looks after her. "Westbrook's a nice girl," he says.

"She is. I'm spending the night with her tonight. It's later than I was expecting."

He nods his head, understanding. "Um, so I don't want to be that guy, but...would it weird if I asked for your number?"

A shiver courses through me. "My number?" He nods, a hopeful look on his face. "Um, sure. I mean, I need friends, anyway," I laugh.

He gives me a slight frown before smiling. "Awesome."

I tell him my number, and he stalks off, me watching him go. This has been a weird summer so far. I've never hung out with the rich crowd in my two years working at the winery. A cute guy asked for my number, and I'm somewhat friends with two rich girls. When—and how—did this happen?

Brushing off these thoughts, I walk to the car. But someone else stops me, and my blood immediately runs cold at the voice.

"I didn't think I'd see you tonight."

Shit.

I turn to find Will staring at me, a blank expression on his face. His eyes scale down my body as they pierce into me. "Yeah, Taylor sort of invited me," I laugh.

But he doesn't return it. He nods, hands still in his dress pants pockets.

"You look beautiful," he says simply.

I swallow, hating the fact that my palms are sweating. "Thank you. So did Mason tonight," I say before I can stop myself. Why did I say that?

He cocks an eyebrow. "Mason's all right," he says, shrugging.

"*Just* all right? I think most guys would disagree."

"I thought we established that I'm not most guys," he says, his tone hard.

The playful smile I had is no more. Clearing my throat, I rub my hands down my dress. "Where *is* the Victoria's Secret model?"

He laughs a rueful one. "Which one are we talking about?"

He's not making this easy. "Will, you know what I mean."

"I don't. There's one standing in front of me, and then there's one that had to leave the dinner party early."

"Oh," I say stupidly, silently beaming about the fact that he just called me a model.

For a few seconds, we're just staring at each other. This is so weird.

"So...you were sitting with Cale tonight," he points out. I was hoping he wouldn't bring that up.

"Yeah, we were just chatting about wine."

His eyes narrow at me. "How would your boyfriend feel about you chatting up Cale Rivers?"

My stomach drops. Cale Rivers? "Rivers, as in—"

"Rivers Country Club. Our competition."

Shit. I wish someone had told me that before. They're in competition with Monroe Country Club. They're both household names, but Monroe beats them in the sense that they own over half of Rose Valley.

But the way he says 'competition' is troubling. It doesn't sound like he just means competitors in business.

"Um, I don't think he would mind," I croak. I need to drop this charade sooner or later. Soon Will might ask if he can meet him.

He gives me a small smile. "Really? Because I think he'd be jealous. Any guy with a *brain* would be jealous of another guy talking to you."

"Will, can we not do this, please?"

"Not do what? I'm just making conversation," he says softly.

I let out a sigh. "Well...I don't think he'd mind."

He's staring at me again, and I'm not sure what to do. He looks about done talking. I give him a small smile, and I'm close to turning around, but a smug smirk grows on his face. "You know...I had to think on it."

"What?"

"I had to think on it," he repeats. "That night I dropped you off, I was confused. Angry as hell, but confused."

"Will—"

"It confused me because you don't seem like the type of girl that would cheat on her boyfriend. Angry because there was a possibility that some other guy had been inside you and had touched you."

For fuck's sake, why is he doing this?

"Can we do this at work?" I croak.

But he's not done. "But what's really is pissing me off is the fact I *know* you're lying."

That's when I freeze.

Literally freeze.

Yet sweat continues dripping down my forehead. "What do you mean?"

"You know what I mean. There's no boyfriend. You lied to me."

Shit. "Will..." I whisper.

"You like me. A lot. And for some reason, that scared the shit out of you to the point you had to lie about an imaginary boyfriend," he growls.

I frown. Now he's just being a dick. "You think too highly of yourself."

But maybe it was the wrong thing to say. Because now he's advancing on me, making my breath hitch. He's inches away from my face, eyes piercing into me.

"Sienna," he whispers. "Look at you. You're a mess, babe. You're sweating. Your skin pales whenever you see me, and you think I don't notice. Your eyes dilate whenever I'm this close to you. Your body is practically burning with heat, and I can feel it. You *want* me to touch you."

He's a freaking sadist. Clearing my throat, I stand my ground. "No I don't."

He cocks an eyebrow, eyes never leaving me.

"Then why haven't you pushed me away yet?" I open my mouth to respond, but I don't know what to say. He's already figured me out, so it's no use. "See, the difference between you and me is, I'm not

97

afraid to claim you and say I want you. Ever since that day I laid eyes on you, Sienna, it was just you. It's *still* you. Forget Mason. I don't fucking want her. Why can't you see that?" His eyes dart across my face in a pained frenzy.

My pulse quickens as his eyes land on my lips. Only because I know what he's wanting to do.

"Will—" My voice quivers. "None of that matters, okay? I have a boyfriend," I lie.

I can't trust him. I can't trust any of these guys in Rose Valley. I have too much baggage, and trying to pursue anything with Will would be emotional suicide. He'd hurt me.

His hungry look quickly transforms into a glare.

"You're such a coward, babe," he snarls, making me flinch. "You know what you're really scared of? Discovery."

I frown. "Excuse me?"

"So *what* if the future is uncertain? You're scared that one of two things will happen. You'll either fall for me or I'll dump you. Is that it? That's what this is about, right?"

"Will," I whisper.

"I'll never be able to tell what's going on in that pretty head of yours, Sienna. But I *know* you're scared of discovery. You don't want to see what this"—he motions between us—"is. And you and I both know it's not just sex," he bites out.

I flinch again. I can't take him yelling at me right now.

"Will, can we *please* not do this? You can yell at me all you want at work, but you're not yourself right now."

He's still staring daggers at me. "Say the word, Sienna. Say the fucking word, and I'll leave you alone."

"Will—"

"Tell me you don't want me, and I'll walk the fuck away."

I open my mouth to say just that, but he's challenging me. He wants me to say that. He *thinks* I'll say that. It makes hating me that much easier for him. But I can't do that. Because it's not true. *Of course* I want him. I want him more than my next breath. But it means nothing. I can't risk getting hurt.

His daggers turn into a smug grin, and I see the Will I met that first day at the winery.

"When you come to your senses, you know where to find me," he says simply, walking away. His back is to me now, and I admire the suit he's in. It's perfectly tailored to his tall body. He's perfect. Everything about him is perfect. But I don't deserve him.

Clearing my throat, I walk to Ashley's car, and she quickly turns around, as if she weren't watching our entire exchange.

I let out a laugh as I feel tears welling in my eyes. "You definitely saw that," I point out.

She gives me a small smile before hugging me. "Sienna, that was hard to watch," she whispers.

I let the tears flow, and they don't stop. "He's really making this harder than it needs to be," I whine.

She pats my head, hugging me tighter. "Honey, why didn't you just tell him? Tell him about your dad."

My anxiety suddenly rises. "No, I can't. That's not his business. He'll want to fix it."

"So? If you guys decide to date, that's a good thing."

"Ashley, I can't let him do that. It's not his place to save me. I've been saving myself and Dad for over ten years now. I can't complicate things by bringing a player into the picture."

She lets out a sigh and pulls back. "Let's just hang out tonight, okay? This was a lot, and I'm sure you just need to sleep on it."

I nod because she's right. Between Cale and Will, things are much more confusing now.

But this is reality.

And neither one of them would make sense.

I'm destined to just take care of my dad and continue with winemaking.

11

WILL

"Dude, are you gonna do it?!" Collin practically shouts in my ear as I put my club away.

It's a sunny day in Rose Valley, and everyone's out on the course. We're on the twelfth hole, with six more to go.

"I don't know yet. The invitational would be great if *I* were great, but I'm only *good*."

Collin gapes at me. "You're shitting me, right?"

Letting out a sigh, I throw my bag on the golf cart. "No, my coach said he can get me in. But I don't know. I don't think I'm good enough to go pro. I never even played in college."

He shrugs, chugging a Bud Light. "You have a powerful swing, and you're a good-looking dude. I'd say you have a chance."

I laugh at his candor. "Thanks, man."

"I think you should do it. Make your own money, if you know what I mean."

"No, I don't know what you mean," I deadpan.

He rolls his eyes. "Look, everyone knows you're gonna inherit the vineyards around the world. But wouldn't it be nice to pursue your own thing? You have a trust account, but making your own money is more fulfilling."

He actually makes a bit of sense. "I guess you're right. But...I don't know, I'd have to practice a lot. I have until the end of summer to let him know."

He nods, and we stop talking about it. There's no use in talking about it if I'm not sure I even want to do it.

It'd be good for you, Will.

There'd be no more relying on my parents, and like Collin said, I'd be making my own money and playing the sport I've grown to love. I smile at the thought.

But I don't have enough time to think about it. Because we're on the next hole, Collin's polishing his club, and I need to focus. He sets the ball up. I watch him as he preps to tee off. The course is silent for a bit as he practices a few swings. As I watch him practice, I look around and lock eyes with the girls. For fuck's sake, they're out today. Mason, Sadie, Willa, and Taylor all strut in their golf skirts, bags in hand.

Rolling my eyes, I look away and continue watching Collin. He does another practice swing before hitting the ball. He watches it go the distance, and I admire it. He looks to me with a smug grin before his gaze lands on the girls. Shit. His smug demeanor changes as he clears his throat and polishes his club. Shaking my head, I polish mine and set my ball up.

"Psst, don't suck," Taylor whispers.

I turn around, and they're all watching me. I roll my eyes. I'm not in the mood to talk to them right now. After last night, I need to forget everything. Sienna looked like sex on legs, and it's fucking with me. Fucking Cale tried to make his move, and I didn't like it.

"What's got your panties in a bunch, Monroe?" Mason's sultry voice sounds behind me. Do these girls not know golfing etiquette? They're talking too much when I'm about to hit.

"Can you ladies look pretty and hush?"

They all raise their eyebrows, and I laugh at how synchronized it is. That sounded bad, but I'm not in the mood for flirting on the course. And Mason talking to me doesn't make matters better where thinking about Sienna is concerned.

Clear your head, Monroe.

Straightening my shoulders, I practice my swing a couple times before hitting. I watch as it goes the distance, smiling.

"For fuck's sake, dude," Collin whistles. "Leave some skill for the rest of us."

I chuckle, packing my bag. Mason saunters up to me again.

"I missed you last night. Sorry I couldn't go home with you. Family emergency, you know?"

"Totally fine, Mason."

I walk with Collin to the cart, but the girls follow us. And Mason continues talking. "What are you wearing to the gala Saturday? Maybe we could match."

Maybe we could match. Shit. I forgot about the gala. The gala I was supposed to take Sienna to. I mutter a curse before taking my hat off and running a hand through my hair.

"I'm not sure yet. I'll text you."

She nods, and the girls walk off. All except for Taylor. She stands there, arms crossed, shaking her head at me.

"You're bringing Mason now? Are you kidding?"

I frown at such a stupid question. "Yeah, what's the problem?"

"You might as well bring Sadie, you dipshit."

Fucking Sadie. "That ship sailed a long time ago."

"I thought the Mason ship did, too."

I narrow my eyes at her. "What are you getting at?"

"I was hoping you and Sienna made up," she mutters.

I was hoping so too. But the girl's fucking stubborn.

"When she drops the act about having a boyfriend, I'd gladly ask her to be my date again. But...she's scared," I croak.

I hate that it bothers me so much. So what if she doesn't want me? Hundreds of other girls do.

"How'd you know she was faking?"

"Because it just didn't make sense. We were having a great time, and then all of a sudden, a 'boyfriend' has an emergency? I don't buy it."

She gives me a look of defiance before letting out a breath. "You're right, she doesn't have a boyfriend."

I roll my eyes at this conversation. I came on the course to get my mind off last night, not rehash it with my sister.

"Then why are we having this conversation?"

"Just give her a break, all right? There really was an emergency that night, just so you know."

I cock an eyebrow. "There was?"

"She told me and Ashley about it. It's very personal to her, though. Just...don't give her such a hard time." She gives me a small smile before speeding up to join the girls.

I look after her, confused as hell. Clearing my throat, I turn to find Collin staring at me. I forgot he was in the cart.

"Lady in red consuming your thoughts again?"

I grunt and nod before driving off to the next hole. We can talk about this another time.

⌒

This week has been pretty shitty. Long hours at the winery and the crowd rushed in *every single day*. I spoke to customers, asking them about their favorite wines. Taylor helped Ashley do back-of-house stuff, like organizing wine and helping out in the bistro kitchen. And Sienna took care of the major customer stuff, like selling wine and answering questions about wine pairings.

It's Friday afternoon, and we're cleaning up. My body's giving me signals it needs to rest. But I don't have time to. Tomorrow night is the black-tie gala, which means I have to help set up at the venue. And there's the Mason dilemma where she wants me to help pick out outfits.

"Willy, stop daydreaming and help us wipe down the tables," Taylor yells.

Rolling my eyes, I walk into the banquet hall and almost stumble when I see Sienna. She's adjusting a white camisole, and I catch a glimpse of a black bra underneath. Her rack looks fucking perfect. She looks up and makes eye contact with me. I quickly look away and join Ashley and Taylor.

"What are we doing?"

"We have to wipe these tables so the staff can set this room up for the gala afterparty tomorrow night," Ashley explains.

I roll my eyes again. The afterparty is *here*? I didn't know that. My mom and dad must've *just* made that decision.

I wipe down tables near the door while Ashley and Taylor wipe down other tables in the middle. Sienna's transporting wine bottles to the back of the room. She walks in with another box of wine, but the door almost closes on her.

I rush over and hold the door open, and she gives me a small smile.

"Thank you."

"Always," I say.

She glances at me one last time before walking to the back of the room. I find myself following her, and I shouldn't be. She drops the box on the floor and flinches when she sees me. "Will," she says softly.

"Sorry, I didn't mean to scare you."

"Why are you following me?"

Honest answer? Because I'm a freaking weirdo. But I don't know, she has me chasing her, and this isn't usual for me.

"I just wanted to make sure you made it to...the back of the room okay," I lie. What the fuck was that?

She looks as if she's worried for my mental health. "Will—"

"Look, I just wanted to apologize for last night."

"Oh, Will, it's okay. We don't have to—"

"I drank a little bit, and I didn't know what I was saying." A huge lie. I knew exactly what I was saying. But I really need this excuse to talk to her.

She gives me another small smile. "It's really okay. We all drank a little bit last night," she chuckles.

"You could say that. Are you still coming to the gala tomorrow night?"

She flinches. "Oh, um, I wasn't planning on it. Would you like me to still go?"

"Do you *want* to go?"

She shrugs. "I don't know. It would weird to go by myself. But...I'll be working the afterparty, so I sort of have to come anyway."

I smile with that new knowledge. She'll be here tomorrow.

"Well, that's good. But you don't have to go alone. Bring your boyfriend."

Her eyes widen. "Oh...yeah. I'll bring him then."

What a stubborn girl. "Yeah, I'll put you two on the guest list."

I love goading her like this. I don't know how long she'll keep it up, but I'll keep playing this game if she wants me to.

"Thank you, I'll...ask him tonight," she says, swallowing.

I take a moment and just stare at her. Her skin is paling again.

"Sienna?"

She swallows. "Yeah?"

"When you come to your senses, you know where to find me," I repeat.

She rolls her eyes and stalks off. My eyes are on her ass again, and I ache for it. The feel of my fingers on those globes are only a mere memory. What I would give to hold them again. Suddenly, Taylor appears at my side.

"Is she coming tomorrow?"

"Yeah, she's bringing her 'boyfriend.'"

Taylor gives me a look of confusion. "She said that?"

"More like she's not willing to drop the act. The girl's as stubborn as a mule."

"Trust me, I know," she laughs. She pats my shoulder and goes back to wiping down the tables.

I'm staring at the beauty that is Sienna. She puts her hair in a messy top bun and continues wiping down tables. I thought I could walk away from her last weekend, but I don't know anymore. Just watching her in her element is the one of hottest things I've ever seen. I miss being able to touch her, feel her...fucking *kiss* her. I have to get some sort of lead on why the hell she's still lying to me.

Taylor told me there was an actual emergency that day I dropped her off. But what was it? And why couldn't she tell me the truth?

Sighing my annoyance, I go back to wiping tables, and then we're all closing down the winery. I need to focus. Tomorrow's the big event. My focus should be on that.

⌒

The next day is an even bigger pain in my ass. My parents are back home early, and it catches me off guard.

"Honey, we're back in Greece tomorrow, but we wanted to be back home for the event. Why do you look upset?" Mom asks.

I don't look upset. I might look annoyed, or even confused, but upset is not an emotion I feel right now. I just wish they would've let me know they were coming home this early.

Mr. Stevens isn't here—he's still out of town—and I know absolutely *nothing* about wine. Sienna was supposed to be teaching me, but that idea sort of went out the window.

"I'm not upset, I just wasn't expecting to see you guys so soon."

She's typing up notes on her laptop and nodding her head, no doubt ignoring my answer.

"How have things been with the winery? Is Taylor helping any?"

I knew she was going to ask this. "Yeah, she's been helping just fine. The winery's been fine. The younger crowd has been the majority of our guests, though. Revenue seems to look good."

I managed to take a look this past week. We're up to $95,000 this week alone in wine sales.

"That's good," she says, adjusting her glasses. "Have *you* been working any?"

I roll my eyes. "Yes, Mom, I've been working."

She gives me a pleased smile before she goes back to typing. I grab a beer from the fridge and run upstairs. I peek into Dad's office, and he's also typing notes on his laptop. For fuck's sake, do my parents work *every single day*? I'm tempted to knock on the door and ask him if he wants to play on one of the courses, but he looks too deep into work. *Save talking for another day*, I guess.

Hours later, I'm slicking my hair back and patting on cologne when my phone rings. Smiling at the caller ID, I pick up and am greeted by a hurricane of screams.

"Just the sounds I like to pick up my phone to," I deadpan.

Willa and Kayla are still screaming in my ear. "Collin told us! You're going *pro*?!"

I could choke the bastard. "Wrong. My coach told me I have the *potential* to go pro and he can get me into a semi-lower profile invitational."

"Will! That's such great news," Kayla says, squealing. "So let me guess. You'll be on to be the next Bryson DeChambeau?"

If only. "Actually, I'm on to be *late* if you two crazies don't let me get dressed."

"Fine, fine, we'll see you at the gala, stud," Willa says.

"See you guys then."

The phone line goes dead, and I go back to getting ready.

My parents and Taylor are already on their way to the venue. Taylor left with some guy I've never met, and I'm on my way to pick up Mason. I'll most likely be the last to show up, but I guess we'll both be fashionably late.

When I pull up outside of her house, she struts out in a white gown. I guess the matching plan isn't happening anymore. I get out of the car and open the passenger door to get in. She smiles at me, and I return it.

"Well, don't you look dapper tonight."

"Thanks," I say, chuckling. "You look beautiful, Mason."

She beams at me, but I quickly look away. This just doesn't feel right. She's beautiful, yeah, but...I find myself comparing her to Sienna. I need to stop thinking about her. It's not fair to Mason. I clear my throat as we head to the convention center.

The venue's set up with black and white balloons and a registration table. We go to the VIP line, and they escort us inside. We walk the red carpet, and the flash of lights almost blind me.

We stop in front of the golden horse statue and pose for the cameras. Minutes later, we continue walking down the red carpet, and the flashes are still coming.

We make our way to our assigned table, but loud gasps behind me grab my attention.

"Who is that?" a photographer asks.

I turn to find Cale Rivers walking down the red carpet.

With Sienna.

Their hands are joined together, and she has the most beautiful smile on her face. My eyes scale down her body, and I admire the bodycon dress. I'm starting to see she likes those kinds of dresses. But it doesn't take away from the fact I feel like the wind's been knocked out of me.

They stop and take pictures, and I overhear the muttering from the photographers. They're all asking who the new girl is. But wait.

Cale's not her boyfriend.

I smile, watching them walk down. She continues to prove me right. They're walking toward us, and I don't miss the frightened look in Sienna's eyes. If it weren't for the dark golden undertone in her skin, I'd have no idea she's blushing. But the pink lightly touches her cheeks nonetheless.

They stop in front us, Cale eyeing me. "Will," he says simply.

"Cale," I say. We both nod, and I feel Mason stiffen at my side.

"Nice dress," she says to Sienna. I frown, looking at her. And the uncomfortable expression matches her demeanor.

"Thank you," Sienna says nervously. "You look gorgeous tonight, Ms. Szuch."

Mason chuckles. "Call me Mason, honey."

Sienna gives her a nervous smile and practically hides behind Cale. The action turns my mood sour.

Clearing my throat, I walk Mason to our table. I don't know what's going on with those two. But I'm not going to stand there and just accept them being here together.

I pull Mason's chair out for her, and she sits down, me sitting next to her. Mom and Dad are chatting with Mason's parents, and all of the other socialites are talking.

The joy of staying in a son's place.

No one cares to talk to me since I haven't inherited the Monroe real estate yet. I don't care for it, but it just bothers me that no one here wants to talk to me. Even though Mason and I are presenting awards to the little girls tonight.

Suddenly, my mom turns to me as if she's heard my thoughts.

"William! Oh dear, I'm sorry I didn't see you." Then her gaze lands on Mason. "And little Mason Szuch," she croons. "You look absolutely gorgeous."

Mason blushes, giving my mom a big smile. "Thank you, Mrs. Monroe."

She then goes back to talking to the guests at the table. This happens every year. Mason and I show up, no one cares to talk to us, we present awards to less fortunate little girls, we eat dinner, and then go to the afterparty, only to be ignored by everyone again. It's the life.

The sound of whistles makes me turn around again. Connor's greeting Cale and Sienna at their table, kissing her hand. My friends are fucking idiots. They keep doing things that *I'm* not even allowed to do anymore.

Clearing my throat, I turn to Mason. "I'm getting a drink. You want anything?"

"Titos and tonic, please," she says.

Nodding, I get up and make my way to the open bar. I order Mason's drink and scotch for me. Something a little harder is definitely what I need tonight.

I turn to the stage and look at the extravagant décor in the room.

"You look really good tonight, Will," a small voice says behind me.

I turn to find Sienna smiling up at me. My heart aches when I see that girlish smile.

"Sienna, hey. You're stunning."

Her smile grows brighter as she orders two Moscow mules. She then turns to me.

"This event is really beautiful. Thanks for inviting me."

I close my eyes. Why did she have to say that?

"Sienna..."

She flinches, finally getting it. "Oh, right. I'm sorry. Sometimes I speak without thinking."

I let out a sigh as the bartender puts my drinks on the bar. I slip a $100 bill in the tip jar and turn to her.

"If only you were my date tonight, Sienna. Things would be so different," I say and walk away before she can say anything. I don't want to hear her response. Anything she says will only hurt more.

I make it back to the table, and Mason's giving me a sad smile as I hand her the drink.

"Thanks."

I nod and sit down, waiting for this damned thing to start. I look at my watch, and it's only thirty minutes now. Thank freaking God.

"Hey, Will," Mason starts. I turn to her, and she has an unsure look on her face. "Is there something you'd like to tell me?"

I frown. "What do you mean?"

She turns around, biting her lip. I follow her gaze and a shiver runs up my spine when I notice she's looking in Sienna's direction.

Shit.

She must've seen me.

"It just seems like there's something going on between you two."

"Not necessarily," I lie. "Well, not anymore, anyway. She... dumped me."

Her eyebrows shoot up. "So you guys *were* dating," she states. "That actually makes a lot of sense," she says, chuckling.

"Mason—"

"Will, it's okay. You clearly still have a thing for her." I can neither confirm or deny that. "And whatever reason she dumped *the* Will Monroe probably has more to do with her than you."

I frown at that. I don't want her to think Sienna has any issues.

"I'm not sure what you mean."

"She's a beautiful girl, but I'm guessing she's pretty unsure of herself. I could tell by the way she blushed. Her skin is gorgeous, by the way," she says, making me laugh.

"Mason, this is weird."

She shrugs, taking a sip of her drink. "It doesn't have to be. Look, I like you. I always have since high school. But I can't make you like me."

I give her a small smile. "I feel so bad."

"Don't," she urges. "If I lose a guy's attention to another girl, I'd rather it be her."

I laugh at this. "Thanks, Mason." I give her a hug, and she hugs me tight. This night already took a weird turn.

She pulls back, smiling. "And for what it's worth"—she briefly looks back at Sienna—"she still has a thing for you too."

I cock an eyebrow at that, excitement coursing through me at that affirmation.

"You think so?"

"I'm a girl. *Yes*, I think so."

I laugh, and we finally talk for the rest of the night until the event starts. I learn about how the equestrian competitions are going for her, and I tell her about the golfing shenanigans.

Thirty minutes go by, and the event starts. The host goes through the program and introduces the little girls that are receiving certificates tonight for a year's worth of free horseback riding sessions at the Louisville Equestrian Center.

Mason and I are called up to the stage an hour and a half into the event. We award scholarships to three little girls, Serena Winthrop, Sally Buchanan, and Maria Shapiro.

We make it back to our seats, and I look at my watch.

One more hour to go.

One more hour, and I can go to the afterparty and hang out with my friends. There's a club downtown that we all want to go to *after* the afterparty. It's been a while since I've been to Louisville—exactly two weeks.

I turn around to Sienna, and her eyes are glued to the stage. She looks so enamored with the graphics. I smile at the look on her face.

The event ends thereafter, and we practically have to jostle around people to make our way to the car in time for the afterparty.

My parents almost never go to it because they know how crazy things can get after the gala. They told me their plane leaves late tonight anyway, so I'm not expecting to see them.

We drive to the winery, and I take the back way inside to avoid the traffic going into the parking lot. We park and walk up the hill to the banquet hall. The décor is already set up when we walk through the doors. Swarms of people are in the corner, already with glasses of wine in their hands. Mason and I sit down at a table, and I go to the bar and order two glasses of rosé.

"Sienna, tell me what's wrong."

I freeze.

Turning around, I come face to face with Cale and Sienna.

"I'm so sorry, Cale. I have to go."

She turns to leave, but he spins her back around.

"What's the emergency? Maybe I can help," he offers.

That damn word *emergency* again. What the hell has happened now?

She makes an annoyed grumble before leaning in and whispering to him, the action making my blood boil.

His eyes widen as she pulls back, a nervous look on her face.

"Let me drive you."

"Cale, please, no. I need to do this alone," she cries, tears welling in her eyes.

"Are you sure?"

She nods, wiping her eyes and running out of the lobby toward the parking lot. What the fuck is going on? Why was she so upset?

"Rivers," I bark. He turns around. "What the hell was that about?"

He runs a hand through his hair, frustrated. "She's dealing with a family emergency. She won't tell me what, but it's her dad."

My blood suddenly runs cold.

Her dad?

Her dad.

Realization stretches across my face as I remember that day I dropped her off.

It wasn't a fucking boyfriend.

It was her dad.

I shake him, needing answers. "What happened? What emergency with her dad?"

"I have no idea, but that scared the shit out of me, dude. I think I should follow her."

I think I should too. Grabbing the glasses of wine off the bar, I turn to him.

"Wait here."

I walk back into the hall and drop the glasses off at the table. Mason's talking to someone as she notices me.

"Will, this is—"

"Mason, I'm so sorry. But I have an emergency I need to tend to."

A look of confusion stretches across her face. "What's wrong? Is there any way I can help?"

I swallow, hating that I'm ending the night this way. "Sienna's dealing with a family emergency, and she needs someone by her side right now." And I'm willing to be there with her.

"I'll come too," she offers, but I stop her.

"Enjoy your night, Mason. It doesn't deserve to be spoiled because of me."

For a second, I think she's going to insist. But she gives me a small smile and nods. She gives me a hug, and I walk back to the lobby to meet Cale. He's pacing as I walk up. He stops when he sees me.

"Let's go."

"Who's driving?" he asks.

I hold up my keys, and he nods. "You're right. The Mercedes looks better pulling up to a hospital," he jokes.

I roll my eyes, but I'm thankful for any attempt to defuse the situation.

12

SIENNA

I shouldn't be upset with him. He's unconscious in a hospital bed, and the only thing giving me hope that he's okay is the heart rate monitor. But the consistent beeping is only more anxiety-inducing.

I'm always waiting for that next shoe to drop at this point.

Story of my life.

"Once you're awake, I'm beating your ass." My voice cracks. "Once you're healthy and able to walk again, I'm never leaving your side."

My dad got into another car accident. Now he's in a coma. His doctor told me the second I walked through the door and saw my dad in a comatose state.

He's in a coma for three weeks, the doctor predicts. It's not always likely, but he's definitely going to be here for a bit. Which means medical expenses will be ridiculous.

Another anxiety-inducing thing.

I can barely stay on top of my therapy visits. How will I afford my dad in the hospital?

I'm lounging in the chair next to his bed, my sweater keeping me comfortable in this damned cold room. I hate hospitals. I hated them when my mom was on life support, and I hate them now. This is all my fault. He was going to the store, and he got hit by a drunk driver.

I should've never left him alone.

I should've never given his nurse the night off.

I should've never left my car.

I should've gone to the gala.

I'm a fucking idiot.

"Sienna," a deep voice sounds at the door.

I turn around and find Will and Cale walking in. My stomach drops as both of their gazes land on Dad.

Shit. They shouldn't be here.

"What are y'all doing here? You should be at the afterparty."

Will swallows, looking at Dad before looking at me.

"We were worried about you. We couldn't let you be here by yourself."

My body quakes as they inch farther into the room. I don't like that they're here. This is so embarrassing. But it does nothing to stop Will from rushing over to me and hugging me tight. And it makes me break down in his arms.

Cale comes up on the other side and hugs me.

"Shhh, it's okay," he whispers.

It's not okay. My dad's in a coma, I have medical bills on top of medical bills, I have rent to stay on top of, and I can barely pay for the therapy that's meant to keep me sane.

Nothing in my life is okay.

I pull back and look at Dad. It's frustrating me that he's not waking up. In some childlike fantasy, he's okay. He's not in a coma. He's going to wake up tomorrow, and I'm going to take him to breakfast. We'll laugh about the whole thing, and I'll work from home.

But he's still comatose.

"Thank you, guys. For coming," I croak.

Will gives me a small smile, his hand on my back. I look at Cale, and his gaze is on Will's hand. Well, this just complicates things. But this is what I needed, and I didn't even know it.

Suddenly, Ashley and Taylor rush in. Shit, does everyone know?

"Sienna, oh my *gosh*!" Taylor shouts, crushing against me. "Your dad had another accident?!"

"Yeah, he's—"

But Will's hand on my back signals me to stop. I look up, and he's giving me a pointed look. He's comforting me. It hurts to talk about it.

"What's the verdict? Is everything okay?" Ashley's breathing is labored.

"He's in a coma," I say, tears welling up again.

They all share knowing looks before hugging me again. All this contact is only making me sadder. I've never had support like this before—outside of my therapist. I'm realizing this is what I've been missing.

The doctor comes in and zeroes in on the party in here.

"Are these close family members?"

"Actually, these are—"

"Yes, we're close family, sir," Will cuts me off. "What's going on? Is he gonna be all right?"

He looks between me and Will, marveling at the difference, no doubt.

"He'll be fine. But we're looking at almost a month-long comatose state."

One month.

I'll be without my dad for one month.

I shiver at the thought.

"And this is based on *what*, exactly? Because I bet if we fly him to a doctor in Atlanta, they'd tell us something different," Taylor argues.

I close my eyes. I don't want them to be difficult.

The doctor raises his eyebrows. "They'll tell you the same thing."

"Are you sure about that?"

"Taylor, please," I say. "That's not necessary."

She gives me a look of defiance. I love that they want to help, but they're not helping by arguing with him.

"So what does that mean for us? We just wait?" Cale asks.

"Unfortunately, yes. I do have some news for Ms. Durham, though." My heart stops at that. "He's not likely to wake up in a vegetative state. But it would be wise to sign a Do Not Resus—"

"I'm not signing that," I say simply. I know what he's going to say, and I'm not doing it.

He gives me a knowing look. "I know it's hard, but I just recommend—"

"She said she's not doing it. What the fuck else do you need to hear?" I calm Will down.

The doctor looks around the room and, resigned, walks out with his clipboard. I'm not planning for my dad's uncertain death. If he can't give me proof that he's dying, I'm not signing shit.

"Asshole," Taylor grumbles, turning to me. "What do you need from me?"

I smile at her. "I don't need anything from you, love. But thank you so much for being here, guys."

"Of course," Cale says.

Will's hold on me tightens. I stay close to him as we all just look at my dad sleeping.

I hate this so much.

I should've stayed home tonight. I shouldn't have gone to that event. I squeeze my eyes shut as tears threaten to escape.

"Guys," I whisper. "I don't understand. My dad's in a coma." The realization suddenly hits me hard.

Will's hand tightens around me again. "It's okay," he whispers. "We're gonna help you get through this."

I shake my head. I don't want to burden them.

"I can't believe you guys showed up."

"Of course," Taylor says, squeezing my arm.

Sighing, I lay my head on Will's chest. I watch my dad for a few minutes and then turn to everyone.

"Thanks, guys. I need to go and pack some clothes," I say, leaving.

"Where are you going?" His voice is filled with panic.

"I'm staying with my dad here." I can't leave him alone. Not for three weeks.

He frowns. "You're gonna sleep on a *chair* for three weeks?"

"Not a chair. There's a daybed behind the curtain," I say, pointing to the window.

He shakes his head, advancing on me. "No, you're not staying here, Sienna."

I let out an annoyed sigh. "Will—"

"Just stay with us."

The simple statement makes me flinch. *Stay* with them? I look at Taylor, and she has a comforting smile on her face. She nods as if to reassure me. I look back at Will, and his gaze is eager.

"I'm not sure if that's a good idea. I wouldn't want to impose."

"You wouldn't be imposing at *my* house," Cale offers.

Will visibly stiffens, his eyes still on me. "She'll be just fine at *my* house, Rivers."

Cale rolls his eyes but gives me a small smile. I have no idea what's going on here.

"I really don't know. That's your...domain."

Taylor chuckles. "Girly, it's okay. We welcome you with open arms. Please, you'll be fine."

I swallow and meet Will's gaze again. He reaches for my hand. "*Please*, Sienna," he begs.

Sighing, I let out a shaky breath. "Okay," I croak. "But only for a week at most."

"You're staying the full three weeks, and it's not a discussion," Will says.

I flinch at his hard tone. And...it's kind of hot.

He offers to drive me to my apartment, so I'm in his car, staring out the window, trying to figure out how the hell my life turned out this way. Will's hand is on my thigh, comforting me. I should be stopping him, but I'm too checked out to even care. It's been a rough month.

He pulls up outside of my complex, and I just sit there and stare at it.

"Sienna?"

I turn to find him staring at me, worried. "I can just stay at home, Will. It's no worries."

"Babe—"

"Really, it's okay. I promise I won't insist on staying at the hospital."

"Sienna, I'm not leaving you alone."

"I wouldn't be alone, though. I'd be visiting my dad."

"During the day, but what about after work? You'll have me or Taylor home to watch over you."

This is so dramatic. "I don't need a babysitter, Will."

"But I'm betting you need someone to talk to," he whispers.

I open my mouth to argue, but it's no use. I hate that he's right. Being home by myself would be lonely.

Sighing, I open the car door and run upstairs to pack clothes. I throw my bathroom essentials, clothes, and shoes in my duffle bag, and I'm downstairs soon after.

Will gives me a satisfied smile, and we're driving back to Rose Valley.

Staying with Will Monroe is probably the worst decision I've made, but clearly I'm not thinking correctly.

⌒

I smile at the large mirror in the guest room. The canopy bed illuminates in the background, the small chandelier shining bright on the gold.

I throw my sweatshirt on and look around the room. Obviously, it's a step up from my closet-sized bedroom. From the dark wooden dresser to the white candles on each side of the bed, I feel like I'm in a royal's room.

A knock at the door drags my attention away. Taylor's smiling at me, and I admire her silk pajamas.

"How ya doing, girly?"

I give a slight shrug. "Doing as best as I can, I guess. Thanks for letting me stay."

"Stop thanking us," she orders. "You're practically family at this point."

I roll my eyes. "You guys have known me for like a month."

"And you're the most normal friend I have."

Laughing, I slouch down on the bed, noticing a mirror overhead. There are two mirrors in here?

"I'm still thankful you guys would let me stay here. It's been a hard month with work and staying afloat. And then *this* happens," I complain. Dad never knows how to stay put. It can be so annoying.

"Dads can be stubborn. But if he's as stubborn as you, I know exactly where you get it from," she says.

Rolling my eyes, I sit up and narrow my gaze at her. "I think you mean '*able-bodied*.'"

"No, I meant 'stubborn.'" I stick my tongue out at her, and she rolls her eyes. "Childish," she laughs, shaking her head. "Get some sleep, girl."

She disappears from the doorway, and now it's just me and my thoughts. Taylor's growing on me. The seemingly spoiled girl just might be my new friend. I only worry that all of this is short-lived.

I take my laptop out of my bag and pull up my application for the winemaking course I've been wanting to take. I've been so focused on work—and the Will drama—to even remember the course at the local community college.

You can't afford it, though.

Well, this is just grand. Sighing, I close my laptop. It's no use signing up.

"Long night?"

My gaze shoots to the doorway, and Will's leaning against it in a T-shirt and boxer shorts. Swallowing, I bring my gaze back up to his eyes.

"How'd you guess?"

His smile eases some of the tension in my body as he strolls across the room, sitting in a chair.

"It was an educated one."

"You know, you really didn't have to allow me to stay here."

He shrugs, fidgeting with his hands. "I'd be a shitty person if I didn't."

"You'd be a cautious person. Which is totally fine."

"Sienna, why didn't you tell me about your dad?"

I nearly get whiplash from the sudden change in subject. I almost joke with him, but his hard expression tells me he's not in the mood.

Clearing my throat, I swallow past the lump. "I...didn't know how to tell you."

"*My dad had an accident, Will. I'm sorry, I have to go.* See? Easy as that," he retorts.

I knew this new revelation would've upset him.

"You wouldn't understand."

His eyebrows shoot up. "Understand what? Here I assumed you just wanted an out from dating me. But it appears you wanted an out from dating me *and* you didn't trust me enough to tell me," he says, the hurt tone not falling on deaf ears.

"Will, you *really* wouldn't understand."

He gets up and moves to my bed, sitting in front of me.

"Enlighten me."

Swallowing, I ponder whether or not I should. "I'm not sure if you want to know."

"Sienna," he starts. "Babe, you barely know me. I barely know you. But goddammit, it feels like I've known you a lifetime. You can fucking trust me," he bites out, making me flinch.

"Okay," I start, my voice shaky. I rub my hands on my pajama pants. "My dad has Parkinson's disease." I wait for a sign on his face. Maybe shock. Maybe confusion. But instead, it's the same pensive expression. He's just listening, so I continue. "There was a bad car accident when I was eight. My mom perished, and my dad was left okay. Up until I turned twenty. I was a college junior when he called me during class one time and told me he was diagnosed with stage 2 of the disease." I let out another shaky breath, and he pulls me close.

He kisses my forehead and rocks me. "Shhh, it's okay."

Gulping, I continue. "It was so hard, Will. It was my fault."

"What do you mean?"

"Dad had been drinking that night. It was after their anniversary weekend. Mom offered to drive, but I really wanted her to read me a bedtime story and be focused on me the whole drive. It was a three-hour drive from Nashville. I loved hearing her voice, Will. I wanted her to read me a book because I was sleepy, and I didn't wanna be awake the full drive."

"Sienna..."

"If I would've just let my mom drive, she'd be alive right now. I'd still see my mom," I whisper, tears falling down my cheeks. I close my eyes to try to stop them, but it's no use.

He's rubbing my back, trying to soothe me. "Babe, you can't blame yourself for that. You were young."

"And stupid." I pull back and look him in the eyes. "You know she brought up wine to me? I was seven, and she used to always tell me... wine is romance. There's something enchanting about a nice glass of wine. I never understood why she was telling me this at such a young age, but it makes sense. Love can withstand any hardship. After she died, I ate grapes...*a lot*. When I turned fifteen, I snuck wine into the house without my dad seeing. It helped me with therapy. It still does. I deal with anxiety. I used to get really bad nightmares, remembering the screams of my mom when the car hit us. She reached for my hand and tried to calm me until the ambulance showed up. But by the time they did...her breathing become...labored. Up until they put her on life support." I shake as the images play in my head. "Wine keeps me sane, Will. I relied on it for so long, and it calms me."

"Sienna, I'm so sorry," he says.

"That's why I want to do winemaking. If wine has helped me through my anxiety and grieving—in moderation, of course—it can help others who are. Therapy doesn't help. I hate it. I can barely afford it."

He wrinkles his forehead. "You can't afford it?"

I shake my head, looking down at my pants. "That's why I drink wine. I can't rely on it all the time. But...I feel better after drinking it." I shake my head. "I can barely afford anything, Will. Our apartment, my therapy, Dad's hospital bills...*everything*."

His sad expression makes my heart break. "Why didn't you tell me sooner? Dammit, Sienna." He pulls me closer again. "I can help—"

"*No*, Will, no. I don't take charity. I've taken care of my dad this long, and I'm not accepting money from anyone."

"It's not charity. Babe, you work your ass off at the winery, but you have so much going on, you can barely enjoy your life. I want to help."

"Will, I really appreciate it, but it's okay. All of this is my fault anyway. If I hadn't been a stupid eight-year-old, my mom would be alive and Dad wouldn't have Parkinson's disease from a car accident injury. In life, there are consequences," I mumble.

He lets out a sigh. "I can't force you, but I just want you to know you can tell me if you need anything."

And yet I won't. But I give him a nod of affirmation anyway. He gives me another hug before walking out of the room. Letting out a shaky breath, I get up and shut the door, locking it. I lean against it, and that's when I let it go.

I slide down the wall as a wave of emotions hits me all at once. My body shakes as I cry, holding myself. I hug my knees and take deep breaths, counting to ten like Ms. Spencer taught me. But it only kind of works.

Because Will changed the entire trajectory of my emotions.

This handsome guy, the guy that I broke things off with, the guy that could have any girl he wants, and the guy that has the cockiest personality I've ever seen.

He's offered to help.

He wants to rescue me.

But I can't allow him.

My ego simply won't allow it. If I overcomplicate things by involving Will in my life, I will just bring him down with me. And I don't want that. He deserves better. And, sooner or later, he'll come to the same realization.

And yet, I find myself getting up from the door and opening it. My legs somehow make the trip to his room. I almost knock on the doorway, but his room is empty.

And so is his California king. It's huge. And it looks so comfy. There are so many reasons I should turn back around and go to sleep. He'll find me in here and wonder what's wrong.

But I don't care. Because the next thing I know, I'm taking large steps toward his bed, and I'm lying down. I get underneath the covers. He'll probably think this is weird, but I don't care.

I might—just *might*—need him to hold me.

I'm crying into his pillows.

And soon, I cry myself to sleep.

13

WILL

There have been wiser men. When they see a gorgeous woman—not to mention the woman of their dreams—sleeping in their bed when they get back home from a night of drinking, they would push said woman out of their bed. They might even pick her up and take her to her *own* bed.

I should've done both of those things.

But I didn't.

Instead, the moment I see Sienna lying in a fetal position on my bed, my heart instantly aches.

I *have* to be hallucinating.

I rub my eyes for good measure, but the image remains the same. She's lying in my bed. Not only is she lying in my bed, but she's clutching my custom quilt. The poor girl was crying in her room, and I sat outside of it for a few minutes just to listen to it. For the longest time, she's been putting on this "tough girl" persona. But it's only barely getting her by.

Her cries were fucking with my head, so I did the only thing a guy in my position could do: I drove downtown and had a few rounds of drinks. I planned on getting drunk, but then I thought better of it.

Coach is going to kick my ass if I come to the course with a hangover.

And then there's Sienna.

Fucking Sienna.

I couldn't get drunk tonight. Not when she needed me the most. And I wasn't even here when she *did* need me.

I change into my sweatpants and take my shirt off, getting comfortable for bed. I slide in on the opposite side and sleep as close to it as I can.

But she has other ideas.

Her hands reach out for me. I almost think I'm imagining it. But I'm not. Her eyes are still closed, her body still relaxed. As if she senses my hesitation, she moves closer to me, hugging me from behind, her tiny body clinging on to me like a life preserver. My body reacts, but not in the way I expect. Her touch eases some of the tension that was there.

Almost like...her touch is home.

I smile as her hands dig into me. And her tiny snores follow thereafter.

Something feels right about this entire thing.

And I'm not about to let it go.

There's something soul-crushing about not finding Sienna next to me hours later. The side of my bed is empty, the ghost of her fingers squeezing me tight. Waves of sadness flow through me as I get up from bed. I guess it was just a pipe dream.

She's not ready.

And it might just take me a while to accept that. I don't know why, but there's something about Sienna that's not letting me let her go. And I don't want that feeling to go away. I want to take care of her. I *need* to.

And it's not some weird primal reaction, either. I just wouldn't be able to sleep at night without talking to her, feeling her, hearing her...fucking smelling her. Her smell is the last thing I sense in the kitchen.

I look around for a note at least, but it's no use. The only thing I find is Taylor, who's slurping down a green smoothie. She vows to me that she'll never miss fencing practice again, and we're off going our separate ways.

I make it to the golf course, polish my clubs, hit a few balls, and I'm on the last hole when my coach drives up on his cart.

"William! So sorry I'm late. My son, Lucas—"

"I think I want to do the Harvey Invitational, sir," I blurt out.

He flinches, a surprised look on his face. "Really?"

"I think it'd be good for me. What do I need to do to get in?"

He shrugs, adjusting his hat and polishing his club.

"I would just need to get you signed up."

"Awesome, well, I wanna sign up."

He cocks an eyebrow. "I thought you said you were going to be busy with the winery this summer. What happened?"

A certain sommelier happened. "Nothing happened. I just...want to start taking golf seriously. So what can I do to get started?"

"Well, first I need to make sure you're ready to start training at the level needed for the professional level. Then you need to start practicing with other golfers. This is seven-day-a-week training. Are you okay with doing that?"

I can barely afford anything, Will. Our apartment, my therapy, Dad's hospital bills, everything.

I squeeze my eyes shut at the mere memory. "Whatever I can do to get into Harvey, I'll do it. Just...let me play."

He eyes me with suspicion. "Not that I'm unhappy with the fact you're expressing interest in going professional, but why *now*, all of a sudden?"

Because if I don't, Sienna will single-handedly fall apart in front of me. And I can't watch that happen.

"I just think it would be good for me. You know, get away from the Monroe fortune for a bit. Make my own money."

He gives me a happy smile before nodding. "Then it's settled. We need to practice every day, William. How often do you go to the gym?"

Is that a serious question? I go every day.

"Going to the gym won't be an issue, sir. I can handle whatever it is you throw my way."

"Well, then. We'll start tomorrow."

And just like that, I'm training every day with Coach Bronson Sanford.

I go to the gym two times a day, practice my swing with Coach, watch videos from the greats, and improve my game like the best of them. Collin and Connor even join me and practically swoon at the newfound knowledge I'm finally looking to compete.

And each time I come back to the house after practice, Sienna's never there. It's been a week since I've seen her. If I didn't know any better, I'd think she was avoiding me.

But maybe she is. She never once stepped foot in my bed after that night. Taylor's been working afternoons at the winery, and she told me Sienna's been visiting her dad on lunch break, checking on him.

It bothers me that she feels like she has no one. It's been her and her dad for so long, she won't accept help. Little does she know, I'll still help her any way I can.

"Sienna will run for the hills if she finds out you're doing this, Willy," Taylor says at the kitchen counter Sunday morning. She's scrambling eggs as I open the fridge, looking for apple slices.

"Then it's a good thing she won't find out until it's too late."

She laughs before stating, "I think it's sweet what you're doing for her. But she won't think so. It's an insult to her womanhood."

I frown. "What does this have to do with her womanhood?"

"It's basically saying you don't think she can take care of herself." She briefly turns around when I don't respond. "Hey, talk to *her*. I'd love for a guy to fight for me once in a while," she mumbles.

I ignore her weird comment. "I'm not trying to insult Sienna's womanhood by helping her."

"You're trying to get into a golf tournament so you can win the purse and put money away for her," she rehashes my plan. "This isn't a romance movie, Willy. Women in real life don't think that's hot."

"Who cares if she thinks it's not hot? I just want to help her."

"Help who?"

We both flinch at Sienna's voice, turning to find her staring at us suspiciously. My pulse quickens at the sight of her.

She's wearing a sweatshirt and slippers. I love how comfy she looks. But it's not her clothes that I'm really looking at. My eyes zero in on those curls. No more loose waves or straight hair.

Her hair is curly.

And it's fucking beautiful.

"Your hair is curly," I blurt out stupidly.

She gives me a shy smile as she absently runs her hand through it. "Yeah, I washed it this morning. It can be a pain in my ass. I'll straighten it later today."

"Don't," I blurt, making her freeze. "It's stunning."

Her smile grows bigger as she stalks toward Taylor. Her eyes land on Sienna's hair.

"They're so cute, girly."

"Guys, please don't gush over my hair," she laughs. "It's just curly."

"It's not *just* curly," Taylor retorts. "I have to get a perm for my hair to get that way."

"You should wear it like that for a while," I offer.

She looks at me, cocking an eyebrow. "I can't do that. It'll get tangled." Well, shit. I can't argue with that. "But since I'm staying here, you guys will see these curls pretty often," she jokes.

"Grab a plate," Taylor tells her. "I made eggs. We're going to work in a few."

Her eyes bulge out of her head. "Crap! I need to make a pitstop before work today."

"Where do you need to go?"

She gives us a sad smile. "I was gonna drop flowers off for my dad. You know, just a reminder that I'm still here and with him."

Taylor and I share a concerned look.

"I'll take you during lunch," I tell her.

"Really?"

"Of course. It's not a big deal."

She gives me a happy smile and quickly grabs a plate. I'm packing lunch, putting on my clothes, and driving Sienna to work. My hand finds its usual way to her thigh, gently squeezing it.

128

I'm pulling into the parking lot of the winery and we're getting out, walking up to the lobby. Eyes are on us as Taylor hops out of her car, running after us.

"Thank you for the ride, Will," Sienna says.

"No need to thank me. It's my pleasure."

I don't know how I'm going to keep this secret from her. She doesn't know that I'm competing professionally. She's said she wants to up her hours at the winery, and I don't argue with her about it. I can't make her rest if she doesn't want to. But it still bothers me that this is how her entire life was since childhood.

Her mom died when she was *eight*, and she thought it was *her* fault. I can't even begin to imagine living with a thought like that. She's had this burden on her shoulders for so long, and I plan to ease it.

For the rest of the shift, we do what we've always been doing: selling wine. We sold three hundred bottles today. Taylor worked her Monroe magic, Ashley helped me—begrudgingly—with the bistro food, and Sienna manned the lobby desk, offering her preferred pairings. We're all a good team. I'd say it was a job well done.

"Well...that went well," Taylor exclaims, slouching down on the couch in the lobby. I sit down next to her. "Three hundred bottles. It's like *we're* running the winery," she laughs.

"We are," I deadpan.

She rolls her eyes. "You know what I mean. Mom and Dad decide to take an eight-week long trip to Europe, and Mr. Stevens sees it as an opportunity to go on vacation," she groans. "We're basically managing this place right now."

"Well, you better get used to it. Because we're inheriting it, stupid."

"Don't remind me," she groans again.

I'm not in the mood for her complaining. I look around the lobby for Sienna, and I see her with Ashley, sweeping the wooden floors in the bistro dining room.

"There you go again, pining."

"I'm not pining." I'm totally pining.

Taylor arches her brow. "You just need to give her time, Willy. I'm willing to bet she's not looking for a relationship right now."

"I *know* that, Taylor."

"And yet you're still staring at her."

"I can't stare now?"

"Well, some people might argue that's rude," she deadpans.

Rolling my eyes, I pick up a box of wine and bring it back to the inventory room. Setting it down on a shelf, I look at my watch. It's almost lunch time. I run back up to the front, and Sienna's waiting, her purse on her shoulder.

Her eyes brighten when she sees me. "Hey."

"Hey, are you ready?"

She nods. "Do you mind if I stop somewhere for flowers?"

"Not at all. Let's go."

I reach for her hand, and we walk to my car. I open the passenger door to let her in, and I walk around to get in. We're pulling out of the parking lot and driving in the direction of Louisville. It's a pleasant quiet in the car. Neither one of us are talking, but the silence speaks volumes.

"Thank you again, Will," she finally speaks up.

I smile, eyes still on the road. "There's no need to thank me."

"Sure there is. You didn't have to let me stay with you guys."

"You really thought that I would let you go home alone while your dad's in the hospital? I know I'm a prick, but I'm not a dick."

Her body shakes with laughter. "Letting me stay at my own *apartment* does not make you a dick. It makes you cautious."

"Yes, Sienna. You're right. I should've been more careful. What am I thinking, letting a hot girl stay at my house? She could be an axe murderer."

She rolls her eyes. "You know what I mean."

"I actually don't. You don't get it. Taylor was right. You're pretty much family at this point. Neither one of us knows you that well, but you're comfortable to be around. I oughta know," I mumble the last part.

Her breath hitches, and I silently curse for being stupid. "Will..."

"Shit, sorry."

She laughs nervously. "It's okay. But again, I'm still thankful."

I smile again and don't respond. If I speak too much, some things will slip out that I'm keeping to myself. If she found out about the tournament, she'd argue with me endlessly. I'm not even convinced she'd accept anything from me.

But I'm doing it anyway.

An hour later, I'm walking with Sienna down the hospital hall, a bouquet of flowers in her hand. She's a few steps ahead of me, and when she stops at the doorway of her dad's room, she freezes. My steps quicken, and I stop next to her.

He's still in an unconscious state, and the heart monitor is consistent. I let out a sigh of relief.

He's still breathing.

I look down at her, and she's still in a daze. I reach down, touching her hand, and she gives me a small smile before putting my hand in hers.

We walk into the room, and she sets the bouquet down on the table next to him. She leans down and whispers something into his ear before giving him a kiss on the forehead.

The scene makes my heart hurt. I have no idea what she's feeling right now, but I can only imagine. My parents barely notice that I exist. And here I am, envying the girl who has the best relationship with her dad.

"He looks so...different," she croaks next to me.

I jump out of my daze and look down at her sad doe eyes.

"Does he like chrysanthemums?"

She shrugs, squeezing my hand. "I don't know. I just think they're pretty."

And that's the only explanation I get. I don't press for more.

We walk back down the hallway, and I notice the stares our way, most of them being on Sienna. I look at her, and she doesn't even notice. She's looking straight ahead, eyes determined on the door in front of us. It could be because she's gorgeous, it could be because we look different. Either way, I'm glad she's not focused on it.

We're back in the car, and I turn my key in the ignition. But she stops me. I turn to find her staring at me with indecisive eyes.

"Sienna? What's wrong?"

She stares at me for another second before moving over to me. My pulse quickens as she sits down on my lap. My hands instinctively trail down her waist, landing on her hips. Her hands go up to my face.

"Thank you for driving me," she whispers.

I swallow. "Of course."

She tilts her head, leaning closer to me. I adjust in my seat, feeling a boner develop. What is she doing?

"Would you be mad if I kissed you?"

I freeze, grunting. This can't be real.

Is she fucking with me?

"Um, Sienna?"

"Hm?" She nudges her nose with mine.

"I wouldn't be mad, but...are you sure you wanna do that?"

She pulls back, eyeing me. Then she nods and slams her lips down on mine. I'm momentarily stunned, but then she deepens the kiss, her tongue seeking entrance. I'm not sure which of us moans, but it's as if a switch flips. I lift a bit to get comfortable, and her lips go to my neck, trailing kisses.

I pull her lips back to mine, biting her bottom lip. She whimpers, the sound sending a shiver through my body. I take a second and focus on her taste. Cherries and vanilla. I could taste her all damn day.

"So," I say against her lips, "does this mean you'll let me inside?" I writhe as I ask the question.

She gently shakes her head, biting my bottom lip. "Nope."

I smile, trailing kisses down the side of her neck. She's going to make me work for it.

Game on.

I toy with the top of her camisole, and she slowly starts grinding on my lap. She's like a fucking cat in heat. She lifts her chest, seemingly giving me permission to do what I want to do.

I slowly pull the straps down, her breathing labored. I smile at the white lace against her skin. The contrast is so fucking hot. I kiss the top of each globe, and I feel her shiver at my touch.

I run my thumbs over both cups, feeling her nipples harden. I groan as I get harder. Her eyes are closed, her lips puckered and plump from our kissing.

She looks like a dream.

She's still slowly grinding as I touch her.

"Touch me," she whines.

I chuckle, pulling one cup down. The hardened nipple grabs my attention. I look up at her, and she's staring back at me, eyes dilated. I run my thumb over it again, and she throws her head back.

"You're really turned on right now."

She nods, her eyes closed again. I reach down and undo her jeans, finding her panties. I need to feel her. I reach underneath and groan at the moisture.

My mouth latches on to her neck, making her moan. I suck at her neck, and she continues grinding on me.

I need to get her off.

I trail kisses down her neck and pull back, looking down at her breasts. I gently kiss one nipple, and she lets out a small cry. I kiss it again as I pull the other cup down. I flick my tongue over her nipple, toying with the other one.

I continue licking and kissing until she cries above me. "Will, please."

And that's enough for my restraint to drop. I suck the entire thing in my mouth, making her squirm. I lap my tongue around her nipple, sucking it in, pushing it to the roof of my mouth.

"Can you get off like this?"

"Yes. *Fuck* yes," she cries.

My pulse quickens, and my hands are shaky as I reach for her panties again. I rub her center, and her body tenses. She begins riding my fingers, my mouth still latched around her nipple. My head is in a frenzy. I'm harder than stone. And she tastes so fucking good.

"Slow down," she urges.

I do what she says, and she slows her undulating down. My fingers slow down on her center, and her face looks flushed. I can't wait to be inside her.

"You're beautiful."

I bite down on her nipple, and her body quakes. I move to her other nipple and give it the same attention, sucking it in as she climaxes. My fingers slow down even more.

I pull back, and she slumps down, her head resting on my neck now. Her breathing is erratic, and I'm still panting, trying to figure out what the hell just happened.

She let go on my fingers.

Again.

For fuck's sake, I never thought this would happen again.

"Baby," I croak. "Are you okay?"

She lifts her head, and my heart aches at the vulnerability in her eyes. "I'm okay," she says with a small smile. "Are you?"

"I'm more than okay," I say, chuckling. "Do you feel better?"

She nods, biting her bottom lip. "You think we're late going back to work?"

"Yeah," I whisper, tucking a strand of hair behind her ear. "You're beautiful," I repeat.

She gives me another small smile. "I'm sorry to...attack you like that," she says, chuckling nervously.

"Don't apologize. I'm sure you just needed a release."

"Yeah, exactly."

Her candor hurts. But I understand it. Her dad's in a coma, and she feels she has no one to lean on.

I cradle her cheek, rubbing my thumb across it. "Are you ready to go back?"

She nods, pulling her bra back up, and moves back to the passenger seat. Clearing my throat, I look around and see we're still in the hospital parking lot.

I glance at her, and she fixes her jeans. Swallowing, I pull out of the parking lot, and we're on our way back to the winery.

14

SIENNA

I attacked Will Monroe in his car. I'm not typically a girl to throw herself at a guy. Nor do I resort to car escapades. Yet I kissed him and let him finger me...again. And for fuck's sake, it felt good. It *always* feels good with him.

I'm thinking about it as I cut potatoes in the kitchen.

It's afternoon the next day, and I haven't seen Will since this morning. We barely spoke. We didn't even talk about yesterday. He only told me he had errands to run and that he'll see me later.

It's almost 5 p.m., and he's still not back.

"Smells good, girly! Whatcha cookin'?"

Taylor strolls in wearing a blue crop tank top and white tennis shorts, her hair in a ponytail, blond strands framing her face.

"I'm making Panamanian Sancocho. It's a stew. My mom used to make it all the time." I pour the corn, culantro, and chicken into the boiling broth.

Her eyebrows shoot to the sky. "That sounds good. What's in it?"

"My mom used to make it with chicken, culantro, peppers, and corn."

"Are you from Panama?"

"My mom's family was. She was half Panamanian. I'm very Americanized." Taylor gives me a small smile as I stir the stew. "She made this all the time when I was little. I remember, we would have Heritage Night at school, and the whole thing would be gone within the first hour."

She laughs, sliding into an island chair. "It smells really good, girly. Can't wait to eat it."

My heart swells at the kindness in her voice. Ever since I moved in with Will and Taylor temporarily, they've been super welcoming.

Taylor's brought me shopping, taken me out for lunch, and we even hung out with Ashley downtown a few days this week. It feels nice to get my mind off things and just relax.

Dad's still in critical condition. It's been a week, and the doctors say it's not looking too hot for him right now. He's slated to wake up in three more weeks, and as the days go by, my anxiety increases.

I'm eating a bowl of the stew with Taylor, and we're laughing about Collin Fairchild's crush on her when none other than Will walks in.

My pulse quickens, my senses heighten, and I already feel a bit of sweat coming on. I hate that he has this effect on me. He meets my gaze, and I feel the blood rush out of my face.

"Hey," he says, eyes still on me.

I swallow, looking down at my bowl of stew. "Hi."

"Where have *you* been?" Taylor asks.

"Working," he simply says, laying his golf bag against the wall.

Working? Doing what? None of us were scheduled to work the winery today.

"Sienna made a bowl of her family stew. Pull up a chair and eat with us."

His eyebrows shoot up as he meets my gaze again.

"You made dinner."

I shrug. "It was the least I could do. You guys have been so nice to me."

"And it's *really* good, Willy. Seriously, grab a bowl," Taylor urges.

He gives me a small smile that I return and grabs a bowl.

Next thing I know, all three of us are sitting and finishing up dinner. We talk about the week at the winery, how the rush will get worse come the beginning of August, and other events coming up this summer at Monroe.

"The Szuchs are having their equestrian auction soon. Are you going?" Taylor's question is directed at me. Why do they keep inviting me to these events?

"Um," I start, clearing my throat. "I don't think the Szuchs would want...the help at their auction."

"I don't think you should give a shit about *who* wants you there," he mutters, still looking down at his bowl.

I can't stop my smile from forming.

"I'll have to see what my schedule looks like, but I don't think I'll be able to make it."

"Sure you will. Just bring Cale or something."

Both Will and I freeze.

We share a tortured gaze.

His body is visibly tense. Taylor has a look that says she has no idea what the hell is going on. The tension in the room is so thick you could cut it with a knife.

I put my bowl in the sink and turn back to them.

"I'll keep you posted," I say.

She rolls her eyes, puts her bowl in the sink, and gives me a tight hug.

"You're a stubborn mule, you know that?"

"It's what I do best."

She says goodbye to both of us, and it's just me and Will sitting in silence. He's finishing off his bowl, and I'm looking around the kitchen, trying to find something to clean. It's weird to be in here with him.

We didn't talk about yesterday. He chalked it up to me just needing a release. That was part of it, but...it just felt good to *feel* him. After seeing my dad in his hospital bed and feeling Will's hand, I got carried away. My brain feels bad for using him. But my heart knows what it wants.

"You don't have to look so weird, Sienna," he jokes.

I'm momentarily brought out of my thoughts.

"Sorry," I mumble, settling on cleaning the dishes.

"You don't need to do that. You cooked."

"It's the least I could do."

He frowns, licking around his lips. The sight sets my core on fire, and I look back down at the dishes in question.

"Sienna, put the dishes down."

I'm not listening to him. I need something to do, and going upstairs, taking a shower, and sitting in bed, thinking about Will's hands is not ideal.

He gently grips my arm, a jolt of electricity shooting through me. "Sienna," he says softly. "Put the bowl down."

Clearing my throat, I slowly put it down and turn to him. He's staring down at me with hooded eyes. I lean back against the counter, looking up at him. For a few seconds, we have a staring contest. There's so much written in his eyes.

What is he thinking?

What are we doing?

What does he *want* to do?

"Will," I croak. "I want to apologize for yesterday," I whisper, the words replaying in my head. I sound pathetic. He probably doesn't even care.

"Why are you sorry?"

"Well, because—"

"Because you kissed me?" I nod meekly. "So? Who cares? It was hot."

I roll my eyes. "Of course you thought it was hot, Will. You're a guy."

"If any other girl kissed me the way you do, babe, it wouldn't have the same effect. It was hot because *you* kissed me, Sienna."

He talks with so much conviction. He has determined eyes, his arms caging me in. I suddenly feel hot, and my core is still on fire. It doesn't help that I'm wearing a push-up bra underneath my camisole. His eyes land on my chest for a few seconds before looking back at me.

"Um, well I'm gonna go then," I say, breaking this weird sexual tension.

It takes him a second to move. A small smile grows on his face before he slowly moves. I take a deep breath and run upstairs. Being near him is dangerous. Now that I jumped his bones yesterday, he's going to be more aggressive in getting what he wants.

And that thought doesn't sound so bad.

I need to get a grip. I'm their house guest. They didn't invite me in to fantasize about Will Monroe. No matter how much I'm tempted to.

And even as I'm taking a shower, the thought doesn't go away.

His lips on my neck, trailing kisses.

He's nipping on the taut skin there as his hand slowly slides down my stomach. I gasp as his fingers linger on my center.

Get. A. Grip.

I grumble at my inner thoughts. This needs to stop. There's no reason I should be thinking these thoughts in the shower.

Letting the hot drops trail down my skin, I turn off the faucet, wrap myself in a towel, and pull out my pajama set from the over-sized dresser. I settle on my white lace panties and do the usual dance into my pajamas.

I need a game plan. I can't stay at their house forever. I'll need to pick up more hours to be able to afford Dad's hospital bills, therapy, and...I've been pondering the idea of putting him in a home. He needs professional help at all hours of the day, and I can't be at home watching him. His fall was a huge eye-opener. If I pick up more hours at the winery and maybe work a second job, I can afford at least...half of that.

Dude, am I fucked.

Closing my laptop, I put it under the bed, turn off the lamp, and lie down. I need to get sleep. But for some reason, I can't.

You know the reason.

A certain blond-haired Adonis won't leave my subconscious.

Those blue eyes send a flash of heat through my core.

Don't do it, Sienna.

Swallowing, I squeeze my eyes shut. But it does nothing to relieve the sudden need I feel. My hand finds its way toward my panties.

My brain is telling me I need to stop and get my ass to sleep. But my hand has a mind of its own. I work myself over, my chest thrusting in the air. Sweat beads on my forehead as I open my legs wider. My hand continues to slide through the moisture until another hand suddenly takes over.

My entire body freezes as my eyes shoot open and I come face to face with the same blue eyes I was just fantasizing about. Maybe I'm still fantasizing?

"Sienna," he breathes.

I gulp as I squint to get a better look. For fuck's sake, it *is* him. What's he doing in here?

"What are you doing?" I manage to ask past the lump in my throat.

His eyes dart across my face, but I can't read his expression. His silhouette body hovers over me, the light in the hallway bouncing off his sweaty skin, only his eyes seen. Why is he sweating?

"I...heard your moans," he croaks.

I arch my back at his voice. He pulls my hand away and replaces it with his. His long fingers rub the swollen nub over and over again.

"What are you doing?" I repeat, groaning as he sticks a finger inside.

He slams his lips against mine.

"You sounded like you needed help," he whispers, biting my lip.

My boobs feel heavy, a bead of sweat slides down my cheek, and my core is burning with desire from Will's hand torture.

He works me over for a few more times before his hand leaves me. I whimper and try to grab him back, but he hushes me.

"I got you."

He lifts my camisole above my stomach, his lips trailing down my stomach, leaving kisses. He hovers over my panties, and the heat from his panting makes me shake. He places a kiss on the center of my panties, and my core throbs in response. He slowly slides them down, his gaze on me never wavering. I swallow, anticipating what he's going to do next.

"Tell me when to stop, okay?"

I nod and grasp the sheets under me as his lips begin their journey. I let out a gasp of surprise at the first contact his tongue makes.

It slides through my moisture, sucking on the nub there. My back arches involuntarily, his mouth becoming too much on my skin.

"Will," I moan, spurring him on.

140

His mouth intensifies, sucking harder on the nub, and I let out a cry of pleasure. For fuck's sake, this is too much. He continues eating me out, a finger joining in. The thickness of it fills me up, and the pain soon turns to pleasure. My body can't take it any longer.

He swiftly comes up for air, wild eyes on me. "Are you getting close?"

When he licks his lip, I throw my head back. God, he's fucking hot.

"Yes," I whimper.

He goes back down and continues devouring me like a man starved. I grip the sheets harder, and my skin grows hotter. As his lips continue their assault, his hands reach under my camisole and squeeze my boobs. Thank God I wasn't wearing a bra tonight.

His callused hands toy with my nipples, and his lips tweak my nub one last time before I slowly fade.

For a second, I feel like I'm floating on a cloud blissfully.

One last swipe of his tongue and I'm brought back to those oceanic eyes.

They're staring down at me, dilated and full of emotion.

"Baby," he croaks. "You came."

I stare at him, stunned. He had his tongue on me for the first time, and it was the hottest thing ever.

"I did."

I wait for him to say something. Anything. Anything that promises that this won't be the last time this happens. This was our next step in intimacy together. And damn, was it good.

But he surprises me.

He takes his shirt off, revealing his pecs.

Shit.

I'm tempted to run my hands over them. But I don't. He hugs me to him and pulls the covers over us.

"What are you doing?"

He kisses my nose and the side of my neck. "What do you think? Sleeping."

Pleasure bells ring within me. "Are you sure you wanna do that?"

"Goodnight, Sienna," he whispers, ignoring my question.

He lies down, pulling me against him, and it takes me a moment to fall asleep.

An hour goes by, his light snores sound in my ear, and I'm still trying to figure out what the hell happened tonight.

~

"Sienna," a small voice says. "Wake up, babe."

My eyes slowly open and instantly regret it. The sun practically blinds me as I sit up. I turn to find Will smiling at me.

My gaze lands on his pecs, and my core heats...again. *Look away.* I just settle on his eyes.

"What time is it?"

He leans over and looks at the alarm clock. "It's 9 a.m."

Shit. I'm late for orientation at the winery.

"I thought I turned the alarm on," I mutter.

"It went off for a bit, but I didn't want to wake you up."

I stop in my tracks. "You snoozed the alarm?" He nods, confusion in his eyes. "No," I groan. "I have to train the new people today."

He flinches, a look of regret forming. "Shit. I'm sorry, Sienna."

"It's fine." I wave it off.

Worse things have happened. Thank God Mr. Stevens isn't back from his trip yet, or he'd give me a hard time for sure.

I'm taking my tank top off and putting on one of my lace bras when I feel Will looking at me. I turn to the bed and catch him.

He has a satisfied smirk on his face as he sits back, hands behind his head, pecs and taut abs on display, looking like every fantasy I've ever had.

"You're staring."

"You're beautiful." I laugh, putting toothpaste on my toothbrush. "I'm serious, Sienna. That color really suits you."

I freeze in place, toothpaste dripping on the counter. I was meaning to talk to him about this. Clearing my throat, I put my toothbrush down and turn back to him.

"Will, I've been meaning to ask you this. Is my...skin color why you're attracted to me?"

He flinches again, the satisfied smile gone. "What? Why would you ask that?"

"I don't know," I say, shrugging. "It just seems like...I'm a novelty to you."

For a minute, I feel like I've said the wrong thing. He's going to tell me to pack my bags and go back to my apartment. I can already feel my face heat.

But he surprises me. Again.

He stands up, walks toward me, and I turn back to the mirror. Gosh, I'm so stupid.

"Your skin is beautiful," he whispers, his lips at my ear giving me chills. "Why would you be a novelty?" His hands come around my waist shortly after.

"Apparently I'm not your usual type."

"You're not. But why would that make you a novelty?"

I let out an annoyed sigh. "Up until maybe a month ago, you had a thing for blondes."

He chuckles, the sound rumbling through me. "I won't argue with that," he admits. "At first, yeah, I thought you were hot as fuck. You still are."

"You're too kind," I deadpan.

"*But*," he interrupts, "I got to know you. You're lippy, and it makes me want to shut you up."

I just stare at him. "Is this your pillow talk? If so, it sucks."

"We'd need to be in bed, doll," he chuckles.

I roll my eyes. "You know what I mean," I grumble.

"Sienna, stop trying to fight me," he retorts. "This is another reason I like you. You fight me all the time. I should fucking hate it, but I don't. I love that you don't agree with everything I say."

I swallow, my heart swelling a bit. "I don't fight you," I lie.

"Yes you do. It's one of the things I've grown to like. And your dedication to my family's winery...I love it. So yeah, I thought you were hot, I still think you're hot, and your prickly personality gives me morning wood. Any more questions?"

Our eyes lock in the mirror. "How romantic," I whisper.

He rolls his eyes, squeezing me tighter. "Just give me a chance, Sienna. Don't blow me off anymore. I like you. And I know you like me. Why are we fighting this?"

"Because it doesn't matter, Will. I don't date guys for short term."

"Who said I want short term with you? No one. You're jumping to conclusions."

"Can we talk about this later? I'm late for work." This is not the time to be having this conversation.

Before I can pick the toothbrush up again, my phone rings. I recognize the caller ID.

Sigh. Cue the morning rush at the winery. I pick up my phone on the third ring. A frantic Ashley is on the line.

"Sienna! Thank God I got ahold of you. *Where are you?!*" she screeches.

I look at Will's smug smirk in the bathroom. "Taking care of personal stuff. What's going on?"

"The Bensons are here to pick up their seasonal wine. They said they spoke to you last week about getting it."

The Bensons of Benson & Herald Dentistry. They always order a seasonal wine that we don't grow at Monroe. It's from an Italian vineyard, and we always have to preorder it before summer each year. I forgot they were coming to pick it up.

"I'll be there in a second. Tell them I'm out running errands."

She says something affirmative, but I miss all of it with all the background noise before the phone line goes dead.

"Everything all right?"

"Work calls," I simply say.

I throw on a T-shirt, jeans, and boots as Will calls out to me, "I'll drive you."

I should say no. But he doesn't give me time to respond. Instead, he slips on his shirt, and we're driving off to Monroe in no time.

His hand finds its way to my thigh again, giving it a comforting squeeze, and I relax. Whatever talk we were about to have has been put on hold for the time being.

Hopefully forever, if I have my way.

15

WILL

The Harvey Invitational is less than three months away, and I don't feel even an ounce ready. My swing is great, but my technicalities seem off. Coach has been having me perfect my hip rotation and getting more time in the gym. It's been a wild few days.

I'm watching my practice tapes in the living room when Taylor runs downstairs in a purple halter top and white jeans. "I'll be back, Willy."

"Where do you think you're going? You promised Sienna you'd help with dinner tonight."

She rolls her eyes impatiently. "I'm going *out*, Willy. I texted Sienna already, and she said it's totally fine."

Fine or not, I don't feel comfortable with her going back on her word. But it's her life, not mine.

"Where are you going all spruced up?"

She brightens up at my sudden interest. "I have a date tonight."

Oh, boy. "Sucking face with another Ivy League boy?"

"My professor went to Auburn, dummy."

"Shocker," I mock.

She rolls her eyes. "And if you *must* know, I have a date."

I snort. "As long as it's not with another Ivy League douchebag," I mutter.

"For goodness's sake, Willy, he went to Auburn! And *you're* one to call another guy a douchebag."

"Excuse me, little sister. I'm not a douchebag."

She cocks an eyebrow and puts a hand on her hip. "Oh yeah? Then why does Ashley hate you?"

I roll my eyes. *This* again. "You'd know better than I do."

She chuckles. "I *do* know. You don't know how to keep it in your pants."

I let out a bored sigh. "You can't please everyone, Taylor."

And if her name isn't Sienna Durham, my heart's just not invested.

"Unless her name is Sienna Durham, right?"

My gaze shoots to her. She's giving me a knowing smile.

Before I can respond, she's out of the door, and I'm left to my thoughts. How the *hell* did she know what I was thinking? Am I that transparent?

I can't think about it anymore, though. Because Sienna rushes in wearing a get-up of white leggings and a crop top. Her curly hair is in a top bun. Makeup free, she's gorgeous.

I just watch as she pulls a protein shake out of the fridge and shakes it. We make eye contact when she realizes I'm staring at her.

"Hi, gorgeous."

Her cheeks lightly blush. "Why were you staring at me?"

"Easy. Whenever you enter a room, my eyes go directly to you."

Something flashes in her eyes, but it's gone as soon as it comes, and it's the same stubborn Sienna.

"I'm wearing my workout gear."

"Your point, babe?"

She rolls her eyes, and I don't miss the playful smile. "I have to go."

"You're going to the gym *right now*? I thought we were having dinner soon."

"I don't think I'll cook tonight. Taylor cancelled on me, and it's been a while since I've gotten a good workout in."

Naturally, my gaze skims down her taut body. "Didn't notice."

"Perv," she says playfully.

She leaves the kitchen, but I need an excuse to be near her.

"Hey, I can join you at the gym, if you'd like."

She freezes and confusion etches her face. "Why would you come with me to the gym? You're already in shape."

"So are you...?"

"You know what I mean."

I can't help the chortle that comes out. "Actually, I don't."

She grows impatient. "Showing up at the gym with you would be stupid. Everyone knows who you are, and they'll be wondering why William Monroe is at the gym with a random girl. That's not great for your bachelor status."

Naturally, I flinch. "Who says I'm a bachelor?"

"Literally everyone," she deadpans.

"Do *you* say I'm one?"

And that's when I know I've got her. She blushes again and clears her throat. "Look, if you're gonna go, just put some clothes on."

She walks through the door, and I'm left wondering why she didn't answer my question.

Does she really think I'm a bachelor?

Yeah, I've been single for a long time. But I wouldn't say I'm a *bachelor*. That makes me sound like I'm a commitment-phobe.

But aren't you?

Frustrated, I run upstairs to get ready for my gym date with Sienna. If she thinks I'm a bachelor, I'm going to have *so* much fun proving her wrong.

~

I wasn't expecting there to be a huge mass of people at the gym. Every machine is occupied, and the platforms have groups of meatheads stacking up on weight. Maybe it wasn't such a good idea to come with her tonight.

"You look like you're freaking out," she jokes.

"I just...didn't think there'd be so many people here."

"It's the gym," she says, slapping my shoulder. She drops her bag on the one platform available.

I watch as she stretches and slips on her weight shoes.

"I didn't know you liked weightlifting."

She shrugs, slipping rubber 25-pound weights on each side. "Wine isn't the only thing that's therapeutic. I love exercise, too. It keeps the blood flowing."

I find myself smiling. "You're really smart."

She chuckles. "I thought that was basic human knowledge."

"It might be. But no one just brings that up in regular conversation, babe. Only you would do that."

She rolls her eyes as she slips under the bar and squats under it. "Spot me?"

I stand behind her, my hands itching to hold on to her hips. Her ass juts up at me, as if to say *hello*. I squeeze my hands briefly to curb the itch. But it does nothing to relieve the urge to hold her.

She steps back and does one squat. And then two. And then another. And then another. And then a few more. She puts the bar back on the rack.

"Nice form," I remark.

She smiles, her forehead slightly glistening. "Thanks. I used to do weightlifting in high school."

"Makes sense."

She flinches and instantly recovers. "You're a giant flirt."

"Of course I am. My turn," I say. It's silly to hide my feelings. She knows how I feel about her. It's up to her if she wants to believe me or not.

I put two 50-pound weights on each side, and she spots me as I start my reps. I do five squats before putting the bar back on the rack.

I wipe my forehead and look up at Sienna, finding her staring at me.

"What?"

She gives me a small smile before clearing her throat. "Nothing, I just admire the weight you just squatted. That was 200 pounds." She laughs a hearty one.

"I go to the gym all the time, babe."

Her eyebrows shoot to the sky. "I figured that. But...200 pounds? Were you a bodybuilder in a past life?"

"It's not that much," I joke.

"It's more than I can do," she mumbles, taking a swig of water. "Why do you lift that much weight, anyway? Did you play a sport in high school?"

"I played football and golf."

"Ahh, yes, right. A true country club boy. *Golf*," she mocks.

I can't help the smile that forms. She loves pushing my buttons.

"Last time I checked, this country club boy had his mouth on your—"

Her hand slapping over my mouth is the only thing that stops me. And the memory of what we did sends a jolt of heat to my crotch... again.

"This country club boy also has a potty mouth," she grits through her teeth.

I smile as she slowly moves her hand. "You seem a little testy, babe. Need me to help you unwind again?" I ask, waggling my eyebrows..

She chuckles, rolling her eyes. "Fuck you, Will."

"When and where?"

She ignores me and does another set of squats.

We spend the next hour on the platforms and then we're walking out of the gym, sweaty and overworked. I'm walking behind her, and my eyes keep landing on those perfect globes.

I squeeze my hands, ignoring the throbbing in my crotch. The golden undertone in her skin is doing something to me—as it always is. I need to get home and get off. My brain can't focus with this girl in front of me.

We make it to the car, and she reaches for the door handle. But my brain isn't operating correctly. I grab her arm, and she quickly turns around.

"What's wrong?"

Those pink, kissable lips. "I shouldn't have come to the gym with you," I whisper.

She gives a throaty laugh. "No shit."

"Can I kiss you?"

She flinches. "What?"

"I want to kiss you, Sienna."

"Will—"

"Sienna." A deep voice sounds next to us. I look to my right and find Cale Rivers taking slow steps toward us. What the hell?

"Cale," Sienna blurts. "What are you doing here?"

"I just came back from getting dinner with my dad. I didn't expect to see you here with...Monroe," he says, sizing me up. I cock an eyebrow.

"We just came from the gym," she answers before I can.

"Are you guys on a date?"

"Yes."

"No," she answers at the same time.

"I'm confused," Cale says.

She and I exchange a look of *What the fuck*? Why would she tell him this isn't a date?

"It's not a...*date*, per se."

"It's definitely a date," I retort. This is fucking stupid.

"Can I talk to you for a second, Sienna?"

I frown at the wiseass in front of me. I look at Sienna and don't miss the caught-off-guard expression on her face. She clears her throat and looks at me. "Do you mind?"

Yes, I fucking mind. "No, I don't mind. I'll just wait."

"Actually, dude, I can give her a ride back if you don't want to wait."

I narrow my eyes at him. A shit-eating grin spreads across his face as we have our standoff.

"Will, please. It'll just be a second. I'll meet you back at the house?"

It's as if someone gave me a blow to the gut. I must be giving a look of annoyance because she hugs me and kisses my cheek.

She walks over to Cale, and I finally know where I stand.

The guy who only gets her off.

16

WILL

I can't stop looking at my watch. I've been home for two hours, and Sienna hasn't walked through the door yet. The time passes, and my annoyance grows.

Where the hell could she be?

What could they possibly be talking about?

Maybe they're making out.

Yeah, that thought doesn't exactly excite me.

Taylor and I are watching *The Bachelorette*—per Taylor's insistence—when the front door finally opens and Sienna struts in. The grimace growing across my face could break it.

Her eyes find mine, and she freezes.

"Hey, guys," she says nervously.

"Hey, girl," Taylor chirps. "Where have you been? Everything all right?"

Sienna throws her gym bag on the couch and slouches down in the chair across from us, avoiding my gaze. "I just went to dinner."

I fist my hands, eyes still piercing into her.

"How was it? Who'd you go with?" Taylor questions.

"Yeah, who'd you go with?" I can't help myself.

She finally meets my gaze. "Uh, Cale Rivers. He just wanted to... discuss some stuff."

I snort. '*Some stuff*' could mean literally anything.

"Oooh, so you guys finally went on that date?"

I roll my eyes at Taylor's excitement.

"It wasn't really a date, but we just talked about...*maybe* going on an official one," she treads lightly, eyes still on me.

That's when my restraint breaks. I jump up and walk upstairs. They can sit and talk, braiding each other's hair if it suits them. I'm not finding any excitement in rehashing the details about the girl I like having a potential date with another guy.

Is that the little green monster, William?

So what if it is? I thought I laid my claim more times than I can count, but every day the girl fucking surprises me.

A hot shower sort of calms me down. *Sort of.* I'm still annoyed that this night went a different way than I was hoping. I didn't expect to go to bed mad at Sienna. Yet here I am.

I wrap a towel around my waist and am looking through my dresser for clean boxers when a knock sounds at the door.

I turn to find Sienna giving me a small smile. Mad at her or not, her cute face does something to me. She looks nervous and uncertain. Kind of how *I* am feeling.

"What's wrong?"

She shrugs. "I don't know, what's wrong? You left us while we were talking," she says, chuckling.

I can't do this with her right now. If she doesn't see the issue with what happened, then she never will.

"Sienna, nothing's wrong."

"I don't believe you."

"It doesn't matter what you don't believe. I don't wanna talk about it," I growl.

She cocks an eyebrow, stepping into my room. "Did I do something to upset you?"

"Are you serious?" She gives me a look of confusion. "Can we not do this please? I don't wanna talk right now."

I step to put my boxers on the bed, but she grabs my arm. "Will, what's the problem?"

"Sienna, please get out," I say softly. She steps in front of me before I can get to my bed. "Sienna—"

"Will, talk to me."

"I *really* don't wanna do this." My voice practically cracks, and I hate it. There's no point in telling her if she doesn't get it already.

"William," she whispers. "Did I do something to hurt you?"

William.

My annoyance grows again. Letting out a sigh of frustration, I blurt, "I guess I just don't get it, Sienna."

She frowns. "What do you mean? Get what?"

"Two nights ago was probably one of the best nights of my life," I admit.

Her eyes widen, a hint of blush hitting her cheeks. "Will, please—"

"The best night being my 26th birthday, babe. Touching you was the best birthday present I ever had."

"I hardly believe that." Her voice cracks.

"You don't have to believe it. But it's the truth."

"Can we do this later?"

"You came in my room, questioning me. Here's your fucking answer."

She swallows, eyes filled with nervousness. "Okay, go on," she croaks.

I let out a shaky breath and pour my heart out more.

"I had my mouth on your tits. Twice."

She flinches. "Will—"

"And I had my mouth on your heat two nights ago. I touched you, tasted you. I want to do both right now." I give a nervous laugh. "But then you give me these damn mixed signals. What, it's okay for a Monroe boy to have a night of fun with you, but when it's time to go home, you get pretty for *that* guy? Cale fucking Rivers?" My mouth is on auto-pilot.

Tears are building in her eyes as she reaches for my arm. "Will, it's not like that," she whispers.

"Then what's it like, Sienna? What the fuck can I do to show that I'm serious about you? Because I'm about close to losing my mind."

She grows frustrated, hands shooting in the air. "You're *William Monroe!* You could have any girl you want. And I mean *any girl you want.* You were dating Mason Szuch, a rich equestrian girl who looks like a freaking supermodel. Not to mention, you also dated a girl who *hates my guts*, Will."

I flinch. "Who hates your guts?"

"Sadie," she mutters.

"Sadie Pritchard? Who cares about her?"

"*I* do, Will! It's not just her either. It's just...everything."

"Sienna, what the hell are you talking about?"

She lets out a sigh and slouches down on my bed.

"I only date guys who I see myself with long-term, Will," she says simply. "I said this before, *I don't do short-term dating*. I lost my mom, and I might lose my dad. Life is too short to waste it with people who don't intend to be in it for long."

This conversation refuses to go away. Sighing, I slouch down next to her.

"Sienna, you have no idea what I'm looking for with you. Why do you keep assuming I don't see you for a long-term relationship?"

She lets out a sigh. "We're just too...different. Different ethnicity, race, socioeconomic background...hell, *personalities*," she jokes.

"None of those things matter to me, babe. I've said this many times. I like you. I like you *a lot*. And instead of giving me a chance to show you, you continue to blow me off and lead me on."

She looks at me, and a look of nervousness etches her face. "That's what I'm afraid of," she whispers.

"What? Giving me a chance?"

She nods her head. "Uncertainty...scares me, you know? What if you decide you don't like me anymore?"

I pull her onto my lap. "That's not likely, Sienna. Every day you surprise me. You challenge me every damn day. I'm not worried about that. Being around you just feels...*right*. I feel comfortable, at peace."

She gives me a small smile. "Will, I like you too. But—"

"No buts. Just say the word, Sienna. Say the word and it's just you and me. No more confusion."

For a few seconds, she chews on the corners of her mouth.

I wait in agony for her response, holding my breath.

Please say something.

But she still ponders.

I'm close to giving up when she gives me a small smile.

"Under one condition."

"And what's that?"

She tilts her head, hands going up to cradle my face. "You said you had your mouth on my tits."

I swallow, eyes going down to said tits. "I did," I croak.

She leans in, kissing my nose. "Can you put it on them again?"

Fuck.

I'm pulling her tank top up in record time, hands going to her sports bra. I run my hands over the two cups, admiring how tight they look in her bra. She gasps, alerting me.

"What's wrong? Am I hurting you?"

She looks down at my lap, and I follow her gaze. "You're hard."

I give her a sheepish smile. "You do this to me constantly," I admit.

She smiles and starts grinding on me. I try to steady her hips, but when she gets turned on, she's like a cannon ready to blow. My hands go back to her sports bra, and I lean in, kissing the top of each cup.

"Lift your arms, babe."

She lifts her arms, and I pull the sports bra over her head. I groan at the stiff nipples. I reach down, adjusting my crotch. I look up at her, and she has her head back. It doesn't look like I need to do much to get her off.

I kiss one nipple, pinching the other. Her whimpers and moans above me push me to kiss it again.

Satisfied with the hardened peak, I lap my tongue around it, savoring her taste.

"Will," she moans. "Baby, that feels so good."

Smiling, I suck it to the roof of my mouth, my hand going down to her Spandex shorts. I reach her wetness, and I grow harder.

She's fucking soaked and ready.

I suck her nipple harder, and she starts squirming, urging me to continue.

"*Fuck*, I wanna be inside you so badly."

"Then do it," she gasps.

I freeze.

I slowly pull back and see her gaze on me. "Sienna?"

"I want you inside me too," she whispers.

And my dick instantly swells. "Baby, are you sure?"

She cradles my face again, nudging her nose against mine.

"I'm sure, Will. Hurry, though. Because I'm close," she whines.

And just like that, I have my towel off and thrown across the floor. She's off my lap and sliding her shorts and panties down. Her giggles sound in my ear as I adjust her on my lap. I reach down again, and she's wetter. Fuck, she's going to feel like heaven.

"Baby," she whines.

I kiss her neck. "Okay, hold on."

I line myself up with her and slowly push inside. I groan at her tightness. She's squeezing me like a vise, and it's never felt better.

I pull out for a second, making her whimper. Then I inch back in, and fuck me, I could stay here all night.

"So fucking tight," I bite out.

She pulls me closer to her, nails biting into my back. The simple sensation makes me pound into her faster and harder. Each thrust makes her whimper, and it's the sweetest sound.

I thrust into her one more time, and she mewls, a sound I'm beginning to love.

"Oh, *fuck*, what is *that*?" she cries.

"That, baby"—I hit the same spot, making her cry again—"is your G-spot."

I hit it again, and her body slightly quakes.

Her lips latch on to my neck, and I inch in and out of her repeatedly until we reach the climax we're both close to.

"Will, I feel it," she cries. "Baby, I feel it."

Her cries send me into a frenzy, pumping into her faster. I pull back, watching her face. She's looking down at where we're joined, her cheeks rosy, jet-black curls mussed. The scene makes my heart hurt.

Our gazes clash, and I'm greeted by those almond eyes. She leans in and kisses me, my hand reaching down to rub her.

Her body goes off like fireworks the moment I touch her center. She bites on to the side of my neck, and it makes me shoot my load into her.

I slow down my thrusting, and her body slowly stops shaking. She's panting into my neck, the heat from her breath comforting me.

She pulls back, eyes dilated. "That was..."

"Amazing," I finish for her.

She gives me a satisfied smile as she nods.

"Amazing is a good word for it."

I give a hearty laugh before leaning in to kiss her. "Baby, you're tight as fuck." The thought makes me groan. "Was that your first time?"

"No," she laughs. "I just...don't have sex often. I wasn't joking when I said I don't have sex with guys who don't see me as a long-term thing."

The candor makes me smile. "If you give me a chance, I promise I won't disappoint you," I say, kissing her forehead.

Her smile is everything. "I trust you, Will."

My heart swells more than it ever has.

I lean in to give her another kiss, but then my brain focuses on a very important detail. We just did it without...

"Babe, while being inside you felt like heaven, I didn't wear a condom." For fuck's sake, I'm usually smarter about this.

She laughs. "It's okay. I'm on the pill."

I let out a sigh of relief. I'm sure I'll have little Monroes running around at some point in my life. But not right now when I'm working the winery and focusing on golf.

The thought of children has me hard again.

My gaze lands suddenly on Sienna, who's staring back at me.

"What? What's wrong?"

Clearing my throat, I shake my head. "Nothing, babe. Here, come on. I'll get you cleaned up."

She smiles as I pick her up, and her legs wrap around my waist. Her softness against me feels so right. I give her a kiss on the neck as we walk into the bathroom and I set her down in the shower.

A few minutes ago, I was thinking about children and Sienna in the same thought. While that should scare the fuck out of me...it actually excites me.

I just might be in over my head with this girl.

And I don't know whether to love it or hate it.

17

SIENNA

Will Monroe is the most affectionate guy I've ever dated. For the past week, it's just been us going on gym dates, dinner dates, movie dates, and going to the park. He's even been giving me more attention than usual at work. If there's one thing I've learned about Will, it's that he's definitely an ass guy.

He never misses a chance to smack mine whenever I'm restocking wine in the backroom, cleaning up after work, and even at home. It's like an entirely different guy. He was cocky before. Now he's just super touchy.

He's touchy even now as he has me cornered in the main bistro at the winery.

"What are you doing?" I ask, his hand squeezing my hips.

"Just holding you."

My heart swells, and my cheeks heat. I'm not used to this type of affection.

"Will, we're at work." I wrap my arms around his neck.

"We're closing in a few," he says, kissing me. "Do you wanna go to dinner?"

I smile. "Of course I wanna go to dinner."

"Good. Because I wanted to ask you something."

This gives me pause. "Is everything okay?"

"Everything's fine, babe. I just have this thing I wanted to run by you."

I frown. "You're scaring me."

He chuckles, giving me a kiss on the forehead. "It's nothing bad, dork. Get out of your head."

I let out a sigh. "Yeah, we can go to dinner. Just give me a minute to close up, and I'll meet you outside."

"Oh no, I'm helping you clean. What kind of guy would I be, letting his girl clean up by herself?"

I hate the giddy feeling I get when he calls me his girl. Obviously, I don't hate it enough because I find myself smiling.

"You'd be my boss letting me do my job."

"Nonsense." He suddenly steps back to let me walk past him. "Get to cleaning, babe."

As I walk past, once again, he smacks my ass. I give him a playful smile, and he gives me a goofy grin. It's going to take a bit of getting used to being around him like this.

Before, we just had sexual tension that would make things uncomfortable. Now that we're seeing each other, things just feel...serene. We're playful and happy. It's refreshing to see. It's made me forget about my dad.

He's still in a coma. They think he'll wake up in a few weeks. I was hoping he'd wake up at the three-week mark, but they said it's still too soon to tell. I don't know what else to do besides visit him every day and stay distracted with work. And Will being around just puts the icing on the cake.

I tell him just that at dinner.

"Thank you so much again for taking me in after...the whole dad situation."

He gives me a small smile and reaches for my hand. "Sienna, you have to stop thanking me, babe."

"But you didn't have to—"

"And we did. Now stop it already."

I don't bring it up again. Instead, we order dinner, and the waitress brings over a bottle of his family's wine. The irony makes me laugh.

I look around the restaurant, and sure enough, we have stares our way. Admiring stares at Will and curious stares at me.

"You're stunning tonight. Everyone can see that."

159

I turn to Will, and he's giving me the same admiring stare others are giving him.

"I'm wearing a plaid shirt and shorts," I laugh.

"You could be wearing a paper bag and you'd still be the most beautiful girl in the room."

I don't know how he does it. He always manages to make me feel like the most beautiful girl in the world even though I know I'm not.

Get out of your head, Sienna.

I keep my gaze on him as he pours me a glass of the Monroe Merlot.

He holds his glass up to mine.

"To a new beginning," he remarks.

We hold each other's gaze over our glasses of wine. Then I remember what he told me earlier.

"You told me you have to run something by me. Is everything okay?"

He lets out a sigh before meeting my gaze again.

"Right. So, babe..."

I smile at the childlike way he starts. "Yes?"

"I play golf."

I can't help the frown that forms. "Yes, I know. You told me."

"My coach thinks I'm really talented, and I even have a few sponsors that are interested in me."

I just stare at him. Sponsors?

"Why would you need sponsors?"

He lets out another shaky breath, and it's freaking me out. Am I missing something here?

I reach for his hand, and it seems to encourage him to continue.

"I'm going professional."

My eyebrows shoot to the roof. "That's wonderful news, Will!" But why is he being weird about it? "That's the thing you wanted to run by me?"

"Not entirely." He hesitates again, and it makes me grip my wine glass. "The first tournament my coach signed me up for is in Scottsdale, Arizona. The Harvey Invitational." His eyes light up the entire time he's talking, and it momentarily distracts me. I like seeing that glimmer in his eyes.

"That's awesome," I say. "I'm not sure why you would want to run that by me—"

"I want you to come with me," he blurts, making me flinch.

My pulse quickens, and my face suddenly heats. "What?"

He nods his head eagerly. "I want you by my side. I'm inviting my friends too, since the tournament lasts for a weekend. But I think it'd be great if *you* were there with me, baby."

Baby.

He is the cutest thing. I can't say no to those piercing eyes. But I'm not sure if I can say yes either. My home is here in Kentucky, and Mr. Stevens would kill me if I left for a weekend with Will Monroe. That wouldn't go over well.

"Will, I don't know. My work is here in Kentucky. And I don't know if I can take an entire weekend off. When is the tournament?"

"It's in August. The 16th to the 18th."

Shit. I definitely can't take time off then. That's the season before our fall season at Monroe.

And it's my birthday.

But more importantly, we have to prep for the rush that comes in September, and Mr. Stevens will be back by then.

"That's the most crucial season before fall, Will," I whisper.

"I'll just have him schedule another sommelier." He shrugs it off. He doesn't get it.

"Babe, I can't just take time off," I laugh. "Especially since Mr. Stevens doesn't know we're seeing each other."

"Sienna," he says, trying to calm me down. "You're forgetting that I'm running the winery until my parents come back. And I can easily approve you for time off that weekend."

"What?"

"It's not a matter of if you *can*, babe. It's a matter of if you *want* to."

And a matter of if I want to be that girl that dates an heir and takes advantage of the privileges that come with that.

"Will—"

"I want you there with me. You don't have to, but I really think it could be good for you. Your dad could be awake by then, and we can even bring him if you'd like. But I think the time away would be great, babe. Please, Sienna. Come with me."

I really don't know what to say. This was a big bomb dropped on me tonight. Will Monroe, my boyfriend, is going to be a professional golfer. And he wants me to join him for his first tournament in Scottsdale, Arizona. He's also giving me this vulnerable, full-of-emotion stare. Almost as if he'd break if I said no.

He was there for me when my dad went into a coma. This is the same guy who insisted on helping me get back on my feet. How can I say no to him?

"Okay, Will."

His eyes light up. "Yeah?"

"Yes, I'll come with you."

He gives me a giddy smile and leans over the table, kissing me. For a second, we're in our own little world.

He pulls back, the same smile still on his face.

"We can finally enjoy our night."

And we do just that. We order another bottle of wine and finish off dinner and talk about his upcoming golf tournament.

As we're talking, I marvel at how his eyes light up when he talks about the sport. It's like watching a little boy play with action figures for the first time.

"Your dad was best friends with *Morris Hensley?*"

He gives me an embarrassed smile. "He was my dad's mentor, really." He takes a sip of merlot. "I would watch them every day after school on the course, and ever since...I just fell in love with the sport." He shrugs.

"That's so cool," I say in awe. It feels so uncanny to be here with him. Will Monroe, larger than life. It doesn't seem real. "Soon you'll follow in his footsteps."

His chuckle rumbles through me. "One can only hope. I love the sport, but...I don't know."

I frown. "What do you mean?"

The usually confident guy suddenly turns tense.

"I just don't know if I'll be any good, you know?"

"What makes you say that? Your coach wants you to go professional. Surely you're amazing."

"Because of my *name*, babe. Hell, I'm sure my sponsors are only interested because they think they'll get in with a Monroe investment. No one's gonna care about my skills on the course. They'll just look at me as the heir of Monroe Vineyards that's finally getting away from the Monroe name."

"Is that such a bad thing?"

"It's *insulting*, Sienna," he says in a pained voice. "I've always been under my parents' shadow. William Monroe VI, son of William V and Lily Monroe. I just want something for myself." He shrugs.

A small part of me wants to say *first-world problems*. But then I look at the sullen pout on his face. This is Will, the guy who's been nothing but genuine and kind to me. He can be a bit of an asshole, but I'm starting to see that just might be a front.

I reach for his hand across the table.

"I've yet to see you play. But I can tell you that there's definitely more to you than being a Monroe. Give yourself some credit, Will. You don't even know how you'll do. You might just kick ass, and none of it will matter."

"But there's no guarantee," he says, eyes piercing into me. "And even so, who will care? My parents couldn't even come to my birthday party. If I win, you think they'll take it seriously and support me going professional?"

"Luckily, I'll be there to support you and take it seriously. I'm no Mr. and Mrs. Monroe—" His laughter soothes a bit of the intensity. "But I'd like to think I'm a good cheerleader. What do you think?"

The boyish smile that always melts my insides appears.

"I think you'd make a *hot* cheerleader." His eyes scale down my body, and I can only smile.

And just like that, he's back.

18

WILL

"I'm sorry, Willy, but you have to watch your sister. Golf will have to wait for now."

I'm staring at her, stone-faced. "But Mr. Hensley got me into this tournament!"

"Well, I'll have to talk to him about that. He's playing in the PGA tour this weekend, Willy. I'm sure he won't notice whether or not you're playing." She brushes it off, packing her suitcase.

The knife in my heart cuts deeper. "Mom...why would you say that?"

For a second, she curses herself and looks down at me.

"I'm sorry, honey. I didn't mean it like that. I just mean...the vineyard has just gotten busy lately, and we're getting a lot of investors who are interested. One is even interested in bringing it out to Napa!"

None of these are things I care about. I just want to play golf.

"Well, that's awesome for you, but what about me?"

"William, you're thirteen. There will be more golf tournaments you can play in. Right now, I need you to take care of Taylor."

She brushes me off again, and that's when I know the conversation is officially over. I'm thirteen. I shouldn't be throwing a temper tantrum. But that's exactly what I'm doing when I stomp into my room and shut the door.

I pull out my phone and text the person I know who would care.

ME: Mom and Dad are giving me a hard time.

164

MASON: *They still want you to take care of Taylor???*

ME: *And it's the big junior tournament that Mr. Hensley signed me up for.*

MASON: *I'm sorry, but that's just sooooo cool your parents know him!*

ME: *Not the point, Mason.*

A knock at the door brings my attention away. Dad's looking at me with a sympathetic smile. I throw down my phone and pick up my TV remote. I'm not in the mood to talk to him right now.

"Don't pout, William. It'll stay that way."

Yes, Dad. Make light of an annoying situation.

"You and Mom never care about what I want. Mr. Hensley told me about the tournament this weekend, and he said he got me in! Why can't I play?"

Sighing, he sits down on my bed. "The vineyard is taking off more than we expected."

"The Monroe name's been around for a few centuries, Dad. I'm sure you're not that surprised that the vineyard's picked up."

"Napa Valley, William. Sophia, Idaho. Even a vineyard in Asheville, North Carolina."

"What's your point, Dad?"

"This is big for us, son. For our family. The Monroe name has potential to live on. A household name."

His pleading eyes tell me everything I need to know. He's right: The family winery has become very popular. But like I said, that was inevitable.

"Dad—"

"How about this, William? I'll talk to Morris, and we'll talk about the next match you can play in. Sound like a deal?"

Ideally, I would be happy. I should be happy. But I have no idea when the next golf tournament for my age group is. Maybe it's just meant to be. I can wait until the next one...I guess.

"Sure, Dad. I was just really looking forward to this one," I mumble.

He gives a sad smile. "I know, son. Just think of it this way: You'll be more prepared for the next one."

Yet, for some reason, that doesn't ease me.

I squeeze my eyes shut of the memory. This is not the time to think about my parents. I'm in a slight crisis.

It's almost July, and Coach has upped my practices from two-hour gym training days to four-hour training days. My knee is starting to feel the new dynamic in practicing, and it doesn't feel the greatest.

"You need to take a break, Will."

Sienna's putting ice on my knee, and I wince in pain.

"I can't take a break, babe. The tournament's in two months."

She rolls her eyes, applying more pressure.

"Do you think you'll be in your best shape if you train on a bum knee?"

I chuckle. "It's not a bum knee. It's just fatigue from all of the practicing."

Her eyes tell me she's not buying it.

"You're taking a break, Will. There are no ifs, ands, or buts about it."

I find myself smiling at this new caring Sienna.

"You know, you're hot when you tell me what to do."

"So easily amused." I take the icepack from her. "Hey!"

"Stop playing doctor for two seconds and play girlfriend for maybe thirty."

"Will, your knee's hurting," she deadpans.

I smile. "Seriously, I'm fine, babe."

"You say that now, but tomorrow afternoon, you'll come home complaining about your knee hurting."

"So what? It comes with the sport." She rolls her eyes and sits back, crossing her arms. "You're adorable," I chuckle.

"No I'm not. I'm annoyed," she grumbles.

"Annoyed with me?"

"*Yes!*" she shouts. "I'm trying to be serious, but you're incapable of doing that."

"Sienna," I try to calm her down. "It's *knee* pain. I didn't tear my shoulder or a hip."

"I know that, but..." She pauses for a second. "It could just get worse if you keep playing on it. Just wait for it to get better, okay?" Those brown eyes peer up at me.

"If I could, I would. But my coach would kill me."

She ponders as if to come up with a solution. I smile at her pensive stare.

"How about *I* talk to him?"

I chuckle. "That's not necessary. Here, I'll talk to him. I'll tell him my girlfriend doesn't want me practicing on a bum knee," I joke.

Her eyes narrow at me. "Are you trying to be funny?"

I laugh, kissing her forehead. "It sounds funny, doesn't it? Babe, I'll be fine. I promise. If my knee ends up breaking, you can kick my ass for it."

She beams, and I marvel at how beautiful her smile is.

"Sounds like a deal to me."

I let out a sigh of relief. "Good. Now do me a favor."

"What's that?"

"Take your shirt off."

She flinches, blushing. "What?"

"You heard me," I say, kissing her. "Take your shirt off."

She rolls her eyes, but her dilated pupils tell me it turns her on.

"We're not having sex when you're injured," she deadpans.

My hand makes its way up her shirt. "I'm not injured." I plant a kiss on the side of her neck, her breathing now labored.

"Will," she moans. "Stop it. Your sister will be back at any moment."

"No she won't." I kiss her neck again and toy with her bra. "She's spending the night with Willa and Sadie."

"Will—"

"Would you prefer if *I* took it off for you?" I pull back, and I groan at her hungry gaze. She wants this too.

Glaring at me, she reaches for the hem of her tank top. I sit in agony as she slowly pulls it over her torso.

"Baby, go faster," I groan.

A mischievous smile touches her lips. "You're bossy."

She tosses the tank top aside, and I just admire her. She's wearing a blue bra, her tits just barely spilling over the top.

I'm on her seconds after, kissing her neck. Her arms come around my neck, and I inhale her scent.

I mumble a curse before asking, "What the fuck do you use? You smell so good."

Her giggle rumbles through me. "It's body wash. I use coconut."

I groan, pulling back. She's giving me a small smile.

"How are you so perfect?"

She frowns, a confused smile growing on her face.

"I'm far from perfect. I'm just a girl," she says, shrugging.

"You're not *just* a girl. You're *my* girl. And that's what makes you special."

She visibly swallows. "Will, that doesn't even make sense."

"It doesn't have to. It's the truth. But you're so much more than '*just a girl*.' You're beautiful, smart, funny, and passionate about what you do. Your eyes light up when you talk about wine, honey. *That's* what makes you special to me."

I don't miss the glistening in her eyes. I wipe a tear away as it escapes.

"I don't know how you do it, Will."

"What do you mean?"

"I don't know how you manage to say things like that and piss me off at the same time," she chuckles.

I smile, kissing her. I don't know how I do it, either. One moment, I'm certain I know what I'm doing. The next moment, I'm a confused mess, not knowing what to say to her. I look like an idiot each time, and I'm not used to being that aware of myself. She brings it out of me.

I'm an idiot, I know I am. Taylor tells me all the time. I know I'm an asshole, too. But Sienna Durham...she changes things for me. Call me crazy, but before her, I was just William Monroe VI, heir to a multi-billion-dollar vineyard. I've been photographed more times than I'd like with supermodels, actresses, and heiresses. I'm a high-profile guy.

And then this girl comes along, turning me on my head. Life has a funny way of showing you what you're missing.

"What?" She's giving me a confused smile. "Why are you staring at me?"

"No reason. Just...you're gorgeous, Sienna Durham. It'll always amaze me."

The appreciative smile on her face gives me chills. I will do anything to keep that smile on her face. I kiss her again, consuming everything that is Sienna.

That's how the next few weeks go. Taking her out to dinner, bringing her on the golf course with me, hanging out with her and my friends. She wins Willa over instantly.

"Your new girlfriend's a peach, Will. Don't screw this up," she whispers to me as I grill burgers.

It's a celebratory barbecue at my house for Collin. Fairchild Resorts now has a hotel in Miami, after months of meetings with contractors and construction. So naturally the guys and I were thrilled.

Miami trips are definitely happening now.

"Trust me, I wouldn't screw it up if my life depended on it," I chuckle.

She rolls her eyes, grabbing a Sprite from the cooler. My gaze lands on the beauty in question.

I admire the yellow floral dress she's wearing as she laughs at something Ashley says. She, Mason, and Willa all surround her.

Can you blame them?

She has this welcoming presence around her, it's hard not to be enamored.

I put the grilled burgers on a plate and yell to everyone that they're done. Mason and Willa hug her before scurrying over to the grill. I make my way to her.

"Look who's making new friends," I say, arms wrapping around her waist.

She rolls her eyes, her arms going around my neck. "Ashley was always my friend, silly." Then she frowns. "Weird. I never thought I'd see the day where I'd call *Ashley* my *friend*."

I chuckle. "See, all you had to do was give her a chance."

She shakes her head, smiling, and reaches up on her tiptoes, giving me a peck on the lips. And just like that, I'm lost in her.

"Can you guys *not* chew each other's faces off in front of guests? How rude."

I pull back to find Cale and Sadie grimacing at us. Sienna instantly stiffens in my arms. Sighing, I back away from her. I forgot about Cale.

"Hey, guys," Sienna says.

Sadie's eyebrows shoot up.

"Yeah, hey," she says sarcastically.

I frown. "What are you guys doing here?"

"Taylor invited us," Cale answers.

Of course she did. She invited my ex-fling and *Rivers.*

Almost as if she were summoned, Taylor skips outside.

"Sadie, Cale! Y'all made it!"

"Of course we did, babe. Where else would we be?" Sadie gives her a hug, and they walk away, talking about Sadie's last trip to Cancun.

I turn my attention back to Cale, and he's eyeing Sienna.

"Everything all right, dude?"

He shrugs, looking me in the eyes. "I'm chill, dude. Just craving a burger." He gives me a curt smile and walks off.

"That was weird," Sienna says before I do.

I chuckle. "Yeah, it might be a bit awkward for a while. You guys were supposed to go on a date, right?" I grind my teeth, thinking about it.

She gives me a sheepish smile. "Yeah, and...I don't think he's taking it well."

"Of course he's not. No dude is stupid enough to be indifferent to dating you."

She rolls her eyes. "If you're saying all of this to get ass, you're barking up the wrong tree. It's my time of the month."

I wince. "Damn, girl. At least let me fantasize," I say, winking and smacking said ass.

She yelps, grimaces, and walks toward the burgers. Willa and Mason quickly pull her aside.

I smile at how right this feels. My heart pangs with a strange emotion. An emotion I've never felt before.

It's a scary emotion. And when she turns around, giving me that girlish smile, the emotion intensifies. I rub my chest. This feeling's not going away. And oddly enough...

I don't think I want it to.

"I think I'll get a dress like that for Willa," Connor says. "If it makes their legs look *that* great..." He then whistles to make his point.

But it doesn't completely escape me that he's commenting on Sienna's legs.

"Yeah, maybe *don't* salivate over my girlfriend's legs."

He rolls his eyes and slaps my shoulder. "I'm obviously kidding, dude. Kind of," he amends.

"Whatever. Look, I think I might need a favor."

He frowns, taking a bite of his burger. "What's up?"

"So Willa and you are endgame, right?"

"Willa's my girl. Forever and always. Why, what's up?"

I let out a sigh of relief. He's the perfect person to ask.

"I think I need your help with something." He raises his eyebrows. I let out a shaky breath. "How are you with surprises?"

19

SIENNA

"**T**hree hours to Kentucky, dear. Are you sure you don't want me to drive?"

"Noooooo, honey. I'm all right," Dad slurs.

I'm rubbing my eyes, hating the slow drive back home. We've been in Nashville for two days, and I'm ready to go back home. It's Mommy and Daddy's anniversary, and they spent it with their rich friends.

"Jerry, you're swerving! Stop the car."

"Wait, Mommy, can you read me a story?"

She turns around, her hazel eyes peering at me.

"Honey, I can't. I have to watch your dad," she whispers.

Those simple words make me sad. I love her voice.

"Jerry, pull over!"

"Stop, Miranda! I got this," he shouts back, eyes briefly leaving the road ahead of us.

I wipe the tears from my eyes, sniffling.

"Enna? Are you crying, baby?"

I wipe my eyes again. "No." My voice cracks.

She gives me a sad smile. Sighing, she looks at the picture book in my hand. "Ahhh, The Home I Knew. You always loved that book, Enna."

"Can you read it to me?" I ask meekly. "I can't sleep."

She takes a fleeting look at Dad and then back at me. Finally, she adjusts in her seat and opens the first page of the book.

"In a land far away, there sat an island that Katie loved very much. It was her home..." *I smile at the words, slowly closing my eyes. Her voice sounds through my head, as I feel myself going in and out of consciousness.* "Katie loved animals because they gave her companionship. It was her happy place. Her safe place. It's her home."

A loud crash, followed by a scream, jolts me awake.

I shiver, watching blood spill down the side of my Daddy's head. His head bobs to each side, almost in slow motion.

I look at Mommy, and she's shaking, face covered in blood, reaching for me.

"It's okay, Enna. Mommy's here," *she says, voice cracking.*

"Mommy," *I whisper, holding on to her arm. The simple clasp of her hand on my arm creates a sense of security, and all worry washes away.*

Until another scream rings out.

"Sienna?"

"Don't worry, honey. Mommy's here," *she whispers, trying to soothe me. But then she lets out another pained scream.*

"Sienna, baby, wake up."

Suddenly, Daddy wakes up at the wheel. And his eyes land on Mom. When I follow his gaze, it lands on her unconscious state. To my horror, her eyes are closed, and blood trickles down her temple, her hand still wrapped around my arm.

"Miranda?"

A weak whimper sounds from her lips.

"Mommy? Mommy. MOMMY!"

"SIENNA!"

I jolt awake to find Will shaking me. I look around, and it's only us in bed. Sweat slides down the side of my face. Will's worried eyes peer down at me.

"Will," I whisper.

"You were talking in your sleep."

"I saw her," I say absently.

"Baby, it's okay. I'm here," he says, hugging me.

"Oh my gosh, I'm so sorry," I say against his chest.

"Was it another nightmare?"

Tears well in my eyes, and I can't stop trembling.

"The book was *The Home I Knew*."

"What?"

I pull back to look at him. "That was my favorite book when I was little. My mom used to read it to me all the time. It was about a little girl who felt at peace on this island in a faraway land. She found companionship with the wildlife there because they were the only ones who accepted her."

He's giving me sad eyes. "Baby..."

"That's why I loved it so much, Will. My mom was my companion. So was my dad, but my mom more so. When Dad was working, Mom was always with me, painting, drinking merlot."

"And that's why you like it," he answers for me.

I swallow the lump in my throat. "It's my therapy," I whisper.

"Sienna, you told me you actually *go* to therapy."

"I haven't seen Ms. Spencer in a few weeks."

"Maybe it's time to see her again, honey."

I roll my eyes. "I've been doing just fine without—"

"Babe, this is probably the third time this week I've had to wake you up because of a nightmare. You *need* to see her."

"I drink merlot," I whisper.

"And I'm sure that's been doing pretty good for you up until now. But I think seeing her again will be better for you."

I wave it off. "I've just run out of my meds, Will. It's not a big deal. I can just get a new batch."

His eyebrows shoot up. "You're *out* of meds?" I nod. "You're seeing her again. Schedule your next appointment."

"Will—"

"No, you're going. I'll take you if I have to. But I don't want you missing out on a good night's sleep."

"Will, if I get back on my meds, I can't drink wine. She says they don't mix."

"Sienna..."

"I *love* merlot. I wouldn't give it up for the world."

For a second, he's peering at me as if he's pondering what to say. Then he lets out a resigned sigh. "How about this? You still go to therapy. I'll take you. When you're not on your meds, I'll treat you to wine. How's that?"

I chortle. "That's what I've been doing."

"But you haven't been finding a balance, babe. You've been off your medication for a while and relying *solely* on wine."

I shrug. "Like I said...it's therapeutic."

"Sienna..."

"If I say yes, will you stop hassling me and maybe we can go back to sleep? I don't wanna fight with you," I plead.

He gives me a smug smile. "Only if you say yes and *mean it*."

I roll my eyes. "*Yes*, babe, I promise I will go back to therapy."

His smile grows as he snuggles me close, pulling the covers back over us. He kisses my forehead.

"Good night. Get some sleep."

I'll try...

The winery is finally in its busy season. We've been getting a lunch rush lately, but the fact that I now have to separate people into two lines in the lobby only solidifies that summer is officially here.

"Do you need me to help out?" Ashley asks.

"Can you manage the second line? Taylor disappeared in the inventory room a while ago."

She nods, hopping behind the counter as I take the next guest's order.

Taylor finally makes it back to the lobby, a box of rosé in hand.

"This is for Mr. Johnson. He said he'll be here in thirty minutes."

I nod, take the box from her, and put it under the counter.

For the next three hours, it's work as usual. Guests order flights of wine, bottles, and Taylor takes care of the guests who have food and wine pairing appointments.

"Another day, another dollar," Ashley jokes.

I roll my eyes, wiping the countertop.

"Yes, says the girl who could retire on her parents' money."

"Hey, my parents' money isn't *my* money. I want something for myself, you know."

"Yeah, yeah. The old *'I don't want to be in my parents' shadow'* speech."

She gives me a smirk. "All right, smartass. Is there anything else you need me to do before I head out?"

"No, you're good. Are you coming out with us tonight?"

"Where else would I be?"

Smiling, I give her an envelope.

"Great, we'll pick you up. Here's your last paycheck, too."

She takes the envelope and heads out. Taylor scurries in, a huge smile on her face.

"What's got *you* so happy?"

She lets out a happy sigh, leaning on the counter.

"I...adore love, you know?"

I snort. "Things going well with the new guy, then?" She gives me a nervous look, and I'm immediately concerned. "What's wrong?"

She swallows, her face paling. "What I'm about to tell you is really confidential, okay? Willy can't know."

"O-kay."

She lets out a deep breath. "The new guy...is my professor," she says quickly.

I frown. "What? You're dating your professor? I thought you went to Brown."

"I did. But he came down to visit me this week since Mom and Dad are out of town. Basically...we've been sneaking around. You can't tell Willy."

I really don't know what to say to this.

"Does your brother at least *know* you're dating someone?"

She rolls her eyes. "Yeah. He just doesn't know *who*. But if he knew who, he'd blow a gasket."

I laugh. "Sooner or later he's gonna find out, love."

"I know. But...I'd rather he find out when the whole...*situation* blows over."

"Situation?"

She waves it off, but I don't miss the blush that hits her cheeks.

"It's not a big deal. But he's great. I just wish things would've gone better with us so we wouldn't have to hide."

I smile at her. "You're really happy then?"

She swoons. "*Oh*, yeah. That guy can *kiss*. And whatever cologne he uses is amazing."

"TMI, girly. But I'm happy you're happy."

She gives me a rueful laugh. "Of course my brother's girlfriend is supportive instead of *him*."

This makes me chuckle. "You know how Will is."

"Yeah, he's annoying."

"*No*, he's just being a brother. He's an *ass*, but he just wants to make sure his little sister is making good decisions."

She waves my words off. "Yeah, yeah. If you ask me, I think he's just projecting."

"What do you mean?"

Sighing, she puts her purse on the counter.

"For as long as I can remember, my brother's *always* made poor decisions. *Especially* with choosing girls."

I think I love her. "Well, yeah, your brother has a type. Everyone does."

"Liking bitchy girls isn't a type, it's a sickness."

I can't stop the laugh that comes out. "No comment."

"Not you," she says quickly. "You're far from that. But—" She looks around, conspiratorial, before lowering her voice. "I love Sadie, but she's prickly."

You're telling me. "Yeah, she definitely doesn't like *me*. Does she still have a thing for Will?" If she does, she can choke.

"Isn't it obvious? Willy's a magnet to girls. He's known for dating influencers and models."

I hate that this makes me sad. "I never asked this, but...is Sadie an influencer? Or a model?" I don't follow too much of entertainment media.

"Sadie Pritchard is Mariska Pritchard's daughter."

I freeze. "Mariska Pritchard as in...the *supermodel* Mariska Pritchard?"

She nods. "Mr. and Mrs. Pritchard live in Rivers Country Club, and Sadie has a home at our country club *and* at Rivers."

Seriously, who the hell *are* these people?

"Two homes? Yeah, why would I think *she's* a threat?"

She waves it off. "Sadie models internationally all the time. She just came back from Berlin Fashion Week not too long ago."

Taylor's not helping my case. "Awesome for her," I deadpan.

She flinches, finally realizing what she's saying. "Shit, I'm sorry, girl. I didn't mean to...make you uncomfortable."

"I'm not uncomfortable," I lie. "I just—"

"My brother likes you. *A lot.* Sadie may be a model, but you're just as beautiful—if not *more*—with a better personality. Don't let who she is get to you."

My heart swells at her kind words. "Aren't you guys best friends?"

She shrugs. "I tolerate her. Ashley, you, and Willa are really the only friends I trust." She clears her throat before leaning in again. "If you haven't noticed," she whispers, "rich people can be kind of superficial."

I laugh at the irony. "I don't think I have, actually," I joke.

She rolls her eyes, smiling, and picks up her purse.

"Well, I need to run some errands before tonight. Do you need a ride downtown?"

"No, Will and I are picking up Ashley. So, we'll meet y'all there."

"Awesome!" She gives me a hug and bolts out of the door.

I look at the door she left out of, finding myself thinking about my life in the last two months.

I met Will Monroe, had a very short fling with him, my dad got into a coma, I started *dating* Will Monroe, and now I find myself hanging out with the rich kids of Rose Valley.

I have nothing in common with these people. I'm not a rich kid, I don't have the luxury to fly to Greece for a day's worth.

I'm Sienna Durham, wine connoisseur.

I'm the girl people go to when they need help with food and wine pairings, the girl who struggles with anxiety and nightmares.

The girl that everyone sees as the help.

This can't last. It *won't* last. It's just fun at this point. And no matter how many times William Monroe will try to convince me, he knows it's true. He's twenty-six, I'm twenty-three. There's a very slim chance he sees me as a long-term thing.

Get out of your head, Sienna. Just go out tonight.

I can think about the outcome of this relationship later.

It's Friday, and I need to let loose.

I log out of the computer, turn off the lobby lights, and grab my purse. As I lock the door, my phone rings. I look at my clock to make sure I'm not late.

It's only 4 p.m.

Pulling out my phone, I look at the Louisville area code. Frowning, I pick it up.

"Hello, this is Sienna."

Papers shuffle on the other side.

"Ms. Durham, yes. This is Dr. Vozzola."

My heart stops. It's Dad's doctor.

"Dr. Vozzola, hi. Is everything okay?"

"Oh yes! Great news, dear. Your father is awake. And he's asking for you."

⌒

Will, Ashley, Taylor, Mason, Willa, Collin, Connor, and I are all packed in the Monroe family Tahoe. Mason and Ashley are whispering something in the background, but my hand fidgets in Will's.

The doctor called, and my dad's awake. Finally. I let out a shaky breath as that realization crosses my mind.

Will's hand squeezes mine. "Are you okay?"

I swallow. "I don't know. He's been in a coma for almost six weeks, you know? It's...weird to hear that he's awake."

He gives me a small smile and plants a kiss on my knuckle. The simple action momentarily soothes me. But it can't do anything to stop the anxiety that rises when we arrive at the hospital.

I unbuckle my seatbelt the moment Will drives up to the entrance door. I give him a quick kiss and run inside, anxious to see Dad. A weird thought suddenly crosses my mind.

That nightmare was a sign.

A sign that, while I lost my mom, I still have my dad. No matter what. With that in mind, my steps toward his room pick up.

When I reach his room, I knock and slowly open the door.

My heart swells when I eye him staring out the window. I inch toward his bed, but his gaze remains outside.

I clear my throat, and his gaze finally lands on me.

"Hi, Dad," I whisper.

He eyes me for a few seconds before his lips start quivering.

"Enna."

That simple word makes me rush over to him, pulling him into a hard hug. He hugs me tighter, like I'm his life preserver. Tears threaten my eyes again, and I let out another shaky breath.

"Sienna," a voice behind me says. I pull back to find Will staring at us.

I clear my throat. "Will, you didn't have to come inside."

"I wanted to be here with you."

Be still my heart.

I give him a small smile, hugging him. I turn to Dad, and he eyes me and Will.

"Um, Dad," I swallow. "This is—"

"William Monroe," he interrupts me, eyes still on Will. "I know who you are, son."

I frown at the blank stare he's giving Will. "Uh, yeah. We're... kind of dating."

Will hugs me closer to him. "It's a pleasure to meet you, sir."

"And it's a pleasure to see you again, son."

Will tenses at my side as my eyebrows shoot up.

"You've met each other?" I turn to Will, his face confused.

"I'm very familiar with William, honey. *Everyone* in Rose Valley is familiar with him. He's a good boy," Dad says.

Relief fills my body. I'm not sure how my dad knows Will, but I'm happy he's responding well to his presence.

"How do you feel, Dad?"

His body is wracked with a large sigh as he shrugs.

"I feel...awake. That's all I can say."

It makes me smile. I give him another hug.

"We're taking you home soon, okay?"

He gives me another smile before he thinks better of it and looks between me and Will. "Enna, can I speak to you for a second? Alone?"

I frown. "Is everything all right?"

"Everything's fine, honey. I'd just like to speak to you without William for a second."

I look at Will, and he gives me a small smile.

"It's okay, babe. I'll meet you outside." He gives me a kiss before walking into the hallway. I turn back to Dad, and a happy grin spreads across his face.

"He's a nice boy, Sienna. He's all grown up."

I frown again. "Do you know Will, Dad?"

"Of course I know William. Bill and Lily were..." He stops himself, and a somber expression etches his face.

"Dad?"

He snaps out of his moment. "Bill and Lily were really good friends of ours," he rasps.

My heartbeat picks up. "You didn't tell me—"

"It didn't make sense to tell you, honey. That's not the point, though. William really is a good boy. Always has been since he was little. You two used to play all the time."

My eyebrows shoot up as I look to the hallway.

"Will and I used to play as *kids*?"

He nods. "William even had a little crush on you," he chuckles. "He drew the two of you together with little hearts around you guys. He did it every year for Valentine's Day."

I smile. "So...what happened? You guys just stopped being friends?"

The somber expression is back, and he's tense.

"It's a long story, Enna. But I think he's good for you. Is he nice?"

More than I hoped. "He's really nice, Dad. He's actually been letting me stay with him and his sister, Taylor."

He chuckles to himself. "Little Taylor's all grown up too, huh? How is she? Last time I saw her, she was so...whimsical."

I laugh at that. Nothing's changed at all. "She's still pretty whimsical. She's been very welcoming."

181

"I'm glad to hear it, Enna. Well, if things are going well, there's no need for you to take me home."

I freeze. "What?"

He gives me a sad smile. "Honey...the moment William walked in here to check on you, your eyes lit up in a way I've never seen before. Like you felt at home with him being here. For a second, I thought I'd never see that sparkle. And I would give anything to put that sparkle back in your eyes. If that means letting you live your life, then so be it."

"Dad," I whisper. "What are you saying?"

"Put me in a home, honey." His voice cracks.

"No," I retort. "I'm not putting you in a home. I can't afford it, and I'm not leaving you alone."

"I wouldn't be alone, Sienna. I'd be where I'm supposed to be."

"Dad—"

"I am almost at *stage 4*, honey," he whispers. "I can't live on like this. And neither can you."

I let out a shaky breath. "But you're not *at* stage 4 yet. Why the rush to be admitted?"

"I'm not rushing, but...I don't want to be treated like an invalid by my own daughter. I'd rather a nurse did that rather than the little girl I raised."

Tears are already streaming down my face.

"I will never forgive myself—"

"Sienna, *please*. Live your life. Live it before you have none left to live." His eyes go to the hallway. "William loves you. I can tell."

A flash of electricity shoots through me. "W-what? No—"

"Yes, he does. And you just might love him too."

"I don't know him," I whisper. "I've known him for two months."

"Love doesn't operate on a timetable, honey. It's an emotion, something you can't control."

My heart fills with something heavy, and it consumes me.

"I can't leave you."

"You won't be leaving me. You'll just be living your life."

"I can't afford a nursing home," I stress again.

He stares at me for a few seconds before sighing.

"We'll figure it out. For now, let them clear me to leave."

I just look at him. Dad's really stubborn. I've been told I got it from him, but I thought they were trying to be funny. Now, as I listen to him, I realize they just might be right. I love him, but having these discussions is frustrating.

I give him another hug before leaving.

I find Will standing near the doorway, and he turns to me with a small smile.

"Everything all right?"

I shrug. "I guess," I say, my voice heavy.

He pulls me into a tight hug. "It's okay, babe. Everything will be okay. Believe me when I say everything's gonna be okay."

I frown at that cryptic statement. "How do you know?"

He peers down at me, tucking a strand behind my ear.

"Because you have me now."

20

WILL

Sienna's dad basically gave us his blessing...without really doing it. *For a second, I thought I'd never see that sparkle. And I would give anything to put that sparkle back in your eyes.*

I was surprised to hear him say that. I was even more surprised when he said he knew me.

I assumed he knew me because of the Monroe name, but something tells me he knows me by another instance.

But where would I have met Sienna's dad?

"You're tense again," Sienna reminds me in bed.

We've been lying in bed all day since it's raining. The weather forecast says it'll be raining with thunderstorms for the next few days, so I can't practice on the course today. And the power went out at the winery, so we all can't work today.

"Nothing, it's just...your dad yesterday. It seemed like he knew who I was, so I was kind of confused," I chuckle.

She lets out a sigh, hugging me closer. She's the big spoon right now as her arms wrap around my neck.

"Apparently, you and I used to play as kids," she chuckles, the sound rumbling through me. Then my ears zero in on what she said.

I lift my head to look up at her. "Wait, are you serious?"

She nods. "Our parents were friends, and you had a crush on me, supposedly. Even as a little boy," she says, kissing my forehead.

"See? I was even into you as a kid. And you say you think this is just a phase."

She rolls her eyes. "Whatever."

"Not whatever." I lean back, propping myself on my elbow. "You're gorgeous now, and you were probably gorgeous back then."

Her brown eyes peer at me.

"I was a kid. So I *definitely* wasn't gorgeous," she jokes.

"How do you know? You don't know how you looked."

"Will, I was a *kid*."

"Well, I have this theory you've been gorgeous your entire life. And you can't disprove it. You can try, but it won't work."

She just stares at me. Those brown eyes pierce into me, and it gives me chills. Did I say something wrong?

"You know...I hate you sometimes."

I flinch. Okay, I wasn't expecting that. "What?"

"The things you say to me...it makes me hate you."

"Did I miss something here?"

She sighs, propping herself on her elbow.

"How can you say stuff like that to me and expect me to function correctly?" Her voice breaks, and it's the cutest thing.

"Sienna..."

"I hate you."

I chuckle and kiss the crook of her neck. "You don't hate me. You just think I'm a piece of shit."

"I do," she says, crying.

"I think you like me."

"Nope, I hate you."

"Well, I don't hate you. In fact, I like you a lot."

She narrows her eyes at me. "No, you like my face."

"Not just your face." I pull her closer, squeezing her ass. "I like these babies too."

"That's why I hate you."

I kiss the crook of her neck again. "Did I say like? I meant, I *love* these babies."

She rolls her eyes, but she's smiling now. "You're such a perv."

I grab her tits. "I love these babies too."

She swallows, her eyes now slightly dilated. "Will—"

"I love your nose," I say, kissing her nose.

She smiles, closing her eyes for a brief moment.

"Will, I think I get it now."

But I'm not nearly done. "I love this little mole above your lip," I say, kissing said mole.

"Can you—"

"I love your lips." I give her a gentle peck.

"So you love my body."

"No, I love *you*."

She freezes, her eyes widened. For a second, we're exchanging gazes, waiting for what the other is going to do next. Hell, I even surprised myself. But...it's all the more true.

After hearing her dad tell her what I already knew, it lit a fire under my belly. I love her. It's a new feeling. And it's a feeling that consumes me.

"Will? Did you just say—"

"I love you. I really do."

She swallows, her eyes darting across my face.

"You can't," she whispers.

This gives me pause. "Why not?"

"'Love' is a strong word. One I'm sure you've never used before. Are you sure?"

"I'm *more* than sure," I say quickly. "And I know I love you. Wanna know why?"

"Will—"

"Because the thought of losing you scares me more than I thought it would."

"What do you mean?"

I let out a shaky breath, squeezing her hand.

"I've dated so many girls. All of them were high-profile and had no sense of reality, if you catch my drift."

"O-kay," she says slowly.

"Not a single one of them has given me a weird tingly feeling when I'm around them. I never once felt the urge to hug them, laugh with them, fucking *kiss* them. I did all of those things with them, but it all just felt robotic. With you, everything just feels...natural. I can't explain it. I just know that I love you. And that's not changing any time soon."

Tears well in her eyes, and I swipe one away as it threatens to escape.

"So my dad was right," she whispers.

I chuckle, kissing her temple. "Your dad was right."

"Well, that just sucks then."

I frown. "What—"

"Because I love you too."

I freeze, my heart thrumming in my chest.

"You do?" For some reason, I didn't expect her to feel the same way. But it's alarming that she thinks it sucks.

"I wanted to be the first to tell you," she whispers, a soft chuckle escaping her.

I let out a sigh of relief, chuckling. "Tough luck, babe."

She laughs, sniffling. "You love me," she repeats.

I nod. "I love you. And thank God you fucking love me too."

"But you don't think this is all happening too fast?"

I shake my head, pulling her closer. "No such thing, babe."

"Will," she sighs. "This is crazy. We've been dating for maybe a few weeks. And we already declare that we love each other? How do we know this isn't just a...phase?"

I consider that she might be right. Maybe I'm just in the moment and mesmerized by her doe eyes.

Maybe I just can't get over how fucking beautiful she is.

Maybe I can't get over how much she despises me.

Or maybe—just maybe—she's the first girl that likes me, Will Monroe, instead of me, William Monroe VI.

"Because I know, in my heart, that there's only room for you in it. And that's all I can give you right now."

For a second, I think she's going to call bullshit. The seconds tick by, and it feels like an eternity.

But then a gorgeous smile stretches across her defined features.

"If you're that confident in this, *us*, then all I can say is...it's you and me."

In that moment, I kiss her. I kiss her like I'm lacking it.

Sienna Durham is too important to lose.

Each and every day, I find myself falling for her.

I love her.

And fuck me, it feels good.

⌒

I might be insane. Any of my friends would call me insane, but the only opinion that matters to me right now is Connor's.

We're looking at diamond rings right now at Hansen Jeweler.

"Thanks for doing this for me, bro."

He shrugs, peering through the glass counter.

"It's no big deal. Dad said their appointment window is wide open right now. For us, this is the wedding season. Everyone has their rings by now."

Connor's dad is the rightful heir of Hansen Jewelers. They're the second largest jeweler in the world right now, and Connor is in line to inherit the name. He's also helping me pick out an engagement ring for Sienna.

"I'm not sure what metal I wanna use. Do you think she'll like gold?"

He gives me a blank stare. "Dude, does it matter?"

"She's not gonna take a platinum ring."

He lets out an annoyed sigh. "How do you know that?"

"It's *Sienna*, dude. She'll think she's not worth it."

"Is she worth it to *you*?"

I just stare at him. I hate when he's right. He gives me a shit-eating grin before looking back down at the glass counter of rings. But the question still stands: *Is* she worth it to me?

She's more than worth it.

Satisfied with this outlook, I decide on a ring. She can scream and yell at me all she wants; I'm getting her the best ring money can buy.

We meet with a man about a potential engagement ring; a 22 carat round cut diamond ring. Simple, but elegant. I think she'll love it. I *hope* she loves it.

First, I want to do something that I feel would be the right thing to do. I need to talk to her dad. I don't have a complete plan yet, but I just need to ask her dad for her hand.

"Son, you came to the hospital to ask me for my daughter's hand in *marriage*?" Mr. Durham is giving the sternest glare I've ever seen.

I swallow, fiddling the box in my hand. "I love her, sir. And...I just didn't think it'd be right to marry her without your blessing."

He narrows his eyes at me. "You want to marry my daughter," he states.

"I can't see my life without her."

He stares at me for a few seconds before clearing his throat.

"Sienna's my baby girl. She's twenty-three and has her entire life ahead of her."

This is where I stop him. "I don't mean to hold her back."

"I'm not saying that's what you're doing. I'm just saying," he chuckles to himself. "You've met my daughter. She likes to be in control of things."

I laugh, running a hand through my hair. "Trust me, sir, I know."

"You really want to marry her, knowing she most likely won't put you first?"

"What do you mean?"

"She wants to be a winemaker. She's spent the last eight years of her life learning about wine."

I frown. "You knew she was drinking—"

"Of course I knew she was drinking wine in the house. She's my daughter, not a ninja."

I can't stop the laugh that comes out.

"Sir, I'm not sure I understand what you mean."

He lets out a sigh, adjusting in his bed. The motion makes me cringe, considering his current state attached to an IV.

"She's stubborn. She may love you, but if there's one thing I know about Enna, it's that she'll do anything to stay close to Miranda."

Realization crosses my mind. "Her mom," I whisper.

He nods, something flashing in his eyes.

"Her mother introduced her to wine. It's helped her...tremendously throughout the years. In her eyes...proposing to her might look like you're suffocating her."

A wave of sadness hits me. It hurts that he might be right.

"So you don't give your blessing."

"I think you're a good kid. I adored you when you were a little boy, and I still do. Standing by my daughter's side is reason enough to like you. But..." The dreaded 'but.' "It worries me that she'll hurt you. Or she'll hurt *herself* by not chasing the one thing she has left of her mom."

I look back down at the hundred-thousand-dollar ring I just purchased. "I guess this will just have to wait then," I mumble.

"Give it a decade," he jokes. "She might come around."

Sighing, I stuff it back in my pocket, give him a tight smile, and make my way out of the room. But not before he stops me.

"And for the record, son, I will *always* give my daughter my blessing to marry you. And you deserve the blessing to marry her."

Another wave of emotion flows through me.

I turn around to Mr. Durham, and I soften at the pleasant expression he's giving me. I let out a shaky sigh. I hoped that telling her I love her would be enough. Maybe it's not.

Mr. Durham's right. She's been an independent girl for most of her life. Taking care of her dad. Working throughout high school. I smile, thinking about that. It just makes me love her even more. But she's...occupied. And I can't get in the way of that.

It's all I can think about at the course. If I got down on one knee, is it possible she'll say no?

Maybe I misunderstood her when she said she loved me back?

"Dude, what are you thinking about?"

I turn to Collin as he takes a swig of Miller Lite.

"Nothing," I say, clearing my throat. "Is it my turn?"

He stares at me, and it makes my skin crawl.

"Are you good, bro? You've been distracted on three holes already."

Collin doesn't know about the ring. I can see it now; he's going to think I'm an idiot. "It's nothing, dude."

I set my ball up, and it's golfing as usual. I have one more month until the tournament in Scottsdale. I've been off my game, focusing on Sienna. It's not exactly a hardship, but I have to think about that too.

"Connor told me you bought an engagement ring for Sienna," he blurts out.

I close my eyes in shame. Well, there goes keeping it a secret from him. "I know. It was dumb. I know that now."

He surprises me by frowning. "Why's that dumb?"

I shrug, throwing my bag over my shoulder.

"I don't know, it's just...she'll most likely say no."

He snorts. "Well, *that's* optimistic."

"I asked her dad for her hand," I remark.

His eyebrows shoot up. "And?"

Letting out a sigh, I say, "He basically told me it's a lost cause proposing to her right now."

"Why the hell would he say that?"

"I don't know, dude. It's Sienna. She already thinks we're moving too fast, but I'm already all in with her."

"So what's the problem?"

We get in the cart, and I lay my head against the wheel.

"I just need to wait, I guess. I wanted to propose to her as a surprise or something. I was gonna have it all planned out. But I don't know anymore."

For a second, there's silence. I lift my head to find Collin staring at me, presumably thinking. I cock an eyebrow, and he suddenly snaps his finger.

"I got it. When's the golf tournament again?"

"The middle of August."

He gives me a huge grin. "Do it that weekend, bro."

"What?"

"When you win! Make it a surprise or something. She'll be so happy for you, she can't say no."

I gape at him. "Dude, that's genius."

He laughs, nodding. "Isn't it?"

"If it weren't also manipulative."

He flinches. "Well, what other choice do you have? If you're so worried that she'll say no, then you kind of don't have any other choice."

Shaking my head, I drive off to the next hole.

"I'll ponder other ideas. But thanks anyway, dude."

He lets out an annoyed sigh, and we're on our way to the next hole.

After a few hours, Collin and I decide to head to the vineyard for drinks. This is the slowest it's been, so we take advantage and walk into the bistro.

Sienna walks in, and I admire her all over again. Long, wavy hair, blue tank top, and white shorts. She looks beach ready, and I adore the outfit on her.

"How is it possible that you get more and more beautiful every day?"

She turns around, large smile stretching across her face. It makes my heart ache.

"I didn't know you were coming in today."

"Collin and I spent some time on the course, and we wanted to get a round of drinks going."

"Oh, okay, what can I get started for y'all?"

"Oh, no. You're gonna sit down and drink with us. Have Taylor or someone else make the drinks."

She rolls her eyes, another smile forming. "Will, I have to work."

"And you will. After you drink with us."

"And tell Taylor to join us, too," Collin chirps.

I roll my eyes while Sienna laughs. "You guys just never give up."

I pull her into my lap. "Babe, just one drink," I whisper, kissing her cheek.

She sighs, kissing me. "What can I make for y'all?"

"Just a Jack and Coke for me," Collin says.

"And I'll have an old-fashioned," I tell her.

She nods and walks off. My eyes, again, are on her pert ass.

"We get it, you're in love," Taylor's voice says behind me.

I turn to find her strutting our way. I look at Collin, and, indeed, he's staring at her, mouth agape. But I go back to what she just said.

"Does everyone know I told Sienna I love her?"

"We all live in the same house. *Of course* I know, dummy."

Collin snickers next to me, and I shoot him a glare. "It's whatever. I don't want to keep talking about it."

"Why are you butthurt? I was kidding, Willy. It's sweet that you told her that." She softens.

"No it's not. Because I can't..."

She frowns. "You can't what?"

I look at Collin, and he gives me a pointed look.

"It's nothing."

She gives me a look of disbelief before shrugging. "Stay secretive all you want, big bro. I don't care. I'm gonna finish planning her birthday party while I'm on break. Talk to you guys later."

This gets my attention. "What? *Whose* birthday party?"

She gives me a confused look. "Sienna's. Her birthday's next month, and the girls and I are throwing a surprise party for her."

What the hell? Sienna's birthday is next month? Why wouldn't she tell me that?

"You're kidding me, right?"

"Please don't tell me you forgot your girlfriend's birthday."

"He doesn't have to. I'll tell you: he forgot his girlfriend's birthday," Collin jokes.

Taylor laughs while I glare at him. "I didn't forget. I just—she didn't tell me, all right?" And it makes me wonder, why?

Because you didn't ask, you dodo.

"If you want, you can help us plan," Taylor offers.

I could. But there's something that's been on my chest. And hearing about her birthday makes me want to get it off. I suck in a breath.

"I was gonna propose to Sienna," I blurt.

Taylor flinches, her face paling. "You were gonna do *what*?!"

"He's got the hots for the sommelier," Collin chirps.

I nudge him, and he grunts.

"Willy? You were planning on proposing?"

I swallow, suddenly feeling my cheeks heat. "It was a stupid idea. I don't even know what I was thinking."

"Willy—"

"Can we not talk about this please?"

"Talk about what?"

Sienna's voice makes us all jump. We all turn to find her staring at us, her steps slowing.

"Everything all right?"

"Everything's fine, babe," I croak.

Her frown tells me she doesn't buy it. "You guys are staring at me kind of strange."

"It's because you're so beautiful, girl!" Taylor says, feigning cheerfulness.

Again, she's smart as hell. She knows something's going on.

"If I interrupted something, you guys could just say that instead of acting like weirdos," she chuckles. She drops the drinks on the table.

"Where's your drink?"

"I had it at the bar." She gives me a fake smile and kisses my cheek.

"You really don't wanna drink with me, do you?"

"Work calls, babe." She gives me a peck this time. "I'll see you guys later. Taylor, you can take a break and hang out with them, if you'd like."

"Awesome! I need to talk to Willy for a sec."

She nods and walks off. And we all just watch her.

"Y'all have no chill," Collin remarks.

But Taylor doesn't care to acknowledge him.

"Willy, you were gonna propose," she recaps.

"'*Were*' being the operative word," I deadpan. I don't want to talk about this. There's no point if Sienna's just going to reject it.

"So let me get this straight: You're playing in your first golf tournament to win a purse for her, and now I hear you're planning on proposing to our cute and stubborn sommelier."

I flinch. "She's my girlfriend, Taylor."

"But no one thought you saw her as a long-term thing."

I frown. "What do you mean? I thought you knew I love her."

"Well...yeah, but come on. You're my douchebag older brother. You don't do serious."

It's almost insulting how highly they think of me. "Well, I do with her."

The concerned look is now replaced with a look of admiration. My little sister is giving me a satisfied grin.

"Well, then. If we're gonna do this, you need to have a plan."

"Wait, I never said I was following through with it."

She frowns as if she doesn't get it. "Did you buy a ring?"

I swallow. "Yeah..."

"*You did*?!" she screeches.

"Only a small one! It's nothing *too* crazy."

She narrows her eyes at me. "How small are we talking?"

I look at Collin, and he drinks his whiskey and Coke.

"A 22-carat diamond ring," I relent.

She gasps, a grin stretching across her face. "*Oh my gosh*, Willy! That's *amazing*! And not even small, dude," she remarks.

I shrug. "I got a nice deal on it. Connor's dad gave me a...Monroe discount."

She rolls her eyes, laughing. "We have to plan this thing, Willy. You're proposing to her. Sienna's my girl. She deserves the best."

I narrow my eyes at her. "I thought you said you didn't know we were a serious thing."

She shrugs. "It was a test. And you passed," she says simply.

I grimace at her. "I hate you, little sister."

"You love me. Everyone does. *Anyway,*" she drags out, "her birthday is August 17th."

I whip my gaze back up to hers. "Excuse me?"

Her eyes widen in confusion. "What?"

"August 17th, as in...the day of my *tournament* August 17th?"

She thinks about it for a second. "Oh. I guess so. Sienna really didn't tell you?"

"No, she didn't."

She shrugs. "Well, I don't have a ton of time to talk. But you can help plan her party. We're throwing it in my suite at the resort."

My eyes bulge out of my head. For the tournament, we all booked rooms at The Phoenician in Scottsdale. Everyone booked a casita suite. But...the casita suite one-bedrooms aren't big enough for a party of maybe ten people.

"How are you throwing a party—"

"I booked a presidential suite," she says quickly.

I flinch, and Collin snickers at my side.

"Why did you do that?! It's only you."

Her eyes widen, her cheeks turning red. "Um, well the guy I'm seeing and I—"

"Forget it," I—and Collin—cut her off. I don't need to hear the details. "I'm helping plan for sure. In fact...I think I have another plan for her birthday, too."

I look at Collin, and he shares my gaze. I see a glimpse of confusion in his eyes before what I mean finally registers. He gives me a look of approval.

And just like that...I'm proposing to my girl again.

On her birthday.

After the tournament.

When—or *if*—I win the purse. The plan has me more excited than I should be.

"William! You sound so excited, honey! What has happened?"

I take a deep, shaky breath as I listen to my mom's voice after a bit over a month.

"Mom...I think I'm in love," I say, chuckling.

She gasps. "No! William, what have I missed?"

I tell her about Sienna—without actually bringing *up* Sienna—and how I met her at the winery. I tell her that she's a sommelier.

"You're dating the sommelier from our vineyard?"

I let out another shaky breath. "I am."

There's a moment of pause on her end. "Is this...the same sommelier that's been training you and your sister?"

"Yes," I answer instantly. "I love her a lot, Mom. I...really think she's it for me."

"Aww, Willy. My baby's in love," she sing-songs. I groan at my mom's squealing. "Honey! William's in love!"

Suddenly, Dad's voice takes over. "What's this about being in love, son?"

I facepalm myself. "Dad, it's not a big deal. But...I'm sort of planning to propose to my girlfriend."

"*Girlfriend*?!" he screeches over the phone, making me pull it away from my ear.

"Try not to sound *too* surprised," I joke.

"We've been gone for maybe five weeks. In that time, you've found a girlfriend? What happened to little Mason Szuch?"

"Mom," I groan. "Mason and I were never...*serious*." They knew this. I don't know why it's such a surprise that I'm not dating her.

"Is she someone we know?" Dad asks.

I take a deep breath and swallow. "She's a...sommelier at the winery."

There's another moment of pause on their side. Why are they being weird about this?

"Well, we'd love to meet the girl that's stolen our son's heart," Mom says.

I let out a sigh of relief. "I think you guys will like her. She's super beautiful, smart, and loves what she does. She even wants to be a winemaker."

"Aww, well we can't wait to meet her! So when are you proposing?" Mom asks.

I tell them about her birthday in a month and how I'm playing in the tournament that has the potential to kickstart my professional golf career.

They're onboard immediately.

"That sounds like a plan, William! We'll be back mid-August, so we'll just take a detour to Arizona."

I freeze. "As in...you guys are coming to see me play?"

"Of course!" Mom exclaims. "It's our son's golf debut. We can't miss that."

I let out a sigh of relief. "Sounds good, Mom. I'll keep you guys posted. How are the meetings with investors going?"

"They're going well! We signed a contract to start building a vineyard here in Santorini. We're scheduled to sign three more contracts with investors in Tuscany, Lyon, and Barcelona."

I smile at this newfound knowledge. "That's great news. Well, I'm looking forward to seeing you guys."

I say my goodbyes, lie back on my bed, and pull out the ring box from my pocket. I open it and admire the shimmer from the diamond.

It's the next chapter in my life.

Sienna Durham.

Damn do I love you.

21

SIENNA

Will is acting like a weirdo, and I don't know how to handle it. It's been a month, and he's been extra affectionate. Even *more* than usual. While it's cute, it's freaking me out.

We've been sleeping in his guest room together, as usual, but he's planned picnic dates, touching me every chance he gets at work...and we've had sex *every week*.

But even so, with his head between my legs right now, it only makes me love him more.

I'm a blubbering mess on the bed, tossing and turning as he holds my hips in place. My hands grab on to his hair, and it gets to be too much. His lips continue sucking, making my hips buck.

He pulls back, sticking a finger inside, hungry eyes staring at my center. "Fuck, you're so wet," he growls. He continues fingering me as he sucks on the nub.

"Baby," I moan.

But it only makes him go faster. My hips start to rock against his mouth, and it makes him chuckle. The sensation sends a wave of excitement through my core.

He sticks another long finger inside, and he sucks harder. And then I see stars. Once again, Will Monroe has put me on cloud nine. This is the most euphoric feeling I've felt with him in bed.

I'm brought back to earth, and my chest heaves as I let out a breath. I open my eyes to find his lips latched around my nipple, blue eyes staring back up at me. His hand trails back down to my core, giving a pat, making me shiver.

He pops it out of his mouth. "You feel good, babe?"

"Mm-hmm," I croak.

His deep chuckle rumbles as he kisses my temple. "Good. Because we have a long day ahead of us."

I let out a groan, pulling my tank top down. "What does *that* mean?"

He props himself up on an elbow, and my gaze lands on his pecs. I absently run a hand over them.

"We leave for Scottsdale in a few weeks, babydoll. I have some last-minute press interviews to do for my debut. And *you* have to figure out how we're even doing the trip with your dad still being in the hospital."

I groan, remembering my dad. He's been in the hospital for a month now after waking up. "Crap, I forgot about that."

He laughs, kissing my forehead. "It'll be fine. If he can't stay there for a bit longer, I can just have him stay at my house and hire a temporary nurse while we're gone."

I flinch. "What? No, why would you do that?"

He gives me a look of confusion. "Why *wouldn't* I?"

"Will, I can't let my dad—"

He lets out an annoyed sigh. "Sienna, you're my girl. If it comes to it, your dad can stay at my house in one of the guest rooms. Or he can come with us to Scottsdale for the weekend. It's totally up to you." And with that, he kisses me and gets up, disappearing into the bathroom.

This is all just...*so* weird. William Monroe, the heir of Monroe Vineyards, is my *boyfriend*. And he insists on being my hero every chance he gets.

He let me stay with him while my dad was in a coma. He drives me to work every day. And he's just offered to bring my dad along with us on our trip for his tournament.

Is this real?

It can't be. I'm not the girl that gets a guy like Will Monroe. I love him a lot. I never thought I would. But, for fuck's sake, he surprised me. This prettyboy heir has somehow managed to steal my heart. And I don't think there's a damn thing I'll do about it.

I give him a kiss when he drops me off at the hospital. I take the walk down the dreaded hall and come across his room. He's sitting up, reading through a magazine. The IV hooked up to him gives me chills.

I swallow, clearing my throat. When he sees me, a large smile stretches across his face.

"Enna! Hi, honey!"

"Dad," I croak. "I've missed you. How are you doing?"

He sighs, closing the magazine. "I'm doing fine, hun. They said I have a few more weeks before I'm ready to go home."

I swallow. "Dad, I have something to tell you."

His satisfied grin is replaced with confusion. "What's the matter?"

"Nothing's the matter, Dad. It's just...Will has his professional golf debut soon."

He flinches. "Oh wow! He golfs? Well, of course he does. He's been golfing since he was a little boy," he answers for himself.

I still feel a bit uneasy that Dad knows Will personally.

"Yeah, his coach thinks he'll do great professionally. So he signed him up for the Harvey Invitational. It's in Scottsdale, Arizona."

His eyebrows shoot up. "Oooh fancy! Scottsdale's beautiful. Miranda and I used to spend time there frequently."

I give him a small smile. "Well, Will's invited me and his friends to support him there. So I'll be in Scottsdale on the weekend of my birthday."

"Aww, that's nice, Enna. See? I knew once you put yourself out there, you'd meet your people." He looks off into the distance, a soft grin on his face. "Remember the book Miranda read to you?"

My breath hitches as the book crosses my mind.

"I do," I croak.

"It was the cutest book for you, Enna. And you found your people," he whispers. "You found your home. I'm sure they love you. Everyone does."

Suddenly, my throat feels heavy. "Yeah, well I just wanted to tell you because Will and I wanted you to be somewhere where you're taken care of."

"O-kay," he says slowly.

"Will came up with the idea of you staying at his house and hiring you a temporary nurse—"

"Sienna—"

"*Or* if you'd like, you can come with us to Scottsdale. We can get you your own suite, but we'd still hire a nurse to take care of you." I hold my breath as I wait for his response. Dad hates feeling like he's a burden. He tries to be low maintenance, but he doesn't understand the gravity of his condition.

"I want you to enjoy your trip, Enna. So if that means staying at the Monroe mansion and being taken care of, then so be it."

I stand there, mouth agape. "Dad—"

"William has big plans for you two, dear. I'm not gonna stand in the way of that. I'll stay here in Kentucky."

I knew he'd say this. But I was hoping against hope that he'd make a different decision.

"You're not staying here."

He flinches, his eyes widening. "What?"

"I'm not letting you stay here. You're coming with us."

"Enna—"

"I'm not *leaving* you here. I'm not letting you out of my sight again. We're booking you a suite at the hotel that we're staying at. And that's final," I say firmly.

He stares at me, and a grin slowly slides across his face. "I wake up, and you haven't changed one bit. I was starting to worry."

I can't help the chuckle that comes out. I give him a hug, and I'm on my way to the winery, via Ashley's car.

"We need to go shopping. A new wardrobe for Scottsdale is imperative," Ashley says.

I roll my eyes. "I don't have 'new wardrobe' money, Ash."

She scoffs, flipping her hair over her shoulder. "I don't believe I asked whether or not you had new wardrobe money," she says matter-of-factly.

I find myself smiling. "I think my summer clothes will do just fine in Arizona."

"I'm sure they will. But I wanna treat you to some cute clothes. I need some new shorts, anyway. You're going with me."

I can't fight the smile forming. Ashley and I became fast friends somehow. Even after the entire debacle between her and Will. Normally, I'd keep to myself. Back in high school, I never thought I'd get along with the people of Rose Valley. I went to high school in Louisville, but everyone knew about the people across the river in Rose Valley: the wealthy bunch.

Like I said before, I didn't always work at Monroe Vineyard.

I've only been working here for two years, and I started out as an intern. I worked at a liquor store downtown, which...had a considerably different crowd. I was used to those people. We had regulars come in that would know who I was. An older man would tip me $50 every time he came in to buy a bottle of Jack Daniels. For a while, the regulars were the people I thought I would identify with. We didn't sell much wine, but it was close enough for me to find my niche.

Until I came across Monroe.

My mom told me about it when I was younger, and I always knew it to be the winery for members who could afford the pricey wine. I remember drinking their Wild Spirit Merlot.

That was the wine my mom drank while she painted. I never knew why she loved it so much. She told me that there was something enchanting about the way tastes dance together in a good glass of merlot. I thought she was nuts. But then when I interviewed for my internship, I asked to taste test the Wild Spirit. It was their bestseller at the time.

One sip, and Mom was right. I fell in love.

It was then that I knew I wanted to work at Monroe.

A few months later, Wild Spirit was discontinued. To this day, I don't know why. But it didn't turn me away from Monroe one bit. In fact, it made me want to stay longer. If staying at the winery that produced her favorite wine in the whole world would keep me close to her, then I wasn't leaving anytime soon.

And here I am driving in a car with Ashley Westbrook. Dating the son of William and Lily Monroe. I've made friends with people I never thought I'd connect with. Yet, in some twisted turn of events,

I find myself traveling with them to Scottsdale, Arizona for my boyfriend's debut golf tournament. Dad was right. I found my people.

Case in point. Will walks up to me at the counter. My eyes zero in on the way his T-shirt hugs his muscles. He's wearing shorts today. There's also the feminine urge to swoon at how tan his skin is today. All those days golfing in the sun.

"Babe! How'd it go with your dad?" he asks, followed with a kiss to my cheek.

"Pretty good. He's going with us to Scottsdale," I say nonchalantly.

He laughs, leaning on the counter.

"Let me guess: He wanted to stay home, but the Sienna effect encouraged him to tag along."

I give him a sheepish smile. "More like forced him," I admit.

Shaking his head, he comes around the counter and wraps his arms around my waist. I tense up, looking around the lobby.

"It wouldn't be a normal day if you let him stay here. It's a good thing, honestly. He needs eyes on him."

But my mind is still on the fact that his hands are wrapped around me. "Um, Will—" I clear my throat. "We're at the winery."

He kisses my temple. "Yes, we are."

"Anyone could walk in right now and wonder what the hell is going on."

He lets out a sigh before turning me around.

"I had my head between your *legs* this morning. But the mere thought of me hugging you has you freaking out," he deadpans.

My face suddenly heats. "That was in private. I thought we talked about—"

"Would you prefer if I shouted in the courtyard and in this bistro that you're mine? Would that ease your mind?"

"No."

He runs his hand through his hair. "Sienna, I—I don't know what you want me to do, doll."

I let out a shaky breath. "I just need you to be patient with me, okay?"

"But I love you," he whispers to me, breaking my heart.

"And I love you, *too*, babe. But this is still new territory for me. Everyone knows who you are. I'm just a sommelier."

"You're *more* than just a sommelier," he argues.

I let out a soft chuckle. "To *you*, Will. I still have a job here. And I can't put that in jeopardy by being public with our relationship."

He reaches for my hand. "Babe—"

"Sienna?" a familiar voice says behind me.

I turn around to find Mr. Stevens, and my heart suddenly wants out of my chest.

"Mr. Stevens!" I exclaim. "I didn't know you'd be back so soon."

His troubled gaze wavers between me and Will.

"The trip overseas was cut short because Mr. and Mrs. Monroe will be back in a few weeks. They said they no longer needed my services at the meetings."

This gives me pause. "Wait, what do you mean? You were with—"

"Mr. and Mrs. Monroe? Yes. They needed me with them in Europe to scope out the vineyard sites and notify them of anything wrong. They hired me as their project manager."

Will and I share a look.

"Oh...okay, well that's great, sir."

"It really is," he says absently, his gaze now on Will. "How have things been with the winery? How have sales been?"

"Sales have been great, sir," Will chirps. "Things have been running smoothly for the most part. I did have one thing I wanted to run by you, though."

His eyebrows shoot up. "And what's that, son?"

Will briefly glances at me. "Sienna will be joining me and my friends on the weekend of the 16th in Scottsdale, Arizona. It's my professional golf debut, sir."

He looks at me, an unreadable look in his eyes.

"Oh, she will, will she?"

I swallow but stand firm. "Will's kind of asked me to join him. It's just for the weekend. I'll be back by that Sunday."

He glances between me and him, and I'm worried he'll say no. But then he surprises me by giving us a friendly smile.

"That's absolutely fine, Sienna. May I talk to you for a second, though?"

I clear my throat and nod. "Yeah, of course, sir." I shoot Will a glance, and he gives me a quick kiss on the temple.

I follow Mr. Stevens to his office. He sets down his briefcase on the desk. I sit down across from him, and he puts his glasses on, turning on the computer.

"It seems you and William have gotten quite acquainted with each other," he says, typing.

I swallow, my palms suddenly sweaty. "Yeah, you could say that," I croak. "He's kind of relentless," I chuckle.

But Mr. Stevens isn't amused. "Of course he is. You're a beautiful girl, and you're not like any other girl he's dated."

I frown. "Well, y-yeah, everyone's kind of told me I'm not exactly his type."

He flinches, his face turning the shade of a tomato.

"Oh, no, that's not what I meant, dear. I just mean, he typically dates amongst the Rose Valley socialites. He doesn't normally entertain the...*help*."

The harsh reality of that hits me harder than I hoped it would.

"I told Will this. But he wouldn't listen to me."

He gives me an easy smile. "Maybe he thinks the relationship is promising. But that's not what I brought you back here for."

"O-kay."

"The vineyard that they're building in Santorini is currently hiring."

My eyebrows shoot up. "Oh?"

He nods, taking his glasses off. "George Galanis will be the celebrity that's managing that vineyard."

A jolt of excitement shoots through me. "The *restaurateur*?"

"Indeed. He's a personal friend of the Monroes. Mr. Monroe has asked him to manage that vineyard, and George is asking for an apprentice to work under him for the fall, winter, and spring quarters."

"Oh, that's cool. What kind of apprenticeship is he running?"

He smiles, crossing his arms. "A winemaking apprenticeship."

My eyes widen. "What?"

He nods. "And he wants to hire someone fresh and new from the States."

"Oh" is all I can say.

"See, Santorini gets a lot of tourists. Many of them are celebrities. They want to make sure they have fresh talent up close and personal."

"Well...that's awesome, sir." I'm not sure why he's telling me all of this.

"I'm not finished. George has personally asked me if I knew of anyone back in the States who would be interested in working in another country for a few months. The person in question must be very talented and knowledgeable in viniculture *and* viticulture." He gives a dramatic pause. "Your name came up."

Chills swim up my spine, and I find my pulse quickening.

"Wait, you brought *me* up?"

"Yes, I did."

"For an apprenticeship in Greece? *Santorini*, Greece?"

He chuckles. "Yes, Sienna, for a winemaking apprenticeship in Santorini. I gave you a rave review, and Mr. Galanis would love to meet you."

"Sir, I—I don't know what to say."

"Say you'll meet with him."

"But—"

"I know you're an aspiring winemaker. You've been doing an excellent job as a sommelier, and we appreciate your work here. Your hard work will pay off, Sienna. Take the interview."

I'm over the moon. The excitement courses through me as so many thoughts race through my mind. An apprenticeship in *Greece*? It's a dream come true.

I'm close to asking how soon we can meet when a new thought crosses my mind: Will.

"Wait. How many months are we talking?"

"He'd ideally like the candidate to be in Greece by the middle of September. That's one of the prime wine seasons there."

That's pretty soon. It's an amazing opportunity, but I'm not sure if Will might think so. I'd be leaving him for months at a time.

"Can I have some time to think about it?"

He gives me a comforting smile. "Is this about William?"

I swallow and nod. "I just...don't wanna hurt him."

"If he truly loves you, he'll understand. Plus, he's a Monroe! If he wanted to see you, he could travel there to see you in a day's time."

I smile. That's true. But that would also mean a long-distance relationship when he's not in Greece.

I shouldn't be thinking that far ahead. I haven't even interviewed yet. I take a deep breath and stand up.

"Thank you for recommending me. When can I meet with Mr. Galanis?"

"He can have a video call with you at the end of this month. Construction hasn't started, so they're not quite worried about it yet."

I let out a sigh of relief. I still have some time.

"Well, that's great, sir. Thank you so much again."

He gives a courteous nod and waves me off. I leave his office, the thought fresh in my mind.

Spending months in Santorini, doing what I love.

How can I turn *that* down?

22

WILL

We finally touch down in Phoenix, Arizona, and I take in the fresh air. The pebble landscaping, the cacti, the bright-as-fuck sun...the Gila monster that just crawled by Collin's foot. It's paradise.

"Bro, it's fucking *hot* here," Connor complains.

"Really? I thought it was actually kind of cold," Sadie deadpans, pulling her hair up in a ponytail.

I roll my eyes at both of them. "Guys, behave. If we're doing this, we're gonna *enjoy* it. Come on! We're in Arizona!"

"You say that like we're in Oahu or something. At least *there*, we can go to the beach," Sadie mutters.

"The Phoenician has pools there," Taylor tells her.

Sadie lets out a sigh of relief. "I prefer a beach, Tay. At least it's clean. Tell me, *why* did I come on this trip again?"

"Because you came to support your friend for his golf debut," Sienna answers.

I look at her and smile. The comment makes my heart swell. I pull her close to me, kissing her temple.

Sadie rolls her eyes. "I honestly don't recall talking to you."

"Sadie, stop. You're on this trip. Stop complaining, or I'm booking you on the next flight home," Taylor threatens.

This shuts her up. She rolls her eyes, putting her shades on.

The limousine finally arrives after standing in the heat. The driver opens the door for us, and we all make our way inside.

Willa and Connor sit on one side, while Sienna and I sit the farthest from the group. Taylor and Collin sit awkwardly on one end of the limousine. Sadie sits next to Cale, and they both look out the window, seemingly annoyed with being in Arizona. Mason and Ashley are giggling at the outside world. What an interesting bunch of people.

Sienna squeezes my thigh, grabbing my attention. "Are you okay?"

I smile at the question. "I *think* I'm okay. Just...nervous, kind of. Two out of these ten don't seem to wanna be here," I try to joke, but fail.

"Don't worry about them. This trip's about you. This is big for you! A lot of things are gonna psych you out this weekend. Don't let them"—she motions to Cale and Sadie—"be one."

My heart swells. God, I love this girl.

"You know what's really psyching me, babe?"

She smiles at me, a hint of confusion etched across her eyebrows. "What?"

"The fact that you didn't tell me your birthday is the day of the tournament," I whisper.

Her eyebrows shoot up. "Because it's not about me. Wait, how'd you find out about that?"

I look at Taylor, who's talking to Mason and Ashley, and Sienna follows my gaze. She rolls her eyes.

"Of course she told you. Look, this weekend is about you, babe. Don't worry about me."

"It's your birthday this weekend, and you didn't think to tell me because 'it's not about you'? I might be new to this whole relationship thing, but I think one of the unspoken rules is to treat your girlfriend for their birthday."

She rolls her eyes, a chuckle slipping out. "Babe. It's fine. Please, this is *your* weekend. Not mine."

I open my mouth to respond, but she has a look of finality in her eyes. I let her have this one. I give her a small smile and kiss her. I turn to look outside at the landscape, but my gaze lands on Sadie.

And she's glaring at us.

More specifically, she's glaring at my arm wrapped around Sienna's shoulder. Well, this is going to be a fun trip.

We check into the resort, and everyone goes their separate ways. Sienna and I drop our bags off as she takes in the room.

The casita suite looks so much more beautiful in person. We have a large window that overlooks the golf course, and a large fountain lies in the center.

Sienna's immediately in awe.

"This is so beautiful," she croons. "I'm definitely drinking a glass on the porch tonight."

I laugh, wrapping my arms around her waist. "It's beautiful, isn't it? Just like you."

She giggles. "You find any moment to be cheesy."

"That's me," I say, kissing her temple. "Do you know if your dad ever checked in?"

"He did. Your doctor texted me and let me know that they flew in last night. He should be squared away. I'll go check on him in a sec."

"I'll go with you if you want."

"No, that's okay. I'm sure you have some press stuff to take care of."

And just like that, I get a phone call. It's my coach.

"That's my cue," I sigh and give her another kiss. "I'm gonna meet him in the lobby. Do you have a key? There's one in my jacket pocket if you need it."

"Great. I'll just check in with him and maybe hang out with Ashley and Mason. Ashley said we need to go shopping, so I guess that's what we're doing."

I smile. I'm glad she's getting along with everyone. It makes this thing—and proposing to her—much easier.

I freeze, remembering the ring box is in my jacket.

The same jacket that has the key in it.

And the same jacket that's lying on the kitchen island.

"Babe, turn around for a second," I say playfully.

She gives me a confused look. "What?"

"Turn around for a few seconds."

She laughs, turning around.

"If this is your way of asking to look at my ass, you could've said that."

I chortle. "You're right, babe. You caught me." I quickly grab the box and slide it in my shorts pocket. "Okay, you can turn around now."

She slowly turns around, looking around the room suspiciously.

"Did you plant flowers somewhere or something? Or a camera?"

I laugh again. "I have to go, babe. But let me know when you're back in here safely. I don't know how long I'll be out."

"Okay, Dad. I'll let you know."

I roll my eyes and give her another kiss. I'm out of the door seconds later, and my pulse finally slows down. I need to be more careful. If she reached into that pocket and saw the box, she'd know something's up and would've booked the next flight home.

And I just couldn't take that chance. I squeeze the box in my pocket and then I'm on my way to the lobby.

Coach is sitting in one of the chairs reading a newspaper, and I notice a man dressed in khaki shorts and a white polo sitting next to him.

"Hey, Coach."

He turns around and quickly slaps the newspaper down on the coffee table.

"William! It's good to see you. How was the flight?"

"It was good. Got some rest. I feel good."

He flashes me a bright grin before he motions the man over.

"William, this is Steven Cartwright. He's a representative from Singleton Athletics."

The man also flashes me a bright grin as he holds out his hand.

"How are you doing, son?"

"I'm good, sir. Thank you for making it out for this tournament. I'm sure you had other promising golfers to see in action, so I'm thankful you chose me."

"It wasn't much of a hardship, son. William Monroe, the heir to a multibillion-dollar cooperation, is *also* a talented golfer? That's music to our ears."

We all share a hearty laugh, taking a seat.

"William here is a very promising player. His name on the course will bring butts to the seats for sure, but we were thinking about the sponsorship offer you've previously mentioned," Coach says.

Mr. Cartwright lifts a finger as if to say *Thanks for reminding me.*

"Yes, the sponsorship. I have the contract here for you—"

"That won't be necessary, sir," I interrupt him.

He freezes, the contract in his hand. "I beg your pardon?"

"Money isn't the issue. I don't need financial support. Not to sound cocky, sir, but like my coach said, my name alone will bring a crowd. I would like to negotiate something more worthwhile."

He frowns, sitting back in the chair. "And what would that be?"

I look at Coach, and he gives me a nod of approval.

"I'm looking at an endorsement deal."

His eyebrows shoot to the roof. "Mr. Monroe—"

"Look at it this way. William Monroe, rising golf star, wearing the Singleton brand. That'll shed more light on *your* company."

He narrows his eyes at me. "You want to endorse Singleton Athletics?"

"It's a better deal for the both of us. We both get the publicity we need. William Monroe gets corporate appearances, autograph signings, licensing. Singleton gets a boost in sales with my name wearing your golf apparel."

For a second, there's silence. Mr. Cartwright's staring at me, and Coach is looking at Mr. Cartwright. We're all thinking about my terms. I may have ruined my chances with Singleton, but it was worth it. I know what I'm worth, and a sponsorship does absolutely nothing for me as a new golfer.

"We'll reconvene tomorrow after the tournament. How does that sound?"

I share a look with Coach before nodding. "That sounds like a plan."

He stands up, his folder in hand.

"Thank you for taking this meeting, son."

I give him a nod, and he walks away. I'm tempted to admit I was fucking stupid for proposing that.

But then I remember who I am.

I deserve more than just a financial backing for a sport that I know I'm good at.

"That was either the dumbest thing you've ever done or the smartest," Coach says, chuckling.

I shrug, and he pats my shoulder, laughing. Then he walks off, leaving me to my thoughts.

Whatever happens with Singleton, it was for the best. It was better to propose that than to be content with the bare minimum. It's all in Mr. Cartwright's hands now.

I get back to the hotel room later after spending time with Collin and Connor on the course, practicing my swing before the tournament tomorrow.

I find Sienna sitting on the porch, drinking a glass of wine as promised. She has her hair up in a top bun, her legs crossed, the light above shimmering against her golden-brown skin. Under the *light*, she's even gorgeous.

I kick my shoes off and get rid of my shirt. I sneak up behind her and plant a kiss on her temple. She jumps.

"Oh gosh, you scared me."

"I'm sorry," I laugh, taking a seat in the chair next to her. "How's your dad?"

"He's doing okay. Your nurse seems like a nice person. He gave him his medication, so he's most likely fast asleep now."

I nod, yawning, and lie back in the chair.

"The jetlag isn't as bad as I thought it'd be."

Her laugh is like music to my ears. "Because the time difference isn't that bad either."

"I know, but it's still fucking with me."

She takes another sip of wine and slides her chair over. "How was the meeting with your coach?"

This is where I tense. "Awful."

She flinches. "Why? What happened?"

I tell her about how I proposed an endorsement deal with Singleton Athletics instead of a sponsorship. Even replaying the words in my head, it's the dumbest thing I could've done.

"I know, it's stupid."

"It's not stupid," she laughs. "You're Will Monroe. Of course you'll get tickets sold."

"It sounds cocky as fuck, but...it's true. And I don't wanna be cheated out of the best publicity possible."

She sets her glass down on the end table and sits in my lap. My hands instinctively go around her hips.

"You're gonna do great tomorrow," she whispers, planting a kiss on my nose. "Stop stressing over the what ifs of your meetings. So *what* if you screwed this one up? There will be plenty of companies that would be interested in giving you an endorsement contract. For now, just focus on kicking ass tomorrow. That's all you can control."

I find myself smiling, looking up at her. "I love you, Sienna Durham."

She gives me a cheeky smile. "I love you more, Will Monroe."

I chuckle, kissing her. "Not possible."

For the rest of the night, it's just me and her, looking over the golf course, the lights illuminating it. She's sitting in my lap, and we talk about this weekend.

She still doesn't know what we have planned for her birthday.

And she still doesn't know about the ring in my shorts pocket.

This *has* to work.

I'm counting on it to work.

In a few short months, Sienna's become more important to me than I expected.

And losing her is the last thing I'd want to do.

The sun is shining through the bedroom window. But the first thing I notice when I wake up is Sienna missing at my side. I pat the side of the bed, but I don't feel her. I slowly sit up, mourning that it's just me.

I quickly hop out of bed, throw on a T-shirt, and walk into the kitchen. There's a plate of muffins and orange juice on the kitchen island. I smile at it. It's a very Sienna thing to see.

I grab my phone from the side of my bed and quickly call her.

She answers on the second ring.

"Good morning, handsome," she says in a sultry voice.

"Happy birthday, beautiful. Where the hell are you?"

She laughs. "The girls invited me to have breakfast and mimosas with them this morning. I knew you'd wake up later than me, so I bought some blueberry muffins and orange juice from the little corner store down the street."

I let out a sigh of relief. The girls invited her out.

"Well, why didn't you just wake me up? I could've had breakfast with you guys."

"It's a *girls'* breakfast, babe. Boys aren't allowed," she jokes.

"Wow, I bring you on my trip and you exclude me."

She chuckles again. "This is *your* day. I'll see you later today, okay? You'll do amazing."

Her words of encouragement soothe me. "It's *your* day, too. And I still wanted to see you this morning before I got too busy."

"I'll see you tonight, love. Get some rest."

And with that, she hangs up. I hold the phone up to my ear for a few seconds before dropping it on the counter.

And then I finally grow some balls. I pick up my phone and call another number.

"Hello?"

"You kidnapped my girlfriend," I deadpan.

Taylor guffaws—fucking *guffaws*—into the phone.

"Stop being a drama queen. Mason, Ashley, Willa, and I are having a girls' morning together before we meet up with y'all later, and we invited Sienna. It's her birthday, so we wanted to treat her. It's not worth a river of tears."

I roll my eyes. "Don't give her a hard time today, okay? Sadie isn't with you guys, right?"

"Sadie hates our guts now that Sienna's in the circle. So it's safe to say she's not joining us this morning. She's probably knocking boots with Cale this morning, for all I care."

I snort and pick up a muffin. "Don't be late to the tournament either. Coach got you guys a front row area at the course."

"Willy, *calm down*. We'll be there. Get in the zone today and stop calling around like a father searching for his daughter. It's weird. She's in good hands."

I give her a grunt, and she hangs up. I throw the phone down again and stuff the muffin in my mouth. I pick up my phone again and see the time. Shit. It's only 8 a.m. Which means it's 11 a.m. back home. It's going to be a long day.

Until it's not. It's already 11, and my driver is taking me to the course. My hands are shaking, my palms sweaty as we approach. There are already people lining the course with folding chairs and coolers.

He drops me off at the back entrance where golfers are asked to enter. I grab my bag and walk through the entrance, and my pulse quickens when I see recognizable faces.

Rodrigo Garcia, the number two golfer in the country, takes a swig of water and swings his club around. Steven Mendocino, a rising golf star out of Stanford University, uses a foam roller on his hip.

Gulping, I walk past them both and place my bag down on the ground. I look around to see if I know anyone.

Thankfully, Coach walks up with a paper in his hand.

"Good afternoon, son. You feel ready?"

I let out a shaky breath. "I...don't know," I chuckle.

He pats my shoulder and hands me a paper. "These are your warmups. Stretch your shoulders and knees. We can't afford any injuries for your golf debut."

I take the sheet from him and start my stretches and warmups. Each stretch calms my nerves, and I find myself no longer shaking.

"Will!" a voice shouts behind me.

I turn around to find Sienna and Taylor smiling at me and waving. I jog over to them.

"Babe, hey. You made it."

She gives me a confused look. "What? Of course I made it. I told you I was going to," she laughs.

"I know, but...my sister had you running around today."

Taylor rolls her eyes. "I thought I told you to stop stressing this morning."

"You told me to stop *calling*."

"Will," Sienna gets my attention. "It's okay. You'll do amazing. This is your first tournament. This is just one of many to come."

I smile at her and lean in for a kiss.

But Taylor ruins the moment.

"Ew! Don't kiss in front of me, please and thank you."

I pull back and glare at her. "Just go claim your spot up front. We start in thirty minutes."

They both nod at me and walk off, but I hold Sienna back.

"Thank you for being here."

Her face softens. "Of course. Now go and do your thing."

And with that, she struts off. My eyes find their way again to her perfectly shaped ass.

"So that's the girlfriend," a voice behind me says.

I turn around and marvel at Rodrigo Garcia. My eyes widen, and I'm momentarily stunned. His look of confusion snaps me out of my trance.

"Um, yeah. She's my girlfriend."

He nods. "Beautiful girl. Almost out of your league."

I flinch, frowning at him. "Excuse me?"

"Oh, I didn't mean any disrespect," he says after disrespecting me. "It's just that a girl like that is a trophy. Why is she wasting her time with a spoiled, rich heir? Especially one that's untalented."

I cock an eyebrow, advancing on him. "Do you have a problem with me, Garcia?"

He raises his hands, feigning surrender. "Whoa, calm down, Monroe. Just friendly advice, man."

"You didn't give me advice," I deadpan.

"Oh, I didn't? Well, let me be clear then. Leave the women to the big boys. And we'll leave the *groupies* to you."

My eyes narrow on him, and he walks away, continuing to swing his club.

Wow. Rodrigo Garcia is a dick.

A *handsome* dick.

But a dick nonetheless.

I find myself glaring at him, but I don't need to put energy in competition.

This is the first tournament of my career. There's so much at stake.

And yet, after that interaction with Garcia, I've never felt more ready.

I look back at Sienna and remember why I'm doing this.

She gives me a smile of encouragement. And I smile back.

I'm doing this for me and her.

It occurs to me that she might say no to my proposal. But it doesn't matter.

Her just being here means the world to me.

And if that means doing something for her, knowing there's a chance it might go unrewarded, then so fucking be it.

She's my girl.

So let the games begin.

23

SIENNA

Will is bummed. And I don't like it. He's sitting down in the grass, rolling a foam roller across his thigh. I walk up and sit down next to him, laying my head on his shoulder. He gives me a kiss on the forehead, but I know he's hurting.

He placed second in the tournament. And while he won $400,000, he's frustrated that he didn't win like he hoped. I follow his gaze as he grimaces at Rodrigo Garcia.

He's doing an interview with ESPN right now, and he briefly glances at Will, giving him a shit-eating grin. I roll my eyes and turn his head toward me.

"Will, it's okay, babe. You did good," I tell him.

He has a pensive look. "Babe, I lost," he grunts.

I can't help but chuckle. "You didn't lose. You got second place."

"You mean I'm the first loser."

"Stop it. It was your first tournament. Against some well-established people. You beat *eight* of them. Most rookies don't do that well."

He sighs, getting up from the grass. He reaches for my hand, and I grab it, standing up. I give him a hug.

"I love you," he says into my ear.

I smile. "I love you, too." I look up at him. "Stop whining. You still got a big pot. You're still richer than me, so what's the problem?"

He chuckles and rubs his thumb over my cheek.

"You'll be rich someday, babe."

I frown. "Hardly. If anything, I'll make six figures as a winemaker. Most aren't rich, though."

He kisses me. "In time. Have faith."

I want to ask him what that means, but we're already leaving and waiting for the limo outside of the course.

Sadie, Cale, Mason, Taylor, Ashley, and Collin left early because they wanted to get booze for Will's celebration party later. But Connor and Willa are still here. They rush over to Will, Willa hugging him tight.

"You did amazing today, love. Stop with the pouty face."

"That's what I've been trying to tell him."

He rolls his eyes. "Can we not talk about it, please? I just wanna party with my friends." He winks at me. "And my girlfriend."

Blush hits my cheeks. "We're definitely partying tonight. What do you guys wanna do?"

Connor, Willa, and Will share weird looks. I stare at them as they communicate telepathically.

Willa finally speaks up. "We're actually gonna hang out at Taylor's suite tonight. You guys in?"

"Oh, we're in," Will says quickly. "We'll be over around five."

I frown, confused about what the hell is going on. Why are they being weird? I look up at Will, and he gives me a smug grin.

"Yeah," I say slowly. "We'll just meet you guys there then. Should we bring anything?"

Connor and Willa share a look and then she gives me a cheesy smile.

"Just bring yourselves."

I nod my head slowly, thoroughly confused. Thankfully, the limo makes it, and Will and I are off, back to the resort. We're snuggled up as he stares outside, looking thoughtful.

I squeeze his hand, and he looks at me, a soft smile growing on his face.

We make it back to the resort, and Will tells me he'll meet me back in the room while I go check on Dad. He's been in the room all day, and his nurse has been keeping in contact with me, updating me on his status. Apparently, he's been doing well all day, but I'd still like to make sure.

I approach his room and knock on the door. His nurse opens it and lets me in.

I look in his bedroom, and he's fast asleep. I lean against the doorway, watching him sleep peacefully. He *is* doing well. I really need to get out of my head. Of course he's doing well. Will hired the family nurse, and he told me he's been keeping the family healthy for over fifteen years now.

I thank the nurse for letting me see him, and I make my way back to the room.

"Will, I'm back," I yell.

But there's no response.

"Will?"

Again, there's silence.

I walk back into our room, and it's empty.

I check the bathroom, and again, it's empty.

Where the hell is he?

I look on the porch, and it's just the chairs and the end table.

Suddenly, I get a text. From Taylor.

TAYLOR: *Hey girly! Would you mind coming over really quick? I need help setting up the party decor.*

ME: *Yeah, no problem! Have you seen Will, though? He's not in our room.*

Then there's a moment of silence on her end.

I frown. O-kay.

I grab my keys and close the door when she finally replies.

TAYLOR: *Oh, weird. Yeah, idk. He might be getting some beer for tonight. See ya in a sec!*

Maybe. He would've told me that, though. *Oh well.*

I'm at her suite minutes later. I knock one time, but there's no response. I knock again, and Taylor opens it. Her hair's curled, she's wearing a bandeau and skinny jeans. And her face is completely made up.

"You're dressed already? Should I have brought my party clothes?"

She looks me up and down. "No, girly! You look fine. You always look great." She lets me in, and I look around the room. I frown because it looks already set-up.

"Taylor," I chuckle. "The room looks alr—"

"*Surprise!*"

I jump when everyone hops up from behind the counter. I'm frozen and in shock as I see the entire gang all looking at me, waiting for me to react. But I can't.

Will is the first one to rush over to me. "Sienna? Babe, are you okay?"

When he touches me, I snap out of it. "Yeah, yeah, I'm fine." Then I realize what the hell just happened. "Guys, what the *hell*?!"

They all chuckle, and Will hugs me. "I'm sorry, baby. We didn't mean to scare you."

"We just wanted to surprise you," Mason says.

"Yeah," Sadie mocks. "Are you surprised?"

I ignore her attitude and just look around the room. They decked it all out with streamers, balloons, and glitter. I look on the counter, and there's a wine bottle-shaped cake on it.

"Thank you guys so much," I whisper. "I don't deserve this."

"Sure you do," Taylor says, hugging me. "You deserve the world."

Tears begin to brim in my eyes as I hug her back. Everyone in the room oohs and ahhs. It makes me laugh as I pull back and wipe my tears.

"I have another surprise for you, babe," Will says.

I turn to him and see the indecisive look in his eyes.

"What is it? Are you okay?"

"Oh, *I'm* fine. But I have something I need to do first."

"O-kay," I laugh.

He swallows and stands tall. "Sienna Sylvia Durham. I love you so much, doll."

My heart swells. "I love you, too."

That affirmation gives him the confidence to continue.

"Ever since I laid eyes on you that first day, I knew you'd be trouble." I laugh at that. "And since then, it's been promising. Sienna, will you—"

A knock at the door interrupts him. We all look in that direction, scared to open it.

"Oh my gosh," Sadie groans. "Stop acting like crazies."

She goes to open the door, and a well-dressed couple walks in. I frown, but Taylor and Will gasp as they rush them.

"Mom! Dad! You guys made it!" Taylor exclaims.

"Did you guys see the tournament?" Will has excited eyes.

The beautiful older woman laughs. "Of course we saw the tournament, dear! We wouldn't miss it for the world. Ever again, at least."

Everyone laughs at that, and it's their cue to go their own way. Taylor squeals and starts cutting the cake. The room is full of murmurs when Lily Monroe's eyes land on me.

She gives me a small smile before something unreadable touches her eyes.

"William, who might this be, dear?" She sizes me up.

Will hugs me to him. "Mom, Dad, this is my girlfriend, Sienna. Sienna, this is my mom and dad."

I swallow and hate the fact that my pulse is going a million beats per minute. This is William and Lily Monroe in front of me. My bosses.

"Hi, Mr. and Mrs. Monroe," I croak.

Lily Monroe's eyes are still trying to figure me out.

"Hello, dear," she says skeptically. "William, she's gorgeous."

He laughs at my side. "Isn't she?"

She tilts her head to the side, and her blue eyes pierce into me. She's like the spitting image of Will, and it's freaking me out.

"You seem so familiar, honey. Have we met before?"

My eyebrows shoot up. "Um, well, my dad told me Will and I were actually friends when we were kids."

She cocks an eyebrow, a small smile touching her lips.

"Is that so? Who's your father?"

"Oh, my dad is—"

"The cake's cut! Sienna, would you like to do the honor of passing out the first slice?" Taylor interrupts.

"Sienna!" Mrs. Monroe exclaims. I turn back to her, and she's giving me a big smile. "Sienna Durham! Is that what you said your name was?"

Will and I share a confused look. "Oh, uh, yes, that's my name."

She pulls Will's dad's arm to get his attention from pouring a glass of wine.

"Bill, honey! Look, it's little Sienna."

He quickly whips his head to me, and a look of familiarity touches his eyes.

"Sienna? Is that you?"

I scratch my elbow out of nervousness. "Yeah, that's me," I chuckle.

"Of course it's you. You look just like your mother."

I swallow as a wave of emotion swarms me. "I've been told that," I try to say over the lump in my throat.

William and Lily both swoon over me as Will pulls me closer.

"Well, this is kind of a strange reunion," he chuckles.

But their attention is still on me. "You've grown up to be a stunning young lady, Sienna," Lily Monroe says.

I only smile back. I didn't think they'd like me this much. It seems almost...strange.

Suddenly, Taylor walks over with a slice of cake. I take it and hand it to Will. "Here you go."

He takes it and gives me a kiss on the cheek.

"Be nice to her. I'll let you guys get acquainted." Then he walks away.

Lily's smiling at the entire interaction. "Our son's fallen in love with the daughter of Jerry and..." Her smile is replaced with a look of terror. She looks like she's seen a ghost. "Miranda," she whispers.

I gasp at the mention of her name. "Yeah" is all I can say.

"Is your father here in Scottsdale?" William Monroe asks.

"Yes, sir. He's staying in his own suite with your nurse. Thank you so much for hiring a nurse for him, by the way."

They both give me a look of confusion.

"Jerry needs a nurse? What happened?"

I squeeze my eyes shut and take a deep breath. "Dad...has Parkinson's disease," I croak.

Lily gasps while William shuts his eyes. They both give me a sad look. And another look of...guilt?

"I'm sorry to hear that, Enna," William says. *Enna*. My mom and dad were the only ones who called me that when I was little. "If Jerry's here...may I see him?"

My eyebrows shoot to the roof, and a feeling of nervousness floods through me. I turn to Will, and he's laughing with Connor and Collin.

"If you'd like to. We can take a walk to his suite." Mr. Monroe instantly nods his head, and it makes me laugh. "Okay then. Just give me a second and we can go see him."

I walk back to the counter and get Will's attention. He ends the conversation with the guys and walks over to me. "Everything okay?"

"Everything's fine. It's just...*your* dad wants to see *my* dad," I chuckle.

He cocks an eyebrow. "Really? Well, that's cool."

I shrug. "I guess. I'll just be a minute." I give him a kiss and lead Mr. Monroe out into the hallway.

We're on our way to Dad's suite, and we talk about the past. Apparently, Will *did* have a crush on me when we were toddlers. We used to hang out all the time, but Mom and Dad moved to Louisville. I ask him why we stopped being friends, and he clams up.

Since that makes him uncomfortable, we're talking about other things such as Monroe and how much I love working at the winery when we reach my dad's room. I knock twice, and the nurse opens the door. His eyes widen when he sees Mr. Monroe.

"Lucas, it's good to see you. Is Jerry doing well?"

He has a look of confusion before nodding. "He's doing great. I just fed him his dinner, and he's watching TV in his room."

Mr. Monroe nods and leads the way, walking toward Dad's room. He seems really excited to see him, and it makes me really happy for some reason.

We're at Dad's room, and he slowly looks up from the TV, a look of confusion on his face. Then something else registers.

"Sienna? What's going on?" Dad asks.

"Jerry," Mr. Monroe starts. "You're here, buddy."

But Dad doesn't look the least bit happy to see him, and it confuses me. He grinds his teeth and looks away.

"Sienna, why is Bill Monroe here?"

I find myself scanning my brain for a response.

"Um, he wanted to see you."

"Well, I don't wanna see him."

Mr. Monroe flinches. "Jerry, it's been over fifteen years."

"You're right, my wife's been dead for fifteen years. Because of you."

This makes me flinch. I shake my head to make sure I heard him right.

"Excuse me?" I intervene. "Dad, what are you talking about?"

"Oh, he didn't tell you on your little stroll here?" Dad's eyes are furious. "The Monroes had the doctors take Miranda off the list for a lung transplant, Enna."

"We did *not* tell the doctors to take Miranda off. We simply brought Morris in and asked them to put him *on* the list for a lung transplant."

"And kicked my *wife* off the list! Because of '*special priority.*'"

"I did *not* want them to take Miranda off the list, Jerry. You know that. You and Miranda were our best friends."

"Well, if that's how you treat your best friends, I don't wanna *know* how you treat your enemies."

"Slow down, please." My voice breaks. I look at Mr. Monroe. "*You* were why my mom died?"

He puts his hand on my shoulder, trying to comfort me. "No, Enna—"

"Don't call her that," Dad growls.

Mr. Monroe's face grows with guilt. "Morris Hensley was a family friend, and he had pneumonia. One day, his lungs collapsed, and he was hospitalized. He didn't have any family. His wife died, he had no children, and none of his golf friends were around. They told us he might need a lung transplant, but the...list was full."

My breathing is labored as I stare daggers at him. "And *then* what?"

He lets out a sigh. "I...organized for them to put him on the list. Which ultimately meant...someone had to be kicked off. And unfortunately"—he looks back at Dad—"that someone was Miranda."

My heart breaks all over again. "What the hell do you mean by '*organized*'?"

He swallows, his face now pale. "Sienna—"

"*What do you mean by 'organized'?!*" I screech.

He goes tense before his jaw tenses.

"He means he paid the doctors," Dad answers for him. "He paid the *goddamn* doctors to take my *wife* off the list to get a lung transplant. To save her crushed lungs."

My body wracks with a sob. "I can't believe no one told me this," I whisper. I look at Dad. "You let me *date* their *son*?!"

Dad flinches. "Sienna, William has done nothing wrong."

"He's their son, right? The son of the two people who killed Mom."

"Sienna, please," Mr. Monroe says. "William loves you. He was planning on—"

"Stop it. I don't wanna hear it."

Before they can say anything else, I storm out of the room and make my way back to Taylor's suite. I left Mr. Monroe there, but I don't care. I need to hear the words from Mrs. Monroe. She would've been closest to my mom.

I knock on the door about ten times before Taylor opens it, a confused smile on her face.

"Hey, girl. What's up?"

I walk past her and approach Mrs. Monroe. She's talking to Will. He looks at me, and his smile brightens. But it breaks my heart. Because I know everything now.

"Sienna, you're back!" He looks behind me. "Where's Dad?"

"Mrs. Monroe," I say, ignoring Will's question. "What happened to my mom?"

She gives me a confused look. "Sorry, honey?"

"My mom. Miranda. What happened to her?"

A look of realization finally stretches across her face, and her cheeks redden. "Sienna, honey—"

"Did you kill her?"

She flinches, and Will suddenly intervenes.

"Babe, hold on. What's the matter?"

"Did you kill her? You took her off the list to get a lung transplant?"

She swallows and advances on me. "Honey, it's not like that."

"Because Morris Hensley was sick, right? He mattered more to you than my mom, right?"

"*No!*" she screeches, making me flinch. "Miranda was my best friend," she whispers, her voice breaking.

I wipe a tear away as it slides down my face. It takes me a second to realize the room has gone quiet.

"She was your best friend. But Morris Hensley was a better friend."

"It's not like that." She's crying now, too. "Jerry didn't even *tell* us that Miranda got into a car accident."

"Mom?" Will finally speaks up, a look of betrayal on his face. "What's she talking about?"

She swallows, embarrassment across her face. "Honey, it—it's a long story."

"I have plenty of time," he says.

She flinches before adjusting her shawl. "Miranda"—she motions to me—"Sienna's mother, was a really, *really* good friend of mine. We went to high school together and spent a lot of moments together as adults. Once we both had children, you and Sienna, we raised you two together. We knew eventually you guys would get together. There was so much chemistry between you two, even as kids—"

"Skip to the part where you killed Mrs. Durham," Will growls.

This makes Mrs. Monroe cry more.

"Remember when Morris was coughing at the dinner table that one time and blood came out?"

He swallows. "Yes, I remember that."

"Well, he came down with pneumonia, and he said it wasn't anything serious. Until he collapsed on the course one time when he and your dad were golfing. We brought him to the hospital that day, and they told us he was dying. They said the only way for him to survive was to get a lung transplant, but..." She swallows. "The list was full. So...y-your father p-p-"

"Paid the doctors to put him on the list," he says, shutting his eyes.

My entire body tenses, a wave of emotion hitting me like a freight train. My pulse quickens, and my anxiety is heightens as I replay what she just said in my head.

Suddenly, the door opens, and Mr. Monroe walks in, shame all over his face. I let out a breath, grab my keys, and walk toward the door.

"Sienna, baby, wait—"

"Will, leave me alone. I need to leave."

His hand on my arm stops me. "Baby, I can't let you leave with all this new information. Let's talk about this."

"There's nothing to talk about," I cry. "My mom is dead, and your parents are the reason why. What else is there to talk about?"

"Sienna, please don't leave, girly. It's your birthday. Let's talk about this first," Taylor says in her small voice.

"I. Need. To. Go."

Sadie snickers in the kitchen, sipping a glass of wine.

"See what happens when you deal with the commoners? *Drama*," she sing-songs.

"Someone tell that cunt to stop talking," I growl.

She flinches, her jaw dropping. "I'm sorry, '*cunt*'?!"

I rush out of the room, my steps angry. I just need to get the hell out of here.

I'm packing my bags, grabbing my dad, and we're taking the next flight back to Kentucky. I can't deal with any of this right now.

His hand is on my arm again. How did he catch up with me?

"Babe, our room is the other way."

I let out an annoyed sigh and turn around, snatching my arm away from him.

"Did you already buy our tickets back home?"

"Yeah, I did."

"Good. Give me mine when we get back to the room."

He turns me around to him, an angry look in his eyes. *He's* angry? "Sienna, stop! *Listen* to me." He takes a deep, shaky breath. "Baby, you can't leave like this. Maybe there's more to the story."

"And maybe there is. I don't really care to hear it right now. And I don't care to be talking to you right now."

"What?"

"Will," I whisper. "This ruins *everything*. We can't be together."

He pulls back as if I've slapped him. "Sienna…" he falters.

"Ever since I started dating you, I knew there was a reason in the back of my head, telling me why we would never work out long-term. I knew this was just a pipe dream. Don't you see? This is reality. We can't be together."

"Sienna, please don't say that. Baby, I love you."

Those three words make the tears in my eyes well up more.

"And I love you, too. But your family and my dad have been keeping this secret from me for over a decade. We can't build a relationship off of this. I'm sorry, but this is over."

His eyes widen, his mouth agape. "Sienna, please don't do this."

"I'm sorry," I whisper. I walk away, but he stops me.

"I was gonna ask you something tonight. Something that would've changed our lives forever. Can I ask it, baby, *please*?"

I frown at that question, confused as hell. What question could he possibly ask?

It doesn't matter anymore. We can't be together.

"Will…just let me go, okay?" I give him a kiss on the cheek and walk away.

I can't be around him right now.

24

WILL

The weekend from hell. I never thought I'd ever see anything like it. I got back to the room that night, and Sienna was already gone. It was mind-boggling to me that she was able to pack up and leave so swiftly. Even so much as a goodbye would've been nice.

Yet here we are. Sitting on the golf cart back home, drinking Bud Lights, watching the girls swing. Collin convinced me to join them on the course since I've been in the house for the last three days. I really don't care to do anything outside of playing golf and finding my girl.

She hasn't gotten back to me. I don't know if she and her dad made it home safely, or if...she really meant what she said.

We can't build a relationship off of this. I'm sorry, but this is over.

Even replaying the words in my head is too much to handle.

"Dude, you gotta stop wallowing. It's making you pout," Collin says.

Sighing, I take a swig and lay my head back. "I don't know what you're talking about."

He scoffs. "You know exactly what I'm talking about. It's *Sienna*, dude. She'll come back to you."

Well, I fucking hope so. "I haven't seen her in three days, Collin. How the hell do you know that?"

"Maybe she needs time."

"Or maybe he needs to get a grip and tee off," Sadie deadpans.

231

I roll my eyes as I watch her walk up to the cart, grabbing a drink from the cooler.

"Aren't *you* a ray of sunshine, Pritchard," I remark.

She scoffs and pops open a White Claw. "I'm just getting tired of watching you wallow over that *sommelier*," she sneers. "I swear, your taste dwindles each year."

"Sadie, what the fuck is wrong you?" Collin barks.

She just shrugs. "I thought I made that clear. I'm tired of him wallowing over the—"

"Yeah, I got it," I cut her off, hopping up from the cart. I grab my golf bag and start polishing my clubs.

And it's back to my days as usual. Golfing and hanging out with my friends, which includes an impromptu trip to Miami. Collin's dad was able to get us a few suites on the house for the weekend.

I drop my bag on the bed, unpack my trunks, and throw on some sunscreen. Maybe getting to the beach will do me some good. My phone beeps, and I chuckle at the text.

CONNOR: *No more pouting, Monroe. Hotties are down here at Surfside and they're looking for the Monroe charm. Get down here, bruh.*

The '*Monroe charm*' couldn't even keep a girlfriend. What would local girls and other tourists do to help me?

Sighing, I throw on my trunks, grab my sunglasses, and make my way down to the beach.

Once I feel the Miami sun hit my back, all my worries go away. Connor, Willa, Collin, and Taylor all lie in the sun on their beach towels. The beach is so freaking busy. As I suspected, but I was hoping to at least avoid a huge crowd.

"Willy!" Taylor's voice bumps me out of my thoughts. "Over here!" She waves me over enthusiastically.

I straighten my back and walk over to them, dropping my bag and towel on the sand.

"You guys didn't tell me it'd be so busy," I mumble.

Connor briefly lifts his sunglasses. "I told you there'd be hotties waiting on the Monroe charm," he says, winking.

Willa flinches at his side. "You're seriously referring to the local girls as '*hotties*'?"

"Don't you ogle a hot guy every once in a while?" Willa rolls her eyes. "That's what I thought."

Snickering at them, I lie down and just bask in the sun. I smile, taking it all in.

This is nice.

When Collin came up with the idea of a trip to Miami, I wasn't game at first. I just wanted to focus on golfing and getting back to my normal life.

My normal life that no longer includes Sienna Durham.

And it's fucking weird. Before her, I was just going through the motions.

Will goddamn Monroe, heir of the Monroe name.

Things didn't matter that much to me. I was the carefree guy that didn't have much going on in his life outside of being rich. And now look at me: heartbroken. And scared to death. Because now it's clear.

She's not coming back.

The thought again hits me like a freight train, and it's almost like déjà vu. I'm flipping through sports channels when I land on the Fidel Cup Golf Tournament. The golf course gives me nostalgia. It resembles the Scottsdale golf course. And another thing I lost: my golf reputation. That's not to say I had one anyway. But I placed second on my first golf tournament.

Singleton hasn't even reached back out to me about my proposition.

So I think it's safe to say I made matters worse.

~

Beep. Beep.

I wake up to my phone going off with a text. Rubbing my eyes, I look at the window, and it's dark. Shit. I must've dozed off. I grab my phone from the side table and see two missed calls from Coach and a text message from Collin:

COLLIN: *Dude, where are you??? Thought we were hitting the nightclubs.*

Sighing, I get up, slip on my T-shirt, and go to brush my teeth. They're probably already at a nightclub. I don't feel totally up to it, but it's why we even came on this trip: to let loose.

I'm wiping my mouth of toothpaste when my phone rings, and it's Coach. What's the problem? I answer on the third ring, and the rustling of papers catch my attention.

"Hello?"

"William, son. I've called you three times."

"Sorry, Coach. I'm in Miami right now, and I was taking a nap."

There's a moment of pause before he starts talking again. "No worries, son. I just wanted to let you know I have some good news. Maybe *great* news."

"What's up?"

He lets out a sigh. "I know you placed second at the Harvey Invitational..."

"Yeah..." *And making me relive it isn't making things better.*

"And while we haven't heard from Singleton yet, you have another sponsorship offer from Trecchian Sports."

I cock an eyebrow. "That's cool. But I'm not looking for a sponsorship, Coach."

"I understand. But you didn't let me finish." He takes another pause, making me nervous. "How does a multi-million-dollar *endorsement* deal sound?"

I freeze, dropping my toothpaste. "Multi-million-dollar?"

"Exactly," he remarks.

I tilt my head to the side. "What numbers are we talking?"

⌒

I'm wearing a Monroe Vineyard T-shirt and cargo shorts as I walk into the upscale nightclub Collin told me about. They let me know that they'll be waiting for me in a booth in the back to celebrate the news. The *big* news.

My face is starting to hurt from the smile that's plastered on it.

An invitation to play at the PGA Maxium Open at Pebble Beach.

A sponsorship offer from Trecchian Sports.

And a hefty endorsement deal *with* Maxium Sports. *Eight fucking figures.* It's a sweet victory to me.

"Monroe! Get over here, dude!" Collin's voice booms as I approach the booth. They let out a chorus of cheers when they see me.

"You got a sponsorship offer?!" Willa sounds surprised.

"*And* an endorsement deal," I emphasize.

Another swarm of cheers surround me. I chuckle, sitting down next to Connor, and grab a whiskey and Coke from the tray on the table.

I take a sip as Taylor wraps her arms around me.

"Congratulations, Willy," she croons. "I'm so proud of you, big brother."

My heart swells. "Thanks, little sister."

For the rest of the night, we drink rounds of whiskey and tequila, celebrating my victories. If there's one thing I learned about life, it's that there's always a silver lining.

"Hey, Monroe," a sultry voice says above me. I look up to find a smoking hot redhead—almost the spitting image of Jessica Rabbit—staring down at me. "You look hot tonight." She gives me a smug grin. My gaze lands on her rack, and it's impressive.

I clear my throat, sitting back in the booth.

"Thanks, babe. How are you doing tonight?"

She chuckles, sitting down next to me. "I couldn't be doing any better than you are. Why do you look so sad? For someone who's scored an endorsement deal for the biggest sportswear company, you sure look in distress."

I smile at her. "You follow sports media."

A cheesy grin grows on her face. "Of course I do. From what I hear, you're not only an heir, but you're also the hottest thing to grace the golf world. That's sexy," she flirts.

I laugh, reaching for my drink. "Thanks," I say, winking at her.

Someone clears their throat, and I turn to find Collin winking at me. "What's going on over there, Monroe?"

I turn my gaze back to the bombshell in front of me. I admire how hot she is. Her centerfold body grabs my attention, and her porcelain skin is flawless.

And yet...there's no groundbreaking attraction. She's a different type of beautiful that does nothing for me, sexually.

She's not *her*.

And it's fucking with me.

I clear my throat and growl at my thoughts.

Sienna Durham has ruined me beyond repair.

And I don't care. I love her. Nothing will change that. It's like I'm incapable of having any form of attraction toward another woman.

The girl sitting next to me has a frown now. "What's wrong? You look sad again," she jokes.

Sighing, I put my drink down and rub my eyes. "It's...nothing."

"You sure?"

I look back up at her, and I see a hint of sadness in her eyes.

"My girlfriend and I just broke up, and I'm...not exactly taking it well,"

Her face drops. "Oh. I'm sorry to hear that. What happened?"

I open my mouth to say something, but then I realize that's probably not the best idea. I don't know this girl, and dredging up these thoughts about my ex—my ex that I'm very much in love with—vocally isn't very productive.

"I blindsided her. And it fucked us up." And that's all I can say.

She nods her head as if she understands. "Ah, I see. Well, if you ever need something to help you get your mind off it...you know where to find me." She winks, gets up, and disappears into the dancefloor.

Not likely. The mere thought of entertaining another woman makes my dick limp.

"Dude, what the hell was that?" I turn to find Collin frowning at me.

"What the hell was *what*?"

He gives me confused eyes. "You had a hot redhead in front of you, and she walked away without you on her arm. What the fuck was that about?"

I roll my eyes, shrugging. "I wasn't attracted to her. She was beautiful, but...I don't know, nothing was there."

He closes his eyes and mumbles a curse. "You mean to tell me you turned down a girl with a *huge rack* because you weren't *attracted* to her?!" I nod my head, not getting it. "Did Sienna turn you gay, dude?"

I chortle. "No, Collin," I deadpan. "Believe it or not, I'm not attracted to every girl with a porn star's body."

He scoffs. "I don't even know who you are anymore," he says, shaking his head. Then Connor whips him upside his head. "Ow! Dude, what the hell?!"

"Worry about your drinking problem and not our best friend's libido," he deadpans. Collin rolls his eyes, scooting back over to the other side of the booth. "Don't listen to him, bro. You're fine. Though it's not healthy to sit here and not *at least* dance with someone."

There's one girl I want to dance with, and she's not here.

"I'm fine, dude. I really don't wanna talk about it, though."

And just like that, he shrugs and scoots back over to Willa. The sight actually makes me rub my chest. I'm sitting here with a couple and Collin, who won't stop flirting with my sister—both of whom are happy as hell. And it's disgusting.

I let out an annoyed sigh and go to the bar. I need another drink.

I order a scotch on the rocks, needing something a bit stronger.

I take a sip and take in the smoky, grainy texture. It's been a while since I've had a good glass of scotch. I take another sip.

And then another.

And then one more.

And then a few more sips.

This shit *hits*.

And I don't realize how much it *does* hit until I wake up the next morning with Jessica Rabbit sleeping next to me.

25

WILL

Two weeks.
Two freaking weeks since I've seen or heard from her.
Two weeks since I've had the pleasure of touching her.
And two fucking weeks since I slept with a hot redhead.
If I looked at my reflection in the mirror four months ago, I'd give myself a fist bump. I should be fucking proud. And instead, I'm counting the days that I've yet to hear from the girl I'm in love with. In fact, I feel like I've cheated on her.

I'm not one to do countdowns of the last time I've seen, heard, or touched a girl. But fuck me, I'm losing my mind.

It's back to work as usual. Well...not really. Now that my parents are back home, I don't need to keep my eye on the winery as much.

Or Sienna, for that matter.

And yet, I'm sitting in the bistro, scouring the walls. I never realized the Italian-inspired architecture my parents chose for this place, along with the murals. It's practically a cathedral.

"William?"

I turn to find Mr. Stevens frowning at me.

I stand up, clearing my throat. "Hi, Mr. Stevens."

"What are you doing here? Why are you staring at the walls?" He gasps. "Do you have an event planned today? I'm so sorry, our event coordinator didn't—"

"No, no, there's no event," I chuckle. "I just...wanted to check out the place. You know, since I no longer work here." I didn't expect to have this sorrowful feeling. It's like she's standing in the room.

I sense her presence.

I smell her perfume.

I even see her hair.

Because it's straightened.

She's staring right at me.

And seeing her takes the breath out of me.

Mr. Stevens says something to me, but I'm too busy walking over to her.

"Will," she says, putting her hands up.

But her face is already in my hands, and I'm kissing her. It's been two weeks since I've seen her. I never thought it'd be this much of a loss.

She's kissing me back, and it gives me the affirmation that she still loves me. Because God knows I still love her.

I give her one last peck before I pull back. And her brown doe eyes stare up at me.

"You're beautiful."

She swallows. "You can't just kiss me," she croaks.

"Baby, it's been two fucking weeks. Where have you been?"

She sighs, trying to pry her head from my hands. But I'm not budging. It visibly frustrates her. "I...needed to get some clarity."

"Clarity?"

She nods. "Your parents dropped a huge bomb on me, Will. I need some time to get over that."

This doesn't sound too hopeful. "If I could change my parents, I would. I promise you, I had *no* idea about your mom, babe. I would've never put you through that by seeing them in Arizona."

Her eyes are suddenly glossy, and I know she's about to cry.

"It's not just what they did, Will," she says, her voice breaking. "For the longest time, I thought maybe I'd found my home. With you. With Taylor. With...*Monroe*. But...everything that happened just proves we're too different."

"We're not that different."

"Your parents paid doctors to get a celebrity friend on the list for a lung transplant. Name one normal person that can do that."

I grind my teeth as I peer down at her. She's right.

"Shit," I whisper.

"And it made my mom perish. We could've saved her." Her bottom lip quivers. Shit. I hug her to me, and she sobs in my arms.

Her quaking body breaks me over and over again. And I hate that I can't do anything to fix it.

But I'll do my best to try. "Can we meet later today? Let's grab dinner. It doesn't have to be fancy."

She has an indecisive look on her face. "Will, I can't. Mr. Stevens told me about an opportunity overseas at the new Monroe location, and...I—I think I'm gonna take it."

My heartbeat pounds in my ears. "You're doing *what*?"

She gives me a nervous smile. "It's a winemaking apprenticeship. I had an interview with George Galanis yesterday. And he offered me the position. In Greece."

I take a step back, taking in what she's saying. "Sienna," I whisper.

"I think it'll be good for me. I need time away from Kentucky for a while."

"So you're just leaving? For how long?"

She swallows, fiddling with her pink nails. "It *was* for seven months. But...he said it could go as long as two years."

I grind my teeth. "So you'll probably be gone for two years."

She nods. "I wasn't gonna take it because of...you. Then I found out about what really happened to my mom. And like I said...it gave me clarity. Doing this apprenticeship will bring me closer to her, Will. Staying here—staying with you—will only remind me of what took her away from me."

I wipe a tear away as it slides down her cheek. "Baby, I never meant to hurt you," I whisper.

"I know you didn't. And you didn't do anything specifically. It's just...a harsh reminder. I need to find my own way, Will."

And with that, she gives me another kiss on the cheek and walks away. I run a hand through my hair. My debut weekend turned out to be the weekend from hell. How do I fix this?

You confront your parents.

And that's exactly what I'm doing. After that weekend, they flew back out to Greece to do a bit more location scouting for another vineyard location there, and they came back today.

I open the door to our house and lay my head against it, feeling the urge to bang my head on it.

"William?" My mom's voice has me opening my eyes. I turn to her, and she has a concerned look on her face.

"Mom," I simply say, walking past her into the living room. "Bring Dad down here, please."

She swallows and nods, running upstairs.

There's a bit of commotion and quiet arguing before I hear them come down the stairs.

Dad's steps slow as he walks into the living room. Mom takes a seat across from me, and he sits down next to her. I find myself staring at a wall before I clear my throat.

"William—" Dad starts, but I hold a hand up to stop him.

"You two...kept this secret from me...for *fifteen* years. And didn't think to tell me," I recap.

"We weren't gonna tell you because we never thought it'd come back up, son. How were we supposed to know little Sienna was the girl you were dating?"

But I'm not thinking rationally right now.

"Sienna's the first girl I've ever fallen in love with. I was gonna propose to her. *Two weeks ago*," I say, my voice breaking.

Mom gives me a sad look. "Honey, we really didn't know it was her you were talking about."

"She was my girlfriend. She wasn't just any girl I was seeing."

"We know that now, son," Dad says.

"So why wouldn't you tell me this? Dad, you really paid to get Morris on the lung transplant list?"

He swallows. "This was around the time you expressed interest in golfing, son."

I flinch. "What?"

"Morris offered to give you golfing lessons when you were nine. You were begging and *begging* him to coach you. So"—he looks at

Mom—"we wanted to do everything we could to make sure he stayed alive long enough to do that for you."

The tears well in my eyes. "No," I whisper.

"It's true, dear," Mom says. "We just wanted to make you happy. And the reason we didn't tell you was because we didn't think it'd be a big deal. Until...we shared what we did to Jerry. We told him, in passing, that you were looking for golf lessons and paid doctors to make sure he would live long enough to train our son. And he put two and two together, figuring out that...Miranda was the unlucky person to get kicked off," she says, sniffling.

For a second, I just sit there and stare into space. My mom gets up, crying into her hands, and Dad gets up to comfort her.

This is the biggest secret my parents kept from me. Not only did it affect my relationship, it's affected how I view them. I saw them as people wanting to make sure their vineyard flourished. They were my superheroes. My parents. But I never thought they'd stoop this low.

They did it to help you, though.

Clearing my throat, I get up and run upstairs to my room. I look through my shorts and find the box. I open it up, and the light immediately finds the diamond. It shimmers in my hand, and I hug the box to my chest.

I spent $100,000 on this ring. And put $400,000 in a savings account set up for her. All of this just feels like a waste now. But such is life.

The girl of my dreams is spending two years in Greece.

My parents kept a secret from me *and* her.

And now...I can't propose to her. It'll just complicate things.

A knock on the door makes me turn around. Taylor stands there, a small smile on her face.

"What are you thinking about, big brother?"

I let out a sigh and slump down on my bed. "Taylor, this seriously fucking sucks."

"I know," she says. "That weekend was...hard to watch."

I sit up and look at the box again. "Taylor, I got a steal on this ring. It's the perfect one for her, too. And I can't even do it because Mom and Dad are so damn secretive," I growl, chucking the box across the room.

Taylor gasps, but thankfully, the box stays closed. There's a chance the ring might be damaged, but I don't care anymore.

Everything's fucking damaged.

"I talked to Mom and Dad and...we're gonna go spend some time downtown today. They want to give you some space, and I asked to go with them."

I let out a sigh of relief. Thank God. I need a break from my family for a bit.

"Okay, great," I say.

She gives me a tight smile. She comes over and gives me a hug, stunning me. She hasn't given me a hug since she was in middle school.

"I'm sorry about Sienna. If she loves you, she'll come back."

One can only hope.

I just shrug, and that's all it takes to get her to get out. She walks out, closing the door behind her.

I run my hands through my hair in frustration when I remember I threw the engagement ring across the room. I get up, pick it up, and open it. I sigh with relief when I find the ring intact. I set it on my dresser and sit down on my bed.

I look through my phone, scrolling through pictures. And I look at photos that we took together. Couple photos at the airport. Photos of her in front of the river downtown. Photos of her kissing me on the cheek.

Sniffling, I turn off my phone and lie face down on my pillow. I need to let this go.

Let. This. Go.

And it seems like I have. Because my eyes pop open, and I forget what the heck just happened. Did I fall asleep? I shoot up and look at my phone.

Sixteen missed phone calls and thirty text messages. All from Willa, Mason, Collin, Connor, and Ashley.

I ignore them all and look at the clock. It's 4 p.m. I took a three-hour nap. Great.

I get up, rub my eyes, and make my way downstairs for a snack. Thankfully, no one's here. I figured they'd be back by now, but Taylor left a note on the counter, saying they'll now be gone until Friday.

I pop open the fridge and grab a beer when the doorbell rings. I look at it, frowning. Who could be here? It's four, so it couldn't be Collin or Connor. They're usually on the last hole at the course by now.

The doorbell rings again.

Sighing my annoyance, I walk over, dreading whoever it is. I open the door, and my eyes widen when I lay eyes on Sienna.

I clear my throat. "Sienna," I say. "Hey."

She gives me a small smile. "Hey. I, um, left some stuff in your guest room, and I just wanted to drop by and pick it up."

My stomach drops. Of course she's here to grab what she left. I don't know why I thought she'd be here for me.

"Yeah, of course," I say, backing up, letting her in.

She walks inside, and I watch her as I close the door. I find myself staring at how perfect her ass is in her jeans. Clearing my throat, I just follow her up the stairs to the room.

She walks into the guest room, and I notice the container of clothes she brought here. She walks over to it, but I stop her.

"I can carry it for you, if you'd like."

She freezes. "No, um, I couldn't ask you to do that."

"It's no problem. I'd be an asshole if I let you carry a heavy container of clothes."

She chuckles, and it gives me chills. Her laugh is still so beautiful. "Well, okay," she says awkwardly.

I pick up the container, and she follows me downstairs to her car. She pops the trunk, and I put it inside. I shut the trunk and turn to find her staring at me.

I swallow. "Is there anything else I can get for you?"

She gasps softly and shakes her head. "No, I—I think that'll be all."

We stand there for another awkward second before she walks around to get inside her car. But I have to stop her.

"Baby, please don't do this."

She flinches, looking at me. "Will, I can't do this with you right now."

"Then...just watch a movie with me or something."

She chortles, surprised. "What?"

"Watch a movie with me. Or have a beer. *Please*, Sienna. Anything."

She just stares at me with sad eyes. "I never thought you, Will Monroe, would be standing here, begging me to stay."

"And I'd do it again in a heartbeat. Because I love you. And I'll always love you. Just don't walk away without giving us another chance."

She walks up to me, hands cradling my face. "Will...I leave for Greece tomorrow," she whispers.

"What? I thought it wasn't for another week."

She shakes her head, squeezing her eyes shut. "It's sort of last minute. They called Mr. Stevens and told him there was some stuff I need to do in person. They need me out there to test out some wines. You know, see which is my favorite. I'm the sommelier, remember?" She chuckles.

"So this is an actual thing? You're really leaving?"

She nods. "I told you I was taking the opportunity, Will. I didn't intend to come here and rub it in your face—"

"Do you know why I fell for you?"

She flinches, swallowing. "Uh-h, n-no, I—"

"You're hot. That was the first thing I noticed."

She glares at me. "Will, can you stop?"

"You told me wine is romance. When you drink a glass of good wine, you know love is just around the corner."

Tears well in her eyes. "You remember," she whispers.

"Of course I remember. I remember everything you tell me, doll. You also told me you found your home. Monroe, baby, is your home. Your mind, babe. Your passions are why I love you. The way you see things is incredibly attractive, and I'll be damned if I let you walk away without fighting."

She swallows, staring up at me. For a minute, I wonder if she's going to drive off anyway. But then she does something that surprises me.

She leans up on her tiptoes and kisses me. My hands instinctively go around her waist, hugging her close to me. She wraps her arms around my neck as she deepens the kiss.

Then she pulls back. "I leave for Greece tomorrow."

I groan. "Fuck, Sienna—"

"But that doesn't mean I can't say goodbye."

I frown at her, earning a smile back. She reaches for my hand and leads me inside my house.

Then it finally clicks. I find myself smiling.

If this is a goodbye—a *temporary* goodbye, I'm hoping—then I won't complain.

As long as I get to love her one last time...

Then I'm game.

26

SIENNA

My core is burning right now. I'm probably a horrible person for using his body one last time, but I love him. So fucking much. But I can't stay here while what I learned is still fresh in my head. Will reminds me of everything I lost.

But if having him one last time can give us both what we need—intimacy—then so be it.

I'm dragging him upstairs behind me, and when we get to his room, he shuts the door. I'm at his bed in record time, and his eyes scale down my body.

"Those jeans are hot as fuck on you, but I need them off, baby," he growls.

Those simple words make my core heat more. I make quick work of my jeans, and I'm just in my tank top and panties.

He groans. "Lace panties," he whispers.

He whips his T-shirt off, and I shiver at his taut abs and pecs. He's gorgeous. He's all mine. But I can't have him.

I shake my head of these thoughts and take my tank top off.

"I decided to ditch the bra today."

He groans again and advances on me. "Smart girl," he whispers.

He plants kisses on my neck, cupping my breasts. For some reason, this is more intimate than him kissing me on the lips. Something about sloppy kisses and gentle nips down my neck makes me hotter.

"That feels so good," I moan.

He chuckles against my neck. "I'll make you feel so good, baby. This body belongs to me."

I shiver in his arms, and he lays me down on his bed as he goes to his knees. His eyes are on my face as he slowly slides my panties down my legs. He licks his lips when he sees my center. He runs a finger over it, and I shiver again.

"I love these tiny hairs," he whispers, planting a kiss on my nub.

"Will," I moan.

He plants another kiss on my nub before spreading my legs more.

"It's okay. I got you."

And then that's when he gets to work. He flicks his tongue over the nub before sucking it in. I squirm above him, but he's holding my hips down. I'm completely at his mercy, and I love it.

"Baby," I moan. "Oh, *God*, that's good."

"Mmm, always so wet for me, baby," he moans, sticking a finger inside. I arch my back, lifting off the bed, and he continues his assault.

He starts devouring me, sucking and gently biting on my nub. I start to undulate against his lips, and he chuckles.

"Fuck, I love seeing you like this. I'm gonna miss this so much."

I look down at him, and he's no longer eating me, but he's still fingering me. He's giving me a look of sadness. I'm close to saying something, but then his finger hits my G-spot.

And again.

And again.

And one more time.

"Are you close?" I nod my head, whimpering. "Play with your tits, babe."

My shaky hands slowly reach up as I tug at one nipple, making me arch my back again. I look down at him, and his eyes are dilated. He starts sucking my nub again and flicks his tongue a few times before his head goes side to side. The sight sends a wave of heat through me.

"Oh, baby, you're so close. I can taste it."

I move faster against his mouth, and he sucks on the nub harder. A wave of moisture coats my center, and he drinks it up. He continues sucking until he drinks up the last bit.

I slow my undulation against his mouth as he places a chaste kiss on the nub again.

He rises to his feet, wiping his mouth. He gives me a wicked smile before leaning down to kiss me.

"That's the most you let go on my tongue."

I swallow, wiping sweat from my forehead. "Your...tongue is really good."

He laughs, kissing down my chest. "I fucking love you," he groans. His tongue flicks my nipple as his hand makes its way down to my center. "You have two options here. I give you another orgasm via fingering and sucking your tits."

I close my legs as another wave of heat hits my core. "Will," I whine.

"*Or* you let me inside you. And I give you an orgasm the old-fashioned way," he teases.

I laugh. "I vote for the second option."

He winks at me, licking my nipple again. "Good choice."

He pulls his jeans and boxers down his waist. He reaches into the pocket and takes out a condom. As he wraps himself up, I swallow and admire how beautiful he is. Those hungry blue eyes really peer down at me.

He wants me. This is the guy I fell in love with. And the guy whose family ruined mine. A lump forms in my throat at the thought.

He immediately notices a change in my demeanor.

"Sienna? What's wrong?"

I clear my throat and shake my head. "Nothing."

He doesn't believe me. He leans down and gives me a kiss.

"I love you, Sienna Durham," he whispers. "Never forget that."

My heart is suddenly heavy. I let out a shaky breath as he lines up with my entrance. He inches inside me and lets out a pained groan.

"Always so damn tight," he says, kissing me.

I slip him tongue, and he groans, intensifying the kiss. "Always a good kisser," I mumble against his lips. He bites down on my bottom lip as he inches in more. I moan, and he starts trailing kisses down my neck. This is the most affectionate he's been during sex. I hate that we have to say goodbye.

He pulls back and looks into my eyes. "I love you."

I swallow. "I love you too."

He thrusts into me a few more times, his lips latched on to my neck.

"I love you."

He inches out and inches back in. "I love you," he says again.

Tears begin to well in my eyes, and the lump in my throat is more prominent. "I love you, too," I croak.

His lips quiver against my neck, and I know he's crying. "I love you," he whispers, his voice breaking.

My heart breaks. "I love you, Sienna," he says.

The emotion and his thrusts are too much for my body to handle, and I feel it coming. He thrusts harder followed with more *I love yous*. The last thrust sends me back to my usual euphoria.

"I love you," he says. He pulls back, and I see the red in his eyes. He sniffles as his eyes dart across my face. "I love you so much," he croaks.

And then he suddenly groans, throwing his head back. One last weak thrust and his head is slumped in my neck. He gives me one last kiss as he tries to catch his breath.

"I love you. Forever and always," he declares.

I close my eyes, silently sobbing, as I hold his body against mine.

I love you always, William Monroe.

TO BE CONTINUED

ACKNOWLEDGEMENTS

Thank you so much to those people who make me feel like I matter. Many thanks to my editor, Kasi, for sticking with me, dating back to my debut novel, *King Larson*. Thank you to my cover designer, Sarah Hansen at Okay Creations, for creating an awesome cover at the last minute and helping me find my vision for this book. Thank you to my interior designer, Elaine, for being patient with me and being flexible with me, being the disorganized new author I am. Thank you to Mom and Dad for supporting me in all things writing and fine arts. Thank you to my sister, Afina, for being there for me as a sister and asking me what inspires me to write. And thank you to you, Zack. You came in later, but I appreciate you for being supportive of me and encouraging me that this is just the beginning. You're truly a gem. I couldn't have done this without you all. And most importantly, thank God for wine. Without you, this story wouldn't have been possible.

COMING SOON

King Larson Series
After Larson (Book 2)

Rose Valley Series (Formerly *Monroe Vineyard*)
The Home I Miss (Book 2)

Standalones
12 Years From Now...

SOCIAL MEDIA
Instagram: allyleeauthor
Twitter: AllyLeeAuthor

CPSIA information can be obtained
at www.ICGtesting.com
Printed in the USA
BVHW031411060922
646321BV00013B/404